BEARDED WOMEN

STORIES

BY TERESA MILBRODT

ChiZine Publications

FIRST EDITION

Library and Archives Canada Cataloguing in Publication

Milbrodt, Teresa, 1978-
Bearded women : stories / Teresa Milbrodt.

ISBN 978-1-926851-46-4

I. Title.

PS3613.I4325B43 2011 813'.6 C2011-905026-9

CHIZINE PUBLICATIONS
Toronto, Canada
www.chizinepub.com
info@chizinepub.com

Edited and copyedited by Samantha Beiko
Proofread by Colleen Anderson

Canada Council for the Arts Conseil des Arts du Canada

We acknowledge the support of the Canada Council for the Arts which last year invested $20.1 million in writing and publishing throughout Canada.

ONTARIO ARTS COUNCIL
CONSEIL DES ARTS DE L'ONTARIO

Published with the generous assistance of the Ontario Arts Council.

Printed in Canada

BEARDED WOMEN

STORIES

For my parents,
who taught me the value of laughter and imagination

Table of Contents

Bianca's Body

My second lower torso grows out two inches to the left of my navel. I call her Bianca. She is at a forty-five-degree angle to my body and an eighty-degree angle to the ground. When I sit down, part of her back rests on my left knee and her legs dangle off the ground. Bianca has her own navel, a crotch, the necessary reproductive organs, and a nice pair of legs. I can move them when I concentrate. She is twenty-nine inches long and if she were a whole person I figure she would have been short, maybe four feet tall. I don't know how much she weighs; it's hard to balance her on a scale, but I'd guess forty-five pounds. Her hips are a bit narrow.

Bianca wears pants and skirts. I have to buy two of everything so she matches my walking legs, but I don't bother with pantyhose or matching shoes. Bianca wears black flats because they go with everything. Over thirty-five years I've grown accustomed to the extra pull on my abdomen, but I have a little rolling cart I rest Bianca on when I'm walking, push it with my left hand like a baby stroller.

It is our third trip to this gynaecologist, the seventh Doug and I have seen. In the office my husband sits on my right, holds my hand. Bianca is supported on a stool to my left. Doug still smells of french fry grease from working the graveyard shift at the diner. I picked him up after I got off work at the television station, have dark crescents below my eyes because I've been up for seventeen hours, since five yesterday afternoon. I do the eleven o'clock news as well as the five AM broadcast. Our newscasts have the best ratings in the state for a market our size, about 500,000 people. The station manager keeps telling me it's because of my bright personality and clear speaking voice, not because Bianca is hidden under the table.

"I think you'll need to have it removed if you want to have a child," says the gynaecologist. "Removal would take the stress of extra weight from your body and improve blood circulation and probably fertility. I wouldn't have advised it ten or even five years earlier, but medical technologies have been improving at such a rapid pace that your risk of serious complications has dramatically decreased."

"But there is still risk," says Doug.

I lay my hand on Bianca's stomach.

We've been having this problem for six years, ever since we started trying to get pregnant. Doug prefers to have sex with Bianca and for a long time I did not mind this. I feel what Bianca feels, and to be honest she has better orgasms. Bianca has gotten pregnant twice and both times the foetus miscarried. For two years we've tried impregnating my walking half. It's not easy since Bianca grows out of my body at a diagonal. She gets in the way if Doug tries to lie on top of me or if I'm on top of him. The necessary parts can't quite reach. We've tried all sorts of alternate positions, none of them comfortable. The one that's worked best so far is when I squat over Doug and move up and down while he thrusts. Bianca has to put her legs on the mattress and bow out her torso. It strains her muscles after a while, but it wouldn't be so bad if my walking half didn't take forever to orgasm. Sex with Bianca is better, easier than with my walking half, even though we have to do it standing, often in the shower. Doug hugs me close to him; I wrap Bianca's legs around his waist, and he supports her with both arms so my side doesn't ache. It works well enough.

But this gynaecologist sings the same song as her six predecessors. Bianca will never be able to bear children because of complications with her uterus—it will always reject the embryo shortly after implantation. If she is removed, there is a greater chance my walking half will be able to become pregnant. The gynaecologist explains this in terms of hormone concentrations. I don't quite understand it, but she seems to suggest that Bianca is leeching estrogen and progesterone away from the rest of my body. I've been injected with hormones and it hasn't worked, but all the doctors say things would balance out if Bianca were removed.

"So I would be able to get pregnant," I say.

"There would be a greater chance," says the gynaecologist.

"But just a chance," says Doug. "You couldn't guarantee anything."

"If it didn't work we could try artificial insemination," says the gynaecologist.

"Just a chance," says Doug.

"A chance." I try to smile.

"They're a bunch of quacks," Doug says in the car on the way home. "They've never dealt with anything like this. They have no idea what would happen if you got it removed."

"They have a pretty good idea," I say. He doesn't know her name is Bianca. No one else does.

"They're still quacks," says Doug. "I don't want you going under the knife and putting yourself at risk for the sake of a baby. We can adopt."

"I don't want to," I say quietly.

"Why the hell not?" he says, though we have had this argument before. "There are lots of kids out there who need good parents. Those doctors are vultures. Do you have any idea how much this will cost? How it'll put them in the news? You're a famous face."

"Locally. Just locally."

"It doesn't matter," he says, "it would still be in press releases all over the country. I don't see why you need to do this whole pregnancy thing. Having a kid is so taxing on a woman's body, and you'll be taxed enough after having surgery. What if they go in there and botch things up with your other uterus? Or what if you still can't have kids even with it off?"

"I haven't decided to remove it yet," I say, "I don't know if I want to try."

"You shouldn't," says Doug. "What would I do if I lost you?"

We lapse into silence. I don't know who to believe. The doctors. My husband. Everyone has an agenda. I know the doctors would be celebrities. I know Doug is afraid for my health. I also think he's afraid of losing Bianca. Sometimes I get jealous. Bianca is sexier than my walking half. Her legs and hips are smooth and slender, belonging to a twenty-year-old girl, while my walking legs belong to a thirty-five-year-old woman. Even though I work out at the gym and my walking legs are muscular, there is a little cellulite and some varicose veins.

I align myself more with my walking half. I don't know why. It has always felt like me, while Bianca felt like someone else. I gave her a name when I was very little, four or five. She is like a younger sibling, a person I love, a person I can envy. If she were removed there are a lot of things I would not miss. Grocery shopping would be less cumbersome.

I wouldn't have to alter all my clothes, make slits in skirts and pants to accommodate her. I wouldn't have to stand leaning over a toilet while Bianca does her business. We wouldn't have to keep ordering special cars with the steering wheel on the right side so I have room for Bianca's body. I wouldn't have a near-constant strain on my left side.

In the car I touch Doug's hand and he doesn't pull away. It is difficult to explain to him why I want a child of my own. It is difficult to explain it to myself, why I feel a need to grow round with the weight of an infant, why I want my body to create another body. I keep trying to come up with reasons but wonder why I have to explain myself to anybody. I always wanted to have a baby, and I wanted to be in my thirties when I did it, have a career and be able to take time off. Sometimes I think my drive to conceive has become stronger the more problems we have encountered, the more gynaecologists we have seen. My body should be able to reproduce. I have all the right equipment. Two sets in fact. But neither works.

By the time Doug and I get home, I'm confused and hungry and not a little cross. Bianca and my walking legs have the same menstrual cycle and it's getting close to their time of the month. It's crazy trying to change Bianca's pad and my walking half's pad in a little restroom stall, even when I use the wheelchair access ones. Doug and I eat cereal at eleven in the morning, too tired to make anything else for breakfast. I keep a little stool beside the kitchen table so I can rest Bianca while I eat. We need to catch a few hours' rest, have to get up at eight in the evening, and by the time we've sorted through the mail and had our cereal it's past noon. We're both tired and irksome. The appointment, the infertility, the possibility of Bianca's removal, is still on my mind. Even though I know it's a bad idea, I want to have sex.

"Can I just do it with your extra parts?" Doug sighs.

"We have to use my walking legs," I say.

"Too early in the morning for that," he grumbles.

"Maybe this time it will work and the hormone shots will finally kick in."

So we end up on the bed—me kneeling over Doug, Bianca arching her lower back and legs with her feet on the mattress, Doug grimacing up at me the whole time. It takes twice as long as usual before he comes. I fall off of him, to the side, hoping to catch it all and clamp it inside me. Become a baby, dammit. Bianca pulls at my side, her legs flailing in the air.

"Feel better now?" he says.

"Sure." We go to sleep, get up at seven-thirty, later than we should, have just enough time to shower and dress and make dinner before heading off to work.

Doug and I met because we were nocturnal creatures. I was in college, a sophomore majoring in communications, and he worked at the all-night diner where I went to study. At first he gave me free coffee when he saw me sitting at the counter or alone at a table. That progressed to donuts, pie, milkshakes if I wanted them, then burgers and fries and even breakfast at five AM. In the meantime I was being prodded into a career in newscasting.

I always thought I'd like to work in television, but never pictured myself in front of the camera for obvious reasons. I figured I would do things behind the scenes, but ended up sitting at a news desk when no one else in my camera-shy television production class wanted to anchor the newscast for our campus station. It was only a half-hour broadcast, aired twice a week, and focused on local and university news. The other students convinced me it would be fine, Bianca would remain hidden, her feet balanced on a milk crate.

I worked for the campus station for five years, even after graduation. Viewership to our program increased tenfold and we expanded to a three-day-a-week and then a five-day-a-week show with me as the primary news anchor. I applied for my current job on a lark. They didn't know about the extra body when I was hired because I sent broadcast demo tapes and did a phone interview. I figured only the upper half of my body would be important to them, anyway. I've had the job for twelve years now and think most viewers know about Bianca even though it's just my upper half on the billboards all over town. Sometimes, though, when I'm at the grocery store or out to eat, someone smiles at me, gives a wave of recognition, and then her jaw drops when she sees Bianca.

The evening newscast is the same as usual—house fires, a gas station robbed, a dog that had twelve puppies and someone assumes it must be a county record. Overnight I'm working on more national and local news developments for the morning broadcast. During a coffee break at two AM, I make the mistake of telling Lottie, the night receptionist, that I'm considering having Bianca removed. She says her lips are sealed.

By five in the morning half the station knows. Lottie swears up and down she only told one other person. I want to strangle her. After my morning broadcast, the station program manager asks if they can do a special on the operation and my recovery.

"But this isn't a done deal," I say. "I don't know if I'm getting the surgery."

"Really?" He scratches his moustache. "I'd think an extra bottom half would be more trouble than it's worth."

"It's dangerous to have it removed," I say before marching out to the parking lot.

Everyone always asks why I don't get Bianca cut off. I tell them our internal organs are mingled, which is true enough, but so many other things are mingled, too. I have always sensed her sexual desire. It is something instinctual, gut-level thinking. I don't know how I would feel without her. Maybe lost. I've read about this happening with Siamese twins when they were separated, how they spent so long feeling what the other twin felt it was a near-devastating absence when that connection was gone. Bianca has always been more passionate than me. If I lost her, lost that, what else might change?

Beside my car in the parking lot I'm approached by a nice-looking man in a trench coat. He hands me a business card and asks if he can buy toenail clippings from Bianca.

"I'd pay a premium for them," he whispers not unkindly. "More if I could watch you cut them, but just the toenails would be okay as well." I stare at him. He smiles, tells me to think about it, touches the brim of his hat. I get into my car quickly and lock the door, sit in the driver's seat for a moment. His business card says he's an accountant. I wonder how he would know which body I sent the clippings from. If they were my toenails at all. There are always a few odd ducks wandering around the studio trying to catch a glimpse of me. There are often a few protestors, too, people who say the only reason I've had this job for twelve years is because of my body, because I am a secret spectacle.

If it were seventy years ago I could be exhibiting myself in a sideshow, painted larger-than-life on a poster on the side of a canvas tent. Freakish people used to be thought of as magical. Bianca could have been an economic asset. Now I'm just made to feel bad.

When Doug and I got married, both of our families were aghast. My mother did not want me to wed someone who planned on a career as a short-order cook, no matter how well-read I said he was. Doug's mother was sure we were going to have kids with three arms. Doug and I had been dating for two years. Our parents met twice before the wedding to have dinner, meals that involved several pointed questions and long periods of silence. His mother asked my mother when I was going to get the extra bits removed. My mother asked his mother when Doug was going back to school. I will never be sure why we didn't elope, why I let my mother insist on a church wedding. I don't think anyone in his family said anything to anyone in my family the entire evening. But I loved Doug because he was a smart person, because we both liked travelling, because he was happy cooking and working nights and reading private eye novels. He didn't mind that we would need to follow my news anchor career, go where I could find work, and he was proud that I had the confidence to keep Bianca. I'd known that I needed to marry a man who saw Bianca as a part of me, not something extra. And maybe that plan worked too well.

I was planning on going to the gym, and after the accountant incident I really need to work out, relieve some of the stress. They're used to me at Perfect Body Gym, appreciate that I can bring people in at six-thirty in the morning. I have a free membership as long as I come in at least twice a week. They keep a little stool for Bianca behind the desk, one with a seat I can raise or lower depending on the equipment I'm using. I do some curls, work on my triceps, and do a few sets on the leg extension machine with my walking half. Then I take Bianca's shoes off, place her bare feet against the wall, and lean all of my weight against her. I bend her knees and straighten them again. It's kind of like doing sideways push-ups, keeps her legs and ass toned. Of course people are always looking at me, whispering behind my back, and over time I've learned to tell myself that I don't care that much.

I get home at eight in the morning feeling tired but a bit better. Doug has been home for an hour at least, made us eggs and bacon and toast.

"The station manager called," he says, squinting at me across the table. "It was about doing a show on you. Some sort of special. He wanted to talk to you about it."

"I tell one person at work about the possibility of an operation and now it's front page news."I shake my head. "I'm still not sure about it."

"You're not?" he says.

"No. I don't know. There's the safety risk and . . . I don't know."

But that afternoon I call the gynaecologist, figure I might as well start going through pre-surgery procedures, just in case. I don't even know which organs are connected where, how they would have to untwist my genitals from Bianca's. While I am on the phone to the gynaecologist's office I wonder how long Bianca could live on her own apart from me. Would it be seconds? Minutes? Hours? Nothing?

At dinner I tell Doug I decided to start preliminary testing but haven't committed to anything. He's mad anyway.

"They're going to hook you," he says. "Once you start down that road, even if you're not sure, they'll force you into it one way or another. Those doctors will lie, tell you it will be easy even if it won't."

"It's still my decision," I say, mad at him for thinking I can be forced into anything. "I can say no. It's my body and I get to decide what to do with it."

It's my body that may conceive a baby. It's my body to detach from

Bianca if I so choose. Sometimes I get tired of making allowances for her. But when I lie awake at night I wonder what is mine and what is Bianca's. Are my breasts her breasts? Is my head her head? Our head? How much does she exist as me and how much is she her own being? I know chickens are supposed to run around for a few minutes after they have their heads cut off. They say it's a muscle reaction, but I've always thought the chicken was still bent on trying to get away. And what is the head on the chopping block thinking once it is independent of the chicken, watching its body in a futile sprint? If the body is still moving, what of the mind?

Doug and I barely talk for a week, just argue. He's mad, says I'm going to needlessly put my life at risk, and he refuses to have sex with my walking half. He just wants Bianca.

"Those parts won't be with us much longer." He slathers his toast with strawberry jam. "Might as well make use of them while they're here."

"But it's a waste of good sperm," I say. "Until I get pregnant, it should all go into my walking half. The extra parts could stay if I conceived. And I'm still not sure if I'm going through with it."

My argument fails to sway my husband and he sleeps on the couch for four nights. When he comes back to bed he's still mad, but mad in a sex-deprived way. We try to figure out a truce—he can have sex with Bianca one night and my walking half the other night. Doug seems okay with this compromise but grimaces when he's under me.

"You could at least look like you're enjoying it," I say.

He smiles a big fake smile.

I sigh because I'm not enjoying it, either.

When he has sex with Bianca it's rougher than before. He thrusts harder, slaps her rear. I wince, tell him to slow down and be gentle. He kind of blushes. We change our strategy. Doug starts out with Bianca, enough to get him excited, then he lies down on the bed and I clamber on top of him while he struggles to hold the juice in. This works a couple times but involves a lot of bumped knees and shins. In the end he's still more turned on by Bianca than my walking half, and this is hurtful though I don't want to admit it.

When I go to have more tests, CAT scans and such, Doug shows his anger in other, smaller ways. He doesn't always kiss me when we leave for work in the afternoon and get home in the morning. He starts doing overtime at the diner, working on weekends and 'til ten or eleven in the morning. He says if I want this surgery and we want a child, we need to save money. I bite my lip and nod.

Bianca's wrath is an even bigger problem. She knows what I am considering, and during the eight weeks of pre-surgery testing I have two of the most painful periods ever. Bianca bloats and it's hard to zip up her pants.

I try to reason with her.

"I'm just checking out options," I say while driving to the hospital for another scan. "This is no done deal." Her hips, her ovaries, her vagina are searing pain. I grit my teeth. All of Bianca hurts, even her knees and feet. I don't know what to do. Part of me worries that even after she is removed the pain will still be there. I have heard stories of war veterans who lost hands and feet but could still feel pain in the absence. A phantom limb seems paltry compared to a phantom lower half.

Protestors are massed every day outside of the television station. They picket carrying signs with black outlines of people with four arms and three legs, say I shouldn't be allowed to procreate at all, regardless of surgery. They believe the abnormalities are hereditary and I'll only birth monsters. Of course I know it's not true, but it hurts to know they think my body isn't fit to produce another. Word also gets out to the local papers, and editorial page letters are devoted to me for three weeks. Some people say I should get the surgery. Some people say I shouldn't get the surgery. The really whacked ones say I should have been killed at birth.

The station manger is mad is because I told him I wouldn't do a television special, whether or not I get the surgery done. He thinks I should jump at the chance for local and national and even international press.

"Think of the fame you'd gain if the surgery were successful and you could conceive," he says.

"If my husband will still have me," I mutter.

The station manager ignores me, says it would be a great career move.

After three months of hassles and tests, I'm more resolute about having the operation than I was before. The gynaecologist says even though it will take me a long time to recover, the procedure itself will be easier than expected—Bianca's liver and kidneys and intestines function separately from mine, and won't be as difficult to detach as they thought.

Of course Doug and Bianca don't want me to have surgery. Even the station manager has changed his mind since I refused to do the television special, says it would be best if I'd just deliberate forever to keep it in the news.

Then Bianca doesn't have her period when my walking half does. I wait a week. Two. At the beginning of the third week I feel a little sick in the evening after I wake up.

"I think I'm pregnant," I whisper to Doug at dinner. Both of us are wide-eyed, as if saying it any louder will make it not true. He hugs me tight and we both hold our breath. I squeeze Bianca's legs tight to keep the baby inside, keep it growing. I don't talk about surgery for days and Doug seems cheery even though he has to have sex with my walking half because we don't want to disturb Bianca.

The foetus miscarries after six weeks.

I sit on the edge of the bathtub, naked from the waist down, my nightgown hitched up over Bianca. I grip her bloody underwear in both hands and cry. This is how Doug finds me. He sits beside me, wraps his arms around my shoulders, rocks Bianca and me back and forth.

"We could always adopt," he whispers.

I cry harder. I want a baby from my body, yet I'm afraid that even without Bianca I won't be able to carry a child to term. What if this pregnancy is Bianca trying to stay with me, trying to conceive to pacify me? I want to keep Bianca. I want to have a baby. I can't have both.

The accountant in the parking lot is still asking for toenail clippings. I see him once a week. Everywhere I go people are watching me. I can feel their prying eyes. Before my possible surgery made news, it seemed like people had almost gotten used to Bianca. Or at least everyone everywhere didn't gape. Now at the gym I think a few dozen people have bought memberships just to watch me work out. They walk on treadmills going one and a half miles an hour and stare as Bianca does her deep knee bends against the wall.

The television ratings are up, haven't been this high since I joined the station.

Doug convinces me to let him have sex with Bianca two days after the miscarriage. He says the pregnancy is a sign that we should keep trying and prove the gynaecologists wrong. Bianca shudders pleasure when he touches her, as if she'd been worried Doug would no longer find her attractive after the miscarriage. He caresses her with a gentleness that is somehow unlike the way he touches my walking legs. I sear with jealously. I know he sees her as a part of me, but how can he understand that she is and she isn't? I feel the hot waves of her orgasm that is mine and not mine. When I start crying Doug hugs me and all I can do is shake my head.

After Doug has fallen asleep I talk to Bianca. I tell her that part of her essence would still be with me even after she was removed. The blood in my body would have run through both of our bodies. She would be a mother along with me. In the back of my mind I wonder wispily if Doug would leave me if I had the surgery. How to explain to him that she would still be there, a phantom pull at my side? In sleep Doug slides his arm over my stomach and across to Bianca, his fingers grazing both of our hips. I wiggle Bianca's toes and wonder what it will be like without her, how long it will take to forget the feel of her legs against bedsheets, Doug's hand on her knee. I grit my teeth, close my eyes, concentrate on wiggling the toes on my walking legs, the ones I know are mine.

The Shell

Martin Wyss had not planned to carve for the dead. He wanted to carve horses and bears and ducks—hooves so hard they could run, fur so soft the chest could rise and fall, wings so strong they could fly. Martin knew he was meant to uncover what was hidden in wood, wanted to pull life from it just as Michelangelo had grabbed David's marble hands and tugged. Michelangelo loved David because he found him in stone, and for the same reason Martin loved the ducks he discovered preening their oaken feathers.

Sometimes, late at night in his garage workshop, Martin was sure he could hear sleepy quacks from the wooden beaks and tired pawing from the hooves of deer. But in spite of his attainment of the near-perfect duck, Martin had to work part time at a hardware store because his art barely sold. Perhaps a dog here or there at craft shows, a fawn from time to time, but most people smiled and nodded and walked by.

His aunt requested the first casket. She was seventy and a chain smoker, knew he was hard up for money, so she asked him to carve a four-foot-high hollow teacup with a hinged lid. It was like she knew in six more months she would need to curl inside. His teary uncle paid Martin handsomely. A librarian aunt asked for a casket shaped like a row of books. A mechanic uncle wanted a toolbox coffin. It did not take long for word of Martin's artistry to spread like a plague. Calls came from eight states, orders for a windmill, a race car, a violin case, all big and with hinged tops. It was too popular, Martin thought, the idea that in death one could lie in what one had loved. He quit the hardware store to carve full-time, but each coffin was labour-intensive, made just enough to pay for his food, mortgage, car loan, and buy materials for the next casket.

"You must be so happy now," his friends said, "able to carve for a living."

Martin shrugged. He still saw deer and bears sitting in the wood, still wanted to carve life but had to serve those who sat nervously at its edge, people who were wilting. Usually he had clients to his workshop twice—once to view his work and place an order, and again for a casket fitting since it was only proper to make sure he had sized them correctly. Martin kept these appointments to a polite fifteen minutes, averted his eyes when his clients rested their wizened legs inside the coffin and either pronounced it comfortable or a little too tight. By the time they left, Martin's fingers had started aching and his knuckles appeared slightly knobbed.

He had the earthy build of a carver, short thick arms and legs and a sturdy torso, but Martin knew even the healthiest of bodies only allowed for so much time, so much completed work. Around the perimeter of his garage, wooden ducks watched him in sympathy.

Odessa Crouch wanted to be buried in a big purple scallop shell. She was sixty-seven and on disability, a recently retired legal secretary at Hummer, Hummer, and Huller. The law firm was downtown, next to the pink marble art museum. Odessa wandered the museum's halls during her lunch hour, strolling past Egyptian mummies and Roman sarcophagi, browsing the gift shop and flipping through poster-sized prints. Botticelli's "Birth of Venus" was her favourite, the goddess rising from the sea in her oversized shell. A lovely way to be born. A lovely way to die. It had been fifteen years since Odessa's body had started hurting, really hurting, and now it always tried to curl in on itself. Her hands, her feet, her arms, her legs, wanted to wind in tight spirals close to her torso, condense into a ball.

Odessa had felt useful at work before pain cut her off. She'd organized legal papers and made phone calls about divorces, custody battles, alimony, and DUI. She was someone who helped sort things out. When Odessa's husband left her for an older woman ten years ago, she got free legal services. Her two daughters were grown, had demanding babies of their own, and Odessa managed to get fifty-five percent of everything because her lawyers were vultures and her husband a wimp. Half of her possessions were willed to her two daughters and three grandchildren, the other half were supposed to be sold upon her death and the proceeds given to the museum. Odessa believed in art and free admission.

She'd heard of Martin Wyss's caskets from a friend of a friend whose aunt had been buried in one shaped like a giant candy bar. The box was white pine but everyone at the funeral swore they smelled chocolate. Odessa wondered if, when she was buried in her scallop shell, people would smell the sea.

When Odessa called Martin to inquire about coffin prices she thought his voice was too high, too weary. Odessa bit her lip. She wanted someone who carved caskets to sound like God.

"I'm thinking of dying sometime soon," said Odessa. "I want a casket shaped like a shell."

"What kind of shell?" said Martin. "Abalone? Conch? Clam?"

"Scallop," said Odessa. "Like Venus."

She wanted to be laid out in the foetal position. Now her wretched spine ached and made her hobble through the grocery store hunchbacked, but she thought that in death the curve would be beautiful, even graceful, once it did not mean pain. She wanted Martin to react to her saying she was thinking of dying soon. Instead he asked where she lived.

"You should probably come to my workshop," he said. "It's not too far, maybe an hour's drive, and you could see a few of my works, decide if it's what you really want."

Odessa agreed even though she didn't drive much anymore, didn't do much of anything anymore without a lot of ibuprofen and sometimes Vicodin on top of her monthly cortisone shots. The pain flowed through her like blood, up her fingers to her arms, down her back to her legs and knees and toes. She'd worked as long as she could at the law firm, longer than her aching body wanted to allow, until the afternoon Mr. Huller brought her a cup of coffee and said quietly that perhaps it was time to take a rest. She was a hard worker, he said, and she'd earned a break after thirty-seven years with the firm. Odessa was certain her arms never hurt more than when she had to clean out her desk. The heat of that pain never left. Odessa hated the way her fingers arched into claws when she didn't take her medication. She hated the way her legs ached in the morning, the way her veins popped out blue against the peach of her skin. She hated the way her feet felt like she was walking on popcorn kernels. Her insides had been replaced, muscle by muscle and bone by bone, with someone else's aching interior, and deceitfully covered with her own skin.

Odessa took a triple dose of ibuprofen on the day she drove to meet Martin. Her doctor said it would harm her stomach eventually. Odessa didn't care, just wanted to keep her body at bay. She focused on the shell, imagined it was just a pen flick away, the writing of one small cheque and she'd figure out the rest from there.

Martin Wyss was one of the most disappointing men she had ever met. Despite his too-weary voice, Odessa had still hoped for a man who looked like he'd been peeled off the ceiling of the Sistine Chapel. Martin was five feet tall if that, had a bit of a paunch, was balding slightly, had arms thick as tree trunks, and not enough wrinkles to be over forty. He was the sort of man she'd expect to come and repair her sink. Martin showed her his garage workroom. It smelled not of wood but dead forests, burned things. One casket was in progress on the wooden bench, a seven-foot-long ice cream cone wide enough for a human body.

"You realise that in a shell they couldn't lay you out to your full height," said Martin.

"Of course," said Odessa. She was five foot nine, taller than he was. Odessa explained her idea for the foetal position.

"When do you plan on dying?" said Martin.

Odessa wrinkled her nose. "One month."

"If you could hold off for one more," he said, "make it two, I would be finished by then. Have to get this one done, you know." He nodded at the cone.

"Of course," Odessa said. She wrote him a cheque, a down payment on her shell.

"I guess that's about it," said Martin, folding the check in half and slipping it in his pocket.

"You don't need to ask me anything else?" said Odessa. "Measure me?"

"I have a good eye for size," said Martin, tapping his head with a sad finger. "I'll remember."

On the drive home, to take her mind off the pain searing back into her fingers, Odessa reconsidered the possible means of her demise. She thought about jumping off a bridge or tall building, but that would be rather disgusting, and they'd have to dredge her body or put pieces of her in the shell. She didn't want to send workmen home retching tales to their wives. There was always a gun or a knife, but those were violent, involved too much blood, and she did want to be presentable when tucked in her shell. As much as she hated her body, she figured that it might as well look halfway decent once it stopped hurting. Poison would taste bad, and there was always the chance she'd vomit it up. She could take sleeping pills, but what if someone found her and took her to get her stomach pumped, or what if she didn't take enough?

Odessa gritted her teeth. She wasn't going to simply lie on her couch and wait for death. She wanted to attend to these matters while she still could, but she finally decided, as she usually did, to put off the question of how she would die until later. The means itself was not that important. What mattered was the shell.

After Odessa left, Martin kept sanding the ice cream cone coffin. It was for a man who'd owned three sweet shops and was not a small fellow. He had heart disease and the doctors didn't give him long. Martin smoothed a sheet of four-hundred-grit sandpaper along the wood grain. Nearly done. It was not a bad sculpture, but all of his caskets felt unnatural, like they were forced out of the wood. They did not flow with the same grace as his animals. He was usually pleased enough with the finished coffin because his customers were happy and that mattered a great deal to him, but carving a casket was not truly satisfying. He opened a can of stain, Satin Woodberry, mixed it with a stirring stick, and began to rub it on the cone with a rag. The wood turned the colour of graham crackers.

He thought of Odessa and her thin knobbed frame. Hers was a body that made one uncomfortably aware of bones and joints. Even though he was not old, he felt the pressure of age, the urge to find things in wood while his hands could still firmly grip the chisel. Martin worried about his body hurting, hardening, paining with life as Odessa surely pained.

He figured she'd probably look better once she passed. Most people did. It was the in-between time that was upsetting, when people had bodies that were withering or oozing and not much could be done about it. Such had been the case with his mother and tea-loving aunt who both died in nursing homes. Martin went to visit his aunt once, his mother twice. They were barely more than skeletons, had machines that breathed for them, fed them, removed waste from their bowels. They blinked at Martin sadly and touched his hand. Their skin smelled peculiar and was slightly sticky, had been claimed by odours and textures no amount of washing could remove. After the initial visits Martin stayed home and worked on the coffins—his aunt's teacup, his mother's pink pump.

His mother loved shoes, fancy ones. She had beautiful feet, ones that looked like they belonged to a forty-year-old even when she was seventy-eight and needed a walker to shuffle around her house. She did so in gold beaded slippers, red sequined sandals, low fuchsia heels, or lavender flats with daisies embroidered along the side. Her neighbours called Martin on the day they found her collapsed on the kitchen floor. The doctors told Martin her insides were failing. The first time he visited his mother, Martin took all her shoes to the nursing home and lined them up in bookshelves along her wall so she could see them from her bed. The second time he visited, the exquisite definition of her bones was too much for him to bear.

While she lay between too-sterile white sheets, he knelt in his garage, glued five thousand magenta sequins on the outside of the pump, and remembered his mother at fifty-five when she was plump and brown-haired and smelled of cinnamon. Martin could not explain why, but the shoe had emerged as naturally as his animal carvings, as if that block of wood had only ever wanted to be a very large high-heeled pump.

Martin made a point to go to all of the funerals where his work was displayed. Even though he was ambivalent about some of his caskets, he felt a duty as the artist to attend the memorials as there were few other places where his art was praised. The deceased always looked pleasant, wore fancy clothes as if ready for a concert or dinner party. His mother and his aunt had been tucked snug in their coffins in nice dresses, their faces made up, their hair neatly permed. Both of them seemed to have gained a little weight and there was a hint of colour to their cheeks. It was reassuring how their bodies had been restored, how they were now caught in a moment of pristine order. Martin could make himself imagine they had died like that.

Martin called Odessa after four weeks, earlier than she had expected. He wanted her to come look at the shell and check the fit.

Odessa still hadn't figured out how she was going to kill herself, but hoped Martin might have some knowledge on the subject of death.

"What's the best way to die?" said Odessa after she pulled into his driveway and got out of her car.

"I don't do consulting," he said.

"I'll pay you extra," she said.

"I'm really not an authority on the matter." Martin turned and started walking to his workshop.

"But you see a lot of dead people," Odessa said, hobbling after him on her sore feet.

"When people come to me," Martin said, "they usually aren't in a situation where they can choose how they're going to die."

"Nobody opts to go out early?" said Odessa.

"If they have plans they don't share them with me," said Martin. "I'm just an artistic advisor. Sometimes they ask me what they should wear after the fact."

He opened the door to his workshop.

"What about how not to die?" she said.

"Drunken and penniless in an alley," he said.

"I hadn't considered that," she said.

"Don't," he said.

The shell was on his worktable, lovely and cream coloured and satin smooth, perhaps five feet long and five feet wide and two and a half feet high when the halves were together.

Martin said, "I still have to sand the inside a bit and screw on the hinge plates, but I figured you should try it so I know if I need to carve out more room."

Odessa's legs were paining, she'd forgotten her pills in the car, but she grimaced only slightly when he helped her up onto the sturdy worktable, lifted the top off the shell. The hollow inside bore slight grooves from Martin's chiselling tools, but despite the roughness Odessa curled herself into a dreamy foetal position. It was perfect.

"I like it very much," she said.

Martin stood by the table.

"Looks good," he said after a moment. "You can stand up now."

"No," said Odessa because the shell seemed to make her elbows and knees ache less. It would hurt to get out. In the shell her insides felt different. Softer.

Martin chewed on his bottom lip for a moment.

"You have to go. I need to keep working on the shell," he said.

"I like it in here," said Odessa. "I don't want to get out yet."

Martin said, "I told you, it's not done."

"You have to work on it right now?" said Odessa.

Martin didn't say anything, stood there for three or four more moments. He'd progressed on the shell more quickly than expected, found once he started working on the scallop it became an obsession. The shell mesmerized him with its contours, the grooves in its smooth surface. Martin studied scallops before he began working, loved how the sea creatures could secrete a hard casing around their bodies, how they lived out the entirety of their lives in the shell.

When he started to carve he found the scallop was already in the wood, smelling of sea, waiting to be released. The shell was not merely a box. It was a creature. He lavished the outside with sandpaper, regretted having to hollow it out as he wanted to carve the scallop itself. It was what belonged there, not an elderly woman.

Martin wanted to line the shell in cream satin, paint the whole thing periwinkle, imagine a three-foot-wide scallop could rest there. He wanted to float it in his bathtub and watch the scallop's massive foot poke out between the two wooden shell halves, flawless and petal-smooth, to explore the ceramic contours of its new home.

But Martin was afraid of Odessa, didn't like looking at her for very long. Partly out of anxiety and partly out of hunger he decided to be nice, have an early lunch and give her a few more minutes in the shell. In the kitchen Martin lingered over his ham sandwich and the newspaper, waited a full hour before returning to the garage to confront Odessa.

"Time to get out," said Martin.

"No," said Odessa, "I'm staying here."

She had been thinking about the shell every day for a month. There was ample time to do so since most of her hours were spent watching television and trying to alleviate her pain through learning about gardening and cooking and needlework. She kept forty bags of peas in her freezer, pulled twenty out each morning after breakfast and put them all over her body while she lay on the couch. There was still pain but it was numb pain, made it easier to separate her mind from her body. Around two in the afternoon she put the twenty defrosted bags of peas back in the freezer and took out the remaining twenty bags of frozen peas, repeated the process.

The wooden shell felt warm and cool, even more soothing than frozen peas. When she concentrated she thought it was rocking her back and forth.

Martin said, "Don't you need to go to the bathroom or eat?"

"I'm going to die here," said Odessa.

Martin flexed his fingers, wanted to protect his shell, haul the scallop to the water where it belonged. He thought Odessa's face had turned a shade paler since she'd arrived, but he could not be left in his garage with the beautiful shell and the husk of a woman. He would not be able to control the drool threading from her mouth, the loosening of her bowels. Usually when Martin carved he did not feel his body, it became part of the wood. He was the wood. If there was an ache in his elbow or a sliver in his thumb it was overlooked, unimportant. Nothing existed but the next stroke of the chisel. Odessa, like his other clients, made him aware of the fragility of his lungs, the stiffness of his fingers, the twinge in his lower back.

"You can't die in the shell," Martin said. "You'll ruin the aesthetic. People are supposed to look nice for their funerals. If you starve there, all covered with shit, it's not going to be pretty."

Odessa winkled her nose and shifted her legs slightly. Martin had a point. If she stayed in the shell to die she might look more like a bag lady than Venus. Not that she'd entertained the thought of looking like Venus. Perhaps Venus' aunt or first grade teacher. Presentable. But in the shell her body curled happily, able to rest as it wanted.

"I'll call the police," Martin said, his words echoing on the concrete floor. "They'll come and dump you out."

Odessa coughed. "Let them," she said.

Martin paused.

"If you don't get out, I won't sell you the shell," he said.

"You have to," she said. "I gave you an advance."

"No contract was signed," he said. "I'll give back your money and keep the shell myself."

This was a wonderful and an awful idea, and one he'd been considering since Odessa arrived and he realised how badly he wanted the shell. If he didn't sell it he might not have enough in his account to pay for his mortgage and food and car loan, but he also knew Odessa couldn't die in his garage and he guessed she had the power to do so.

Odessa was quiet for a moment.

"Bring my pills from the car," she said.

He found her purse. He found her keys. He found a small bottle of pills on the passenger seat, gave Odessa the four she requested along with a glass of water and a half hour to get ready.

Odessa knew she needed something to drink. Even more importantly, she believed Martin when he said he would not sell her the shell.

Pain surged as she stepped out of the scallop. She lost that sweet peace with her body. When she went to the bathroom she had diarrhoea. Martin was good enough to make her some mint tea, though, and when she held the warm mug her fingers hurt a little less.

"The shell could be finished now," she said. "Just tie it to the top of my car and I'll take it home and pay you in full. It would be less work for you."

Odessa knew that if she had the shell, if she could lie inside it without pain, it wouldn't matter so much if she lived or died.

"No," Martin said. "It isn't done. I have to paint it."

He couldn't part with the shell, didn't know if he could find another piece of wood that would contain a shell so lovely. Better to go into debt while he made Odessa another scallop. He wanted this one.

Odessa finished drinking her tea. They walked back outside to Martin's garage and stood by the worktable.

"If you're not going to let me take it home yet," Odessa said, "let me get back inside. Just for a little while. I don't ache as much now. I'll be able to get out."

"You need to go home," Martin said.

Odessa put both of her hands on the lip of the shell. Her fingers were thin as crab legs.

"Please," said Odessa.

Her nails dug into the wood. Martin grabbed the other side of the shell and pulled. The shell was heavy, moved a few inches across the wooden tabletop. Odessa didn't pull back, her arms were not strong, but her fingers were set, her muscles locked.

"You're supposed to have more compassion for the dying," she said.

"Dying people aren't supposed to be belligerent," he said. "They're supposed to be sickly and meek."

"Forget meek," she said. "If I really wanted to I'd make myself drop dead right here, and then what would you do?"

Martin stared down at the floor and imagined Odessa's insides leaking out.

"I'll give you twenty percent extra if you let me get back inside," she said. "Just for a moment or two. I promise."

Martin gritted his teeth but nodded. He'd carve a second shell and charge her more for that one.

"Two more minutes in the shell," he said. "That's all."

Odessa asked if he could put the top on the shell first, attach the hinges.

Martin wrinkled his nose.

"It'll be harder to finish the inside and paint it," he said, but eventually he agreed because he was eager to see the shell together, too. He hurried through the half hour it took to position and screw on both brass hinge plates. When he was done, Martin raised and lowered the top half several times before helping Odessa back on the table.

Odessa curled herself inside the shell. It still felt warm.

"Close it for a minute," she said.

Martin obliged, lowered the top half gently onto the bottom.

Odessa heard him count to five before opening it again.

"No," she said, "I mean a minute."

Martin rolled his eyes but closed the shell again. It was dark and warm and Odessa heard him whispering one-one thousand, two-one thousand, three-one thousand. She heard the sea. Her joints loosened and she felt floaty, as if she was immersed in a pool of water that wasn't wet. Too soon the crack of light at the opening of the shell widened to an annoying brightness.

"Okay, that's it," Martin said, tapping the side of the shell.

"No," she said.

"If I have to push the shell off the table to get you out," said Martin, "I will."

"It might break," said Odessa.

"Get out," said Martin.

She didn't.

It was too much. Odessa's skin smelled medicinal. Martin imagined her hands caught in a clench, her face becoming paler and harder, her chest ceasing to rise even the tiniest bit, her cheeks caving in. There could be no dead things in his shell.

Odessa heard a door open and close. After a couple minutes she heard it a second time. Then she felt the shell start to move. She still didn't believe him, figured it must be an empty threat until the scallop slid off the edge of the table, dumped Odessa onto the couch cushions Martin had arranged on the garage floor. The shell gaped over Odessa like a huge open mouth, just missed hitting her arm. Odessa started sobbing.

"You didn't give me much choice," Martin said quietly as Odessa lay on the cushions.

The smell of the sea filled her nostrils, soothed her slightly so her eyes did not burn so much. Martin walked around the table and eased the shell off Odessa, centred it on one of the couch cushions.

She stopped crying. Her face relaxed. Her bones ceased to ache. Odessa rolled to her stomach and planted her hands on the floor, stood up. Something around her body had been lost, a sense of grounding, gravity. She felt a release in her legs, her hips, her spine, sweet and sudden. The smell of the sea was potent. New strength surged in her arms. Odessa knew that for at least a few minutes she could be powerful outside the shell. She pictured herself carrying the scallop to her car, driving home with the trunk cracked open slightly.

When she grasped the edge of the shell with her thin fingers, she saw her veins were growing brighter, nearly glowing through her skin. The shell slid more easily than she had expected, off of the cushions, onto the concrete garage floor. Martin gaped at her.

Odessa pulled it down the driveway, paused for a moment when she felt her arms ache, but a second wave of strength rolled through her body, and she kept going.

"I'll send a cheque," she called to Martin.

Martin could not move. He winced at the sound of the wooden shell grating against the concrete driveway, but shoving it off the table with Odessa inside had drained him. He could not chase her. As Odessa lugged the giant scallop to her car, her power was mythic. But when she was halfway there, Martin noticed her pace beginning to slow. Her body bowed over, closer to the ground, but she kept lumbering backwards, even as her fingers loosened incrementally. He knew what was coming. The slow motion tumbling forward as if into a pool of water. But not just yet. Odessa pulled the scallop along.

For a moment the driveway dissolved, the harsh cement went blue, the shell floated along and Martin envisioned the barest shimmer of a young woman's gold hair, hands covering herself in modesty, then he saw the second figure, the silver grey of an old woman's hair, her nakedness without apology as she tugged the shell through the waves.

Mr. Chicken

I'm taking inventory in the walk-in freezer, have my hat and gloves on and am counting packages of sandwich buns, when one of my employees barrels through the door to tell me Mr. Chicken is back. She shivers in her green Golden Lotus blouse, grabs my elbow, drags me from the freezer.

"I can't very well do much about him," I say, taking off my hat.

"But he scares us," she says. "You're the manager. Manage him."

By the time she and I reach the front counter, Mr. Chicken already has his first box of chicken bits in hand and is waddling back to a table to start eating. I don't know who first started calling him Mr. Chicken. Probably one of the high school boys who works the fryers. Mr. Chicken is maybe fifty years old, balding, has salt and pepper hair, wears a white shirt and dark pants and a tie. He weighs about five hundred pounds and his stomach avalanches over his waistband like the extra is going to drop off at any moment.

Mr. Chicken's gaze wanders around the room, staring hard at Golden Lotus customers and employees alike. We all watch his ritual from the corners of our eyes. He eats the first box of chicken bits then returns to the counter and orders a second twenty-piece box, lumbers back to his table and eats them all. He returns a third time, a fourth, a fifth, until he has eaten one hundred chicken bits. Then he orders a cherry turnover. An apple one. A vanilla fried ice cream. A chocolate. We watch him for twenty-five minutes. The way he keeps eating is scary, mechanical. Some of my employees think he must have four stomachs like a cow, that he's not really human. In the past month, more than a few customer survey cards have come back with "Get rid of the weird fat guy" written in the comments section.

Mr. Chicken stares at two little kids sitting at the next table until they cry. There is no expression on his face. I know I have to say something to him. I scratch the stubble on my chin. I'm not a very big woman and I like to go by the traditional idea that the customer is always right, but upsetting children is going too far. I take a deep breath and plod into the dining room area toward his table, hear my employees hold their collective breath.

"Pardon me, sir," I say. "I'm the manager at this restaurant."

Mr. Chicken stares at me. "The food's fine. Good food."

I don't know why I get mad at the staring. His eyes are a little sad, a little angry, a little like they're daring me to do something.

"Some of our customers reported that you were looking at them intensely," I say in my most polite manager voice. "They worried if you were okay."

Mr. Chicken stuffs the end of a cherry turnover in his mouth. "This a restaurant or a shrink's office?"

"Those kids you were staring at got upset," I say.

"Not my fault." Mr. Chicken wipes his mouth with a napkin. He smells of sweat and grease.

"I see," I say. "Thank you for your time, sir. I hope you continue to enjoy your meal."

I trudge behind the counter feeling rather like an idiot. All of my employees are biting their lips. I was unable to save them from the stares of Mr. Chicken. But I don't feel right kicking someone out of the restaurant and I'm too stressed to be assertive. I had an awful date last night. James. We'd been out three times before and after dinner I figured I had to tell him that I was a closeted bearded lady. Because I'm blonde and shave every morning it's really not noticeable, but relationships are always a problem. I explained the beard to James as we sat side by side on the couch in my apartment. He stared at me, then said he had to leave. When I asked about another date, he said that if he wanted to date someone who shaved his face he'd date a guy. Of course it hurt. Of course I cried after he left. But I've heard worse. Women with beards are scary. We cross that line between masculine and feminine. Maybe the men I date figure I'm going to run around hammering nails and fixing toilets and lifting weights and doing all of those stereotypical guy things and make them feel like pussies. Or at least less like guys.

Mr. Chicken lumbers out of Golden Lotus at two-thirty and my employees breathe a collective sigh of relief.

"Can't you call the police on him or something?" says one of the guys who works the drive-through.

I try because I'm not sure what else to do. The dispatcher's "hello" sounds bored and unhelpful but I tell her the story anyway, how there's a man staring at the customers in my restaurant and I'm not sure what to do.

"I'd like to take legal action," I say.

"Is he disturbing the peace?" she says.

"Not really," I say. "He's quiet, but he's making little kids cry."

"We can't do much about that, ma'am," says the dispatcher, "not unless your fat man is trying to eat somebody."

"What am I supposed to do?" I say.

"If he's really fat," she says, "you could sell tickets."

I relay the call to my employees who are not amused. My afternoon is only mildly redeemed because I get to take off work a little early at four so I can make it to my haircut at Hairyette's by six. Even though Hairyette's is two hours away it's worth the drive. My stylist, the only other bearded lady I know, has a beautiful silky brown beard that she keeps neatly trimmed.

"I keep hoping you'll come back with a lovely blonde beard," she says while she shampoos my hair.

"It looks good on you," I say. "It would look silly on me."

"You need to try it," she says, wrapping a towel around my head. "Get used to it."

I tell her about James so she can give me sympathy.

"You have to grow out the beard and then start looking," she says. "Some men love beards. My ex-husband for instance. Now there was a man who always said, 'If I can have a beard, my wife might as well have one, too.'"

"But he's your ex," I say.

"Honey," she says, "there's a lot more to a marriage than facial hair issues."

I nod, but in the end it's too easy to shave every morning and keep myself looking normal. One of my ex-boyfriends suggested electrolysis, but it's too expensive, too painful, and I'm afraid of scarring. I might end up in a worse place than I am already.

I feel better after the haircut at least, good enough to visit Mr. Yamoto and give him the weekly report on the restaurant. Mr. Yamoto owns Golden Lotus, cooked there for a number of years before his joint pain got too bad. He doesn't get out of the apartment much now, weighs about three hundred and fifty pounds, but says he used to be two hundred pounds heavier. He was a sumo wrestler back in Japan, a celebrity, but after he injured his ankle and retired his fan club dissolved, the letters slowed to a trickle. He wallowed in a thick depression for a few months before deciding to come to America. Once he whispered to me that the restaurant saved him.

"Cooking," he says. "That was the answer." He designed the menu to be based around tempura fried foods. Everything is lightly battered and then bathed in hot oil, which explains why many of our regular customers aren't that much smaller than Mr. Chicken, although they are quite a bit nicer.

When I get to Mr. Yamoto's apartment he nods at me, a tiny bow, and invites me in for really strong Japanese coffee. As we sip I tell him I'm not going out with James anymore. Mr. Yamoto turns his coffee cup around in his large hands and shakes his head, tells me I'll find the right person soon enough. He doesn't know about the beard.

I open my mouth to tell him of Mr. Chicken, but I can't. I don't want to whine. I want to show Mr. Yamoto that I can be in control of the restaurant. And getting special attention makes me queasy. So I tell him that the new tempura wasabi mushrooms are selling really well.

"I knew it," says Mr. Yamoto who is always trying to develop odd new menu items.

He pats my hand when I leave and tells me to keep up the good work.

When I open the door to my apartment the air smells heavy and greasy even though I just had a ham sandwich for dinner. I rub my slight chin stubble, the prickly bits that are apparent around this time in the evening. Sometimes I shave twice a day, once in the morning and once after dinner, even if I'm just going to stay home and watch television.

It's reassuring to stand in the bathroom with my electric razor and run my hand over my smooth chin, know that a moment before it had been rough.

Mr. Chicken is back at Golden Lotus the next day, staring at people with a renewed sort of meanness. After he buys his third box of chicken bits I approach his table again.

"Sir," I say, "we value you as a customer but ask you stop staring at people."

Mr. Chicken squints up at me. "If I want to look at other people and have them look at me, what's wrong with that?"

"We do not tolerate hostility toward other customers in this restaurant," I say.

Mr. Chicken harrumphs.

Ten minutes later, when Mr. Chicken is on his second apple turnover, a woman comes up to report that he's been looking at her so intensely that she lost her appetite.

I march back to his table.

"Sir," I say, "I'm going to have to ask you to leave."

"No." He glares at me.

"Sir," I say again, "if you don't leave we may have to resort to more drastic measures."

"Go ahead," he says.

We stare at each other. His eyes are hard and the colour of cocoa. After a few moments I nod at him curtly.

"Very well," I say and troop back behind the counter. Half of my employees are cowering in the break room and worrying over what he is thinking, what he might do, if he looks like the sort of guy who'd drive his car into a fast food restaurant. I tell them that they watch too much television and give myself one more day to think of something before calling Mr. Yamoto.

In the morning I'm running late and don't shave, go through the day with a bit of blonde stubble. I'm a little nervous about it, but the beard is pretty much invisible even to me, the roughness only apparent when I touch my face. During my lunch break I decide to start staring at Mr. Chicken. He wants people to look at him so I do, sit at a table across from his and fold my hands and focus my gaze on his flushed face. He glances at me and then looks away, stares at others who are more willing to become uncomfortable. I rub my stubble as I stare and for once it feels kind of neat, rough and scratchy, mirrors my mood.

The next day I hit the snooze button three too many times, can't do anything but throw on clothes and run out the door, so the stubble stays. It itches a little and is visible if someone is standing really close to me. Mr. Chicken doesn't look at me but seems angrier than usual. I swear he's the reason why five customers get out of line and go to the restaurant next door. While I watch them walk out without buying anything, I decide to grow out my beard. I will make Mr. Chicken stare at me so he won't look at anyone else. I'll shock him, scare him, show him I don't look like everybody else, either, but that doesn't mean I go around and make little kids cry.

This plan seems perfectly brilliant for four hours until I leave work and am standing in line at the grocery and realise that the rest of the world will see my beard, too. I glance from side to side to see who is watching, but the cashier doesn't even give me a second glance.

I have been shaving every day since I was fourteen years old, since the beard started growing and my mother found me in the bathroom rubbing my chin. She screamed and dragged my father in. He showed me how to use an electric razor. My mother bought me one of my own the next day.

"You're already shaving your legs," she sighed. "We'll try not to think of this as being that different."

Mom was always the optimist.

I had friends in high school but never dated. Easier that way. I never wanted anyone looking at me, knew the girls who didn't shave their legs and arms were teased something awful. They didn't care, but I did, fretted constantly about what people would say if they knew I had a beard. When you look like everyone else, you don't really think about how you can stand in a group of people and have no one pay much attention to you. Maybe some days you want to dye your hair pink or wear weird clothing but it's easy to take off, easy to fit in again when you want to. When you need to. It's when you don't look like everyone else that you realise how important it is.

By day four I'm getting used to not shaving even though the beard still isn't that apparent. Every time I reach for my razor I bite my lip, tell myself just one day longer. I've always had a certain pride in being able to conceal my beard, in knowing that nobody's the wiser unless I go out of my way to tell them about it. But it's rarely good when I do. I repeat to myself that maybe my stylist is right and I just need to get used to it.

Mr. Chicken is still averting his gaze from me and making customers uncomfortable. I worry that if my plan doesn't work soon we'll start losing a lot of business to the fast food restaurants on either side of us. We're the only one with fried ice cream and fried wasabi mushrooms, but they aren't worth braving the glare of a fat guy.

After I haven't shaved for a week, my employees are so freaked out that they forget to be scared of Mr. Chicken. I have to call a meeting after the lunch rush and explain it, how the hair started growing when I hit puberty and I've just recently stopped shaving.

"I think it's cool," says one of my female employees.

"It's kind of gross," another mutters.

"I'd date a girl with a beard," says one of the guys, but he's the sort who always brown-noses so I don't know if I can take him seriously.

When Mr. Chicken comes in for lunch I sit one table away and glare at him over my coffee. With the beard slight but apparent he keeps glancing at me, blinking, looking away, looking back. Other customers are looking at me, too, but I hope I'm not as off-putting as Mr. Chicken. No one seems to leave because of me.

After work I go to have a drink at the bar two blocks from my apartment. Part of me wants to try out the beard. The other part really needs a drink. I order a cosmopolitan and sit at the bar watching guys watch me. Because it's a little dim they can't see the beard at first. I know they've spied it when their eyes get wide.

The guy who sits next to me and orders a Guinness is wearing a polo shirt.

"So," he says, "is that a beard or just really good makeup?"

"It's a beard," I say.

"Wow," he says and pauses. "Wow."

This is the extent of our conversation, but to his credit he sits beside me until he's finished his beer. We're both watching the soccer match on the television above the bar.

"Well," he says, "have a good night."

"You, too," I say. I order another cosmopolitan and glance sideways at this group of three guys sitting in a booth at the far wall, whispering and looking over at me every once in a while. I start wondering what kind of guy is going to find a beard attractive on a woman. I could either find the really open-minded ones or the weirdos who think it would be cool to have a bunch of kids with beards.

After a couple more minutes one of the guys from the booth comes over and nods at me. "We really like your beard," he says. "Very well trimmed." He's smiling.

"Thanks," I say and nod. I have no idea whether he's being serious or sarcastic but I've always been terrible at judging such things. The guy returns to his friends and they all look over to me and one of them gives a little wave. I wave back and then watch more soccer. I don't leave the bar until after they've gone. They were probably sincere but I don't feel like taking chances.

At home I wash my face and brush my teeth and wash my face a second time to get out the toothpaste that stuck in the beard. It's an odd sensation to be growing it out. A weight has been lifted. I don't have to hide it anymore. A weight has been added. The way most people look at me now, I might as well have hair growing all over my body.

On my day off I go to Hairyette's for advice on beard maintenance. It's still a little stubby and I have a sort of lumberjack look. My stylist tells me that in another week or two it will look much better, silkier. It just takes patience.

"You may never want to be clean shaven again," she says.

Her clients say the beard suits me, but they are the sort of people who are used to bearded women and probably like the aesthetic.

When I look in the mirror I'm still not sure. I'm getting used to it the way people get used to a new haircut. It looks really strange at first, but somehow starting the beard, having it, makes it easier to keep growing.

Mr. Chicken grimaces the next day when I sit at the table next to him. Customers are now looking at him and me. I'm stealing his limelight. This wasn't what I'd originally intended, but perhaps if Mr. Chicken gets pissed enough, he'll leave my restaurant alone and find someone else to bother.

Even though many of my employees say they don't mind the beard, a week after our chat in the break room, the girl who didn't like the beard quits.

"It isn't about the beard," she says, but she doesn't look at me while she's saying it.

I don't work the register anymore, don't even fill in when we're short, just keep myself in the background except when I go on break and sit next to Mr. Chicken. Some customers smile at me. Others look horrified. Most of those are female. Women are scared of facial hair. We must bleach it or shave it or pull it out. I know that all too well.

When I go to Mr. Yamoto's apartment for my weekly restaurant report I can feel every heartbeat in my fingertips. He opens the door and smiles then frowns then cocks his head.

"New look?" he says and steps to the side so I can walk in. I explain how I've always had facial hair but kept it shaved. Mr. Yamoto plops gracefully in a pea green overstuffed chair.

"You don't think it will make the restaurant lose business?" he says. "It might prove distracting to customers."

"Or it might bring them in," I say with a hopeful smile even though it's a dumb idea.

Mr. Yamoto deepens his frown.

"I'm staying in the background, really," I say. "The employees aren't bothered by the beard. I've never grown it out before. I want to try this."

"Can't you try it when you have a week's vacation?" he says.

"It's not a problem for anyone," I lie. "Really."

Mr. Yamoto folds his thick hands together and looks down at them for a moment.

"I'll have to think about this," he says. "It's a restaurant and appearance is important."

"Okay," I say, "okay."

Mr. Yamoto is a believer in consistency, you have to be if you own a restaurant, so I'm glad he's giving me a chance. If I hadn't been working for him for so long I know he'd make me shave it off without a second thought.

The following day, Mr. Chicken and Mr. Yamoto arrive at almost the same time. They both order a box of chicken bits and sit with two tables between them.

I go out to speak with Mr. Yamoto when I take my break.

"I haven't been down to the restaurant for a time," he says. "I wanted to see how things were doing." Meaning he wanted to see how people were reacting to me.

Mr. Chicken is glaring at both of us, his angry eyes boring holes into our table. All attention in the restaurant is focused on us—the former sumo wrestler and the bearded lady—and away from him. After a few minutes Mr. Chicken stands and plods to the counter. He's there an awfully long time. When he returns he's carrying two trays, both towers of cardboard boxes. It's more food than he usually eats—eight boxes of chicken bits, four fish sandwiches, three apple turnovers, three cherry turnovers, three sides of wasabi mushrooms, three cartons of spicy onion rings, six fried ice creams. Mr. Chicken unfolds a napkin with a snap of his wrist, lays it across his lap, and starts eating, really eating, cramming chicken bits and onions rings and mushrooms into his mouth with his fat hands at such a rate I wonder if he's even chewing. Everyone is staring at him—me and Mr. Yamoto and all of the employees and all of the customers and it's so disgusting and so fascinating no one can look away. He rips the turnovers and stuffs half in each cheek, eats the fried ice cream in three large bites, smearing food across his face. We're all gaping, can smell the cloud of sweat and grease around his body.

I don't know how long it takes Mr. Chicken to finish everything. Maybe two minutes, maybe five or ten. It feels like a really long and really short period of time and there is complete silence in the restaurant. No one is placing any orders. No one else is even eating. We're all just staring. When Mr. Chicken has finished everything and there is just a pile of boxes on his two trays, he wipes his mouth with a napkin, stands up, and promptly throws up everything on the golden tile floor.

We're still staring.

Mr. Chicken plops back down and starts crying, his mouth gaping in soundless sobs.

Half of my employees run for gallons of ammonia and bleach and mops.

Mr. Yamoto stands up and walks around Mr. Chicken's table, touches his shoulder, and it may be my imagination but I think Mr. Chicken leans toward him slightly. Mr. Yamoto daubs Mr. Chicken's eyes very gently with a grease-stained paper napkin.

I finger my beard. It is starting to become silkier as it gets longer, the hairs not so short and hard. I don't know how long I'll keep it, probably shave it off eventually, but for now it feels kind of nice.

Cyclops

Usually cyclops babies don't live very long. This is why you never hear about them, why the cyclops woman is the only one to have reached thirty. Two people besides her parents know she has just one eye—the family ophthalmologist and the midwife who delivered her in her parents' bedroom. Her mother wanted to keep the process as natural as possible, worried about strange things drugs were supposed to do to newborn babies.

The cyclops woman's father makes her wear a shade, a crescent-shaped sunglasses lens that fits around her head, so the world looks a little dark to her. Her father's world is also getting darker. His glaucoma is worsening and the ophthalmologist says he'll be blind in a matter of months. He won't stop working, though. At the counter of Drogo's, the family coffee shop, he explains to customers that his daughter wears the shade because she has a condition that makes her extremely sensitive to light.

"I think it's very becoming," says Cynthia Liss, one of the regulars. She says the eyes are the most intimate part of the body and the shade lends an air of mystery like Japanese women with their fans.

The cyclops woman thinks the shade makes her look like a washed-up Hollywood starlet that happens to be working at the family coffee shop.

Her father boasts that Drogo's is the only coffee shop in the world with a reliquary. Drogo is the patron saint of coffee house keepers and unattractive people. His finger and six eyelashes rest across from the counter in a tiny glass coffin etched with gold curlicues. The coffin is attached to the wall and surrounded by a big gilded frame. The finger looks like a piece of beef jerky, and the eyelashes could be anybody's, but some of the regular customers make a habit of touching the coffin every time they enter. Cynthia Liss leaves small offerings—dime store rings, single fingers cut from gloves, and red nail polish because she says red is the most Catholic colour. On Drogo's feast day, April 16th, the cyclops woman's father has her festoon the frame with ribbon.

He brought the finger and eyelashes back from a trip to Belgium three months before he opened the coffee shop. At least once a month he stands behind the counter and tells the story of how he found them in a little apothecary shop in Brussels. He says, "The apothecary whispered to me that Drogo's finger had been taken from St. Martin's in Sebourg, where Drogo died and where the rest of his relics are kept. That old man said Drogo's finger had worked miracles for others who had come into his shop. It had made an old woman's gnarled hands straight, a little boy's deaf ear hear, a dog's lame foot strong."

When her father finishes the story, he nods and smiles at the cyclops woman. She smiles back, knows he bought the finger hoping it would manifest a miracle, give her a second eye. When that didn't work it became an attraction. Sometimes she wonders exactly how her father looked when he walked into the apothecary shop, if the way he squinted at objects suggested he had the loose wallet of a desperate man. Other times she figures that if she is a cyclops woman with brethren who taunted Odysseus, surely the finger could have belonged to a saint.

There are little cards with Drogo's picture and biography next to the gilded frame and customers can buy them for a dollar. The picture is a painting really, a man with a huge nose, uneven lips, and eyes looking in different directions, a man Dali would have loved. The cyclops woman reads Drogo's biography every night even though she's memorized it, how he was the son of a Flemish nobleman whose mother died when he was born. When he grew older he became obsessed with the idea that he'd killed her, so he sold everything he owned and became a shepherd and a hermit and made nine pilgrimages to Rome. Later he contracted an odd disease that made him very ugly, and he spent the rest of his life living on barley bread and warm water. People said he was able to bilocate, be in two places at once, tending sheep and attending Mass. The Cyclops woman wonders if that is true with his remains as well, if he actually has twenty fingers, twenty toes, four eyes, and two noses roaming the world. She cleans the fingerprints off Drogo's finger's glass coffin every night. The cyclops woman knows the finger well, all its joints and creases, and likes it in the way that people like something because it is familiar.

At night the cyclops woman's mother frets over the books, how the small shop is barely keeping afloat even with the reliquary. Her father claims Drogo is why they're still in business. The cyclops woman has been watching his latest ritual, how he stands in front of the finger before the shop opens and after it closes. She wonders how fast the glaucoma is progressing. The family ophthalmologist says she has the same disease, but he doesn't know how long it will be before she is blind. It could be a year, five years, ten. She worries what will happen to her family when neither she nor her father can see. The shop isn't making enough to hire extra help. Her father wants to keep working in the store, despite his impairment.

"I'm perfectly fine," he says. "Not blind yet. I can tell how much coffee is in the cup."

"You're getting steam burns from the espresso machine," says the cyclops woman.

"I am not," says her father, but she watches him run his hands under cold water for a few minutes in-between customers, wincing. She knows he is moving slow, trying not to bump into things. He misses the counter when giving a customer her coffee. The cup shatters on the floor, sloshes hot liquid behind the register.

"It slipped out of my hand," he hisses to his daughter while she gets another cup of coffee and helps her mother pick up the ceramic shards.

At dinner he reaches for the salt and pepper shakers and knocks both over.

The cyclops woman's mother bites her lip.

"I don't know what we're going to do about the finances," she whispers.

"What we've always done," says the cyclops woman's father. "We're going to sell coffee and get a business loan to tide us over."

"I want to go on the road," says the cyclops woman.

Both her parents stare.

"Talk shows," she says, "book deals, maybe a movie. People will pay to see me."

"You will do no such thing," her father says, stabbing his meatloaf. "That is what we've worked to help you avoid. Nothing good comes of that sort of fame."

"But it would be easy," says the cyclops woman. "We'd be set forever."

"I will not have my daughter prostituting herself," says her father. "I'd rather go on welfare."

"I'm not stripping in front of people," says the cyclops woman.

"You're not taking off your shade," says her father. "You can't know what would happen after that."

"You can't either," says the cyclops woman.

"What if doctors got hold of you," says her father, "and you spent the rest of your life with needles in your arms and a tube up your rear?"

The cyclops woman's mother doesn't say anything, just puts her hand over her mouth.

The cyclops woman decides to let her father think he's won for the time being. They all keep chewing. She knows she won't let her family go on the public dole.

That night she lies in bed and dreams her usual dream about serving coffee at the counter when a customer snatches her shade away. She stands there blinking her one eye. Sometimes nobody notices and sometimes everyone does, but it is pleasant to feel the cool air on her eye, not to have it closed behind the stuffy sunglasses lens.

In the morning the cyclops woman's mother has a headache. She has been complaining of headaches more often lately and the cyclops woman knows it is because of stress. The cyclops woman's head hurts sometimes, too, and she finds herself squinting more, getting eyestrain. She knows the vision loss, the blurriness, will only progress until the day there is nothing. No black. No white. As if she'd never had an eye to begin with. When she cleans the glass on Drogo's coffin that night she reads the information card for the five thousandth time and feels sorry for Drogo for the five thousandth time. He endured so much pain, so much misery, so much sacrifice, and his mother was still dead.

The cyclops woman finds the key to the locked glass cabinet. Her father thinks no one but him knows it is hidden behind the counter in a five-year-old box of Earl Grey tea. She opens the glass case and touches the finger with her small hand. It feels hard and leathery, like it sat in the sun for centuries. She thinks she feels a slight warmth and a slight pain in her own fingers, stands there for a moment with that warm ache before locking the case again. The cyclops woman sits against the wall and slips the shade off her head, stares at her hand. It seems to be glowing slightly.

Because she knows her father would never agree to it, the cyclops woman and Drogo's finger leave at three-thirty in the morning after she makes a few phone calls, packs a bag, and tells her mother her plan. Her mother nods and takes a couple aspirin.

"Everything will be fine after your father stops having a tantrum," she says.

At first the cyclops woman figures she'll be gone for a couple of weeks, travelling to a few coffee shops several hours away, displaying Drogo and charging a small fee to touch him and buy an information card. The coffee shops she called were a bit sceptical, but agreed when she said she wouldn't charge them for the display and she'd work the counters if things got busy.

In Indianapolis the cyclops woman stands beside Drogo, her shade in place, reciting the story of his life until she is hoarse. She is tired and her hands ache from the long drive, but Drogo's finger looks content in its temporary new home, a clear glass jewellery box she bought for five dollars and lined with red velvet. Coffee shop patrons gladly ante their dollars to touch the finger for ten seconds, pay an extra buck for a Polaroid snapshot beside the relic. Some people mutter that it looks like a piece of beef jerky and they're certain they can smell pickling spices. Others say they feel a slight heat or ache or calmness after rubbing the first digit. The cyclops woman smiles and adjusts her shade. A young acne-stricken reporter from the local paper comes to do a story for the religion page.

"There aren't very many touring relics," she says.

"I guess not," says the cyclops woman.

The reporter says, "His mother died?"

"He never got over it," says the cyclops woman. She thinks of her own mother at the cash register trying to ring up customers and keep her father calm as he rants about the missing finger and mistakenly pours scalding coffee over his hands instead of into a mug.

"Those are neat sunglasses," says the reporter.

The Indiana coffee shop owners are an elderly couple who let the cyclops woman spend a few nights on their uncomfortable couch. She wants to take the shade off when she goes to sleep but thinks the better of it.

"I have a disease that makes me sensitive to light," she tells them at breakfast, her back still aching from the flat couch cushions.

"That's some finger," says the old man, spreading marmalade on his toast.

"Once I thought I saw a vision of the Virgin in some sugar I spilled on the floor," says the old woman.

The cyclops woman does not like the endless black cord of road. She does not like peeing in gas station bathrooms, eating peanut butter sandwiches two meals a day because she wants to live on the cheap, sleeping in her car when she can't find anyone to loan her their couch for a night. In the morning she neatens herself best she can in fast food restaurant restrooms, wets her comb and ties her hair back into a neat bun before driving to the next venue. Many of them are tiny places like the ones her father owns, coffee shops where the owners are struggling and sympathetic, eager to try any new scheme as long as it's free. She stays three or four days at each, long enough for word of mouth to get out and for the crowd of sceptical and curious visitors to be exhausted. Many people compliment her on her shade. Half of them ask where they can get one before asking her to snap a photo of them standing beside Drogo.

The cyclops woman keeps her arm tense and ready at her side, wondering and worrying and almost hoping that someone will try to snatch off the shade. Sometimes she puts her hand on the black half-moon lens, her fingers tugging gently, wanting both to greet and prevent revelation. In the end she keeps it on because worrying over the consequences, the might-bes, gives her a headache. She could be invited on all the talk shows, or doctors could cut her up and put parts of her in test tubes.

She calls home twice a week to tell her parents of her travels.

Her mother says the touring finger has made the local news and business has increased in the shop. More people are visiting the six eyelashes still safe in the glass case across from the counter. The cyclops woman's travel-weary body aches less to hear of her successes. Then her father gets on the phone.

"You need to come home," he yells so loudly that she has to hold the receiver away from her ear. "How is Drogo? Have you taken off your shade?"

"No," she says. "Dad, don't worry. This is going to save us. I'm keeping the shade on and keeping close track of Drogo."

"I just know someone is going to steal him," says her father.

"We'll both be home soon," she says, "and things will get better. Business will pick up. This is just the sort of attention the shop needs."

"People are wondering when the finger will be back," her father mutters. "Six eyelashes just don't cut it."

In San Francisco people start claiming to have visions after touching Drogo's finger. They imagine themselves in multiple, having divided like a cell.

"I could knit a scarf from both ends," says one elderly woman.

"I could play golf with myself," says a middle-aged man.

"I could hold twice as many ice cream cones," says a pudgy kid.

The cyclops woman tilts her head. No one ever had visions in her father's coffee shop. Maybe they just weren't attracting the right crowd. But her father never let anyone touch Drogo. Every night the cyclops woman runs a slim finger over Drogo and notices his wrinkles are a little less deep. Drogo is wearing away. The cyclops woman bites her lip and tells herself that she is imagining the change. But she thinks of her own bones, if they will exist like this after she is gone. Even now, what would people see if they touched her? What sorts of visions might erupt after they gazed into her single eye? She wants to know. She doesn't want to know.

The cyclops woman holds her breath as patrons whisper prayers to the finger, asking for the wart to be removed from their big toe, the bald patch on their scalp to fill in, their right arm to grow an inch so it's the same length as their left, their lips to get a little fuller, their hair to be straightened. They peer in wall mirrors or tiny compacts dug from the bottom of purses, wrinkle their noses at their too-freckled, bushy-eyebrowed, eyes-too-close-together faces. The cyclops woman squints at them, those who decree themselves unlovely, and knows that no one would look at them twice in a crowd.

After four months, two weeks, and five days on the road, the cyclops woman drives home from Orlando, twenty hours straight, because she just wants to get back. She arrives at three in the morning, her body cramped and car-weary. Her father appears at the front door. He has always been a light sleeper, probably heard the car engine. His face glows red in the streetlamp light.

"I'm home," she calls from the driveway.

"I'm sure you were discovered," he yells. "I'm sure someone knows about you now and they'll come pounding on our door tomorrow."

The cyclops woman walks closer and sees how her father grips the doorframe too tight, how his legs waver, how his eyes focus somewhere over her head.

She takes off her shade.

"It finally worked," she says. "I have two eyes now. I don't have to hide."

"Really?" he says. For a moment she sees a glow in his vacant stare. Then his eyes dull again.

"Don't lie to me," he says.

"How do you know I'm lying," she says, "you can't see."

"Of course I can see you," says her father. "I'm fine."

"Fine," says the cyclops woman.

"I don't want you working at the shop anymore," he says. "It's too much of a risk."

"Don't be silly," says the cyclops woman.

"You shouldn't have gone," he yells, his hand shaking against the doorframe.

"We have more business, don't we?" says the cyclops woman.

Her father marches back inside.

The cyclops woman goes back to her car, grabs Drogo's box from the passenger seat, stomps in after her father.

"He wouldn't let me tell you he was getting worse," her mother whispers later. "And he kept telling me he was fine, but then he'd miss the door and bump into a wall."

"But I should have been home," says the cyclops woman, smacking her hand against the kitchen table. "He should have been able to see me just a little longer."

"The tour was going so well," says her mother. "I didn't want to tell you, didn't want to upset you. There was nothing you could have done if you had come home. We needed those articles in the papers. We're doing better now."

The cyclops woman grimaces as she watches her father walk down the hallway, his fingertips skimming the wall until they hit the doorframe and he turns into his bedroom.

In her dream the cyclops woman is beside her father in the coffee shop, removes her shade and has sprouted another eye.

"It worked," she says. "Drogo worked."

"No, he didn't," says her father.

The cyclops woman holds her shade and knows in the end this miracle didn't matter. Her father can't see both her eyes. And now that she has two of them, they are both going blind.

Before the shop opens in the morning, the cyclops woman rests Drogo's finger back in its glass case, the creases worn smooth. Cynthia Liss and a few other regulars are standing at the front door, anxious for the shop to open. There will be more customers for a while, but the cyclops woman wonders how long it will last. Will people keep coming when her father is blind? When she is blind? Four months on the road was not enough. But maybe there isn't anything that would be enough. She thinks of her father at home trying violently to see and knocking into the kitchen table. There is more money in the family bank account and her mother bought her father a new white cane he is refusing to touch. The cyclops woman knows he will use it in time, just as in time he will be less angry with her. She locks Drogo's glass case and imagines how Cynthia would beam if she knew the cyclops woman was a cyclops woman. She imagines the gifts Cynthia would bring—single contacts, bottles of mascara, eyeshadow in every colour of the rainbow.

Outside the customers press their fingers against the glass, leave temporary smears the cyclops woman will have to wash off in the evening. Her eye hurts as she squints at them through her shade. The world is blurrier than it was before she left. She will have to remove the black lens eventually. It will not be a choice. Now she is simply prolonging that moment, that revelation. Maybe she will wait until she can no longer see faces.

Snakes

They are slim and brown and look like dreadlocks. The longest ones trail halfway down my back. I wrap a scarf around the snakes and tie a loose knot to keep them in a ponytail and out of the way, especially when I'm bartending. They can't be close to the half-empty beer glasses because they'll get drunk if I let them. When I'm not paying attention they try to sip beer on the sly. The snakes and their tiny primal brains are connected to my instincts, my subconscious, so I can't always control what they do. They're like seventy-eight little siblings. I love them, but they're annoying.

"Am I going to turn to stone?" slurs one guy at the bar after polishing off his fourth gin and tonic in an hour.

I give him a granite stare, say that he's reached his limit and I'm cutting off his booze. If someone hadn't come up with that turn-to-stone bullshit, I would have been able to get a better job, maybe in a high-end retail store, and not have to work two part-time gigs. Understand that I'm bitter.

Tips have been bad tonight, which doesn't improve my mood. I'm hoping to make enough this week to finish paying down my credit card bill. Between tending bar and shelving books at the library I can get by, but the tips give me a little room to breathe and buy a couple chocolate bars at the grocery.

It's April, a rainy night, and I have to walk home. The snakes don't like getting wet, and when they're too cold or warm I get a headache. My car gave out six months ago and it wasn't worth repairing, but winter was hell. I had to walk around with a big fleece head wrap that kept the snakes warm enough for the ten-minute walks from my apartment to the bar and the library.

I budget as I walk, figure this month I'll have just enough. So much for the credit card bill. Last year I was optimistic about the future, bought a new couch, then I had to get the brakes and heater on my car replaced. A waste of money since it died a few months later.

I'm also paying for one class a semester at the college, which means no new car soon, just books and tuition. I want to get a degree in biology and a job doing plant research. I like studying cells and reproduction, started taking classes four years ago, but I'm only a sophomore. I remind myself I don't have to be in a hurry to finish, but it feels like I'm not going anywhere. I don't want to quit my jobs and get student loans and end up paralyzed by debt I might not be able to pay off. A couple friends of mine who work at the bar tell me every night how they're never going to be in the black.

"Just because you go to college doesn't mean you'll have a great career," Katie says. She has a degree in history and fifty thousand dollars in loans. Before I got the job at the library and just worked at the bar, I was really scrimping. Ran up two credit cards in the process. Every night my snakes got headaches as I thought about the bills I couldn't pay off. I don't want to be in that position again.

But night after night I collapse in my apartment, too tired to study because I've been working all day, but if I don't study I won't be able to pass my classes and get a degree that might win me a better job (though Katie is quick to remind me it's not guaranteed). Tonight I have reading homework for my Greek mythology class. (It's one of my electives. I took it because I hoped I could dispel a couple myths, mostly ones about me.)

My upstairs neighbours have decided to throw one of their parties. I have to be up at eight, and it sounds like my ceiling is about to give because of the boozy thumping. I stomp to the second floor and feel like a crotchety old woman, but dammit, I need to get work done. Intoxicated people loll out the apartment door. One of my upstairs neighbours (there are two guys and a girl) wavers towards me, stepping over a couple of bodies.

"Would you keep it down," I say. "I have to work in the morning."

"Sure thing," she says. She's wasted. I hear someone vomit.

Back in my apartment I still can't concentrate, decide I might as well sleep, but I have to lie in bed with a pillow over my head. I want to break the damn lease and move because all the other people in the building are twenty-something college students whose parents are paying for their degrees. They could care less about studying. But this is the cheapest apartment I could find that's within walking distance of both my jobs. I don't have extra money, can only hold the pillow more tightly over my head. The snakes lean against the wall, feel the vibrations from the partygoers upstairs.

My snakes are cranky in the morning, nip at each other as I dress and wash my face. I give them bits of toast and grape jelly. They nibble pieces out of my fingers but are still in a sour mood, so I buy a double mocha for us on the way to work. Whatever they eat goes into the rest of me, whether it's toast or coffee or mosquitoes, but I only taste what I put into my own mouth. By the time I get to the library my snakes are so hyped up on caffeine they bump into the big glass door at the entrance, reminding me why I don't give them coffee too often. When my snakes get nicked or squeezed it hurts like hell.

In the afternoon I go to City Park to help the Garden Society with our annual weeding and planting. Being outside cheers me a bit, and it cheers my snakes because they get to eat the little bugs that circle my head. I love plants but can't have many in my apartment because there's too little light and not enough room.

I scare new Garden Society members, older ladies who are nice enough when they get to know me, but sometimes it takes a while for them to be cordial. It helps if I keep the snakes mostly covered by a big kerchief. The ladies and I have plenty to chat about since we all love plants and have to budget carefully. We all have low incomes so we're the same sort of almost-desperate, get exactly enough money to survive each month, our hands clenched around every dollar. We all pray nothing will go wrong and force us to pay more money that we don't have.

On Wednesdays my Garden Society friend Violet takes me grocery shopping. She knows I don't have a car, and she's happy to give me rides. Wednesday is senior day so she gets fifteen percent off everything.

"My oldest girl wants me to move into one of those assisted living places," she says, "but they're so expensive. I want to stay in my apartment. It's pricey enough."

I sigh. "My rent just went up. I don't know how I'm going to balance that and my class fees and books. I can't take time off work and just go to school."

Last night my friend Katie was complaining about her debt again, saying that if she'd known she wouldn't be able to do much with a bachelor's degree in history she wouldn't have gotten it in the first place.

"Now I have to worry about car payments and house payments and kid payments," she says. Katie and her boyfriend just had a son, and children don't come cheap.

Too many people who frequent the bar have student loans they've been supporting for ten years, which is part of the reason they want to drown their worries in beer. I can't end up like that. I have to think about the stress I'd be causing myself and the snakes. I have to keep plugging away at my coursework. At both jobs. At my lingering credit card debt. But every time I push the stone up the hill, it rolls back down.

My Greek mythology class meets on Thursday nights. The prof is an older guy. At first I thought he was nice, but when I stopped by his office to discuss my paper on how Odysseus was a total jerk, my prof asked if I wanted to chat about our course readings over drinks.

"I didn't think they let students and professors do that," I said.

"It would be strictly academic," he said, "just in a more relaxed environment."

I told him I'd think about it.

Tonight in class he asks my opinion on the story of Orpheus and the Greek concept of the afterlife. I hate how he acts like I'm an authority on everything Greek, mumble something about the River Styx and Charon and how I picture him as a surly New York cabdriver. My prof nods and smiles and says that's a very interesting idea. The other students roll their eyes.

"Are you fucking him or something?" mutters the guy who sits beside me.

This rankles my snakes. They start hissing, which turns the heads of everyone who wasn't already staring at me. Shit. I slide down in my seat and leave right after class, before my prof can ask my opinion on anything else. I paid hard-earned money to take this course, and I'd drop it if I could afford to take the loss, but I'm financially committed to a creep for the rest of the semester.

I complain about him to Violet when we tend the City Park gardens on Monday.

"He sounds like my ex-husband," she says. "He was a bastard and a flirt besides. Do you know if this professor of yours is married?"

"Don't think so," I say because I haven't seen him wearing a wedding band, but sometimes people take those off if they want to give the appearance of singlehood. I work in a bar so I know all the tricks.

"Just keep away from him," she says. "No private meetings in his office."

I nod. I'm careful not to let him catch me alone, though it won't do anything to relieve my in-class embarrassment.

After our gardening session Violet drives me to the store so I can buy bread and milk, then she drops me off at my apartment. I grab my sacks from the back seat and Violet closes the car door for me, but she doesn't notice that one of my snakes is in the way.

The pain in my head is excruciating. I'm glad I can't see the blood.

"My sweet Lord," Violet says, grabbing a hankie from her purse and wrapping it around the end of the decapitated snake. "Doctor or vet?" she yells, shaking my shoulder.

"Vet," I say, almost woozy from the pain.

The next half hour blurs. I wish someone would cut off my head along with the snake's. The vet only has to use a local anaesthetic, but it knocks me out.

I wake up sitting in a padded chair in the vet's office, listening to dogs barking in the next room. Violet sits beside me, twisting a clean hankie in her fingers.

"Oh goodness," she says. "How do you feel? I'm so sorry."

My head doesn't hurt, feels like it's full of lead marbles. The vet called my doctor and explained the situation. My doctor called a prescription for Valium in to the pharmacy.

The vet had to remove the snake at its base and put in a few stitches. She says I'll have to be off work for a few days to give the wound time to heal. I want to protest, say I can't afford to be away from my jobs that long, but the anaesthetic makes my tongue thick.

A nurse gives me a small cardboard box containing what's left of my snake. It's wrapped in a little baggie, the kind they use for pets that have been put to sleep. I stare down at the box and get weepy again. Violet pats my shoulder until I've exhausted my tears, then she drives me to her apartment and has me lie down on her bed. She says she'll pay for my medical bills.

"But it was just an accident," I say. I think of that little cardboard box, my lost snake, and start weeping again. Violet hugs me. I don't have names for all my snakes, but there were seventy-eight of them and now there are only seventy-seven. The remaining ones will be traumatized.

Lying on Violet's bed with a glass of ginger ale on the table beside me, I ask woozy questions. If a snake got cut off at the base, near my skull, would it die or just grow a new tail? Could the snakes exist independently of me? My snakes have been injured, my snakes have received small cuts, but none of them have died before. Maybe I'm a burden to them. Maybe they don't want to be attached to my head, forced to breathe smoke every evening at the bar. Maybe they'd be happier writhing around in the City Park gardens, eating bugs on their own accord, not subject to my whims and part-time jobs.

I take more pills when the pain rises in my head. Violet brings me toast and eggs and sandwiches and meatloaf. The snakes and I don't feel like eating. I can feel their sorrow, their confusion. They nip at each other, upset because they don't know what to make of the floaty feeling we all have from the Valium.

Violet tells the Garden Society ladies about the accident and they send cards. Some bring casseroles and small potted plants to her apartment. I smile and try to thank them, but it's difficult. The snakes and I are too depressed and dopey because of the painkillers. That haze quells some of our sadness, at least for now, but I have too much time to think. I have a responsibility to my snakes, these seventy-seven living things on my head. I have to make sure they are safe and healthy, but sometimes I don't know how to best care for them. It makes me a little mad; I didn't ask to be given these snakes, but now I have them and I have to negotiate that.

My snakes are like little kids. Defenceless.

The Garden Society ladies come to Violet's apartment for a meeting, cluster around my bed and chat in quiet voices. We mourn with Olivia—she's in a rental agreement she can't break but her apartment is so full of dust it's making her allergies worse. No amount of sweeping seems to help. So many of us Garden Society members are in that situation, a state of trapped. We have fixed lives—fixed incomes, fixed rental agreements, fixed expenses—and none of us can break out. We feel hopeless. Like there are no good options.

My prof leaves messages on the answering machine at my apartment (how did he get my number?) wondering why I was absent from class and saying he missed me and he hopes he didn't do anything to make me upset. It's too creepy.

After a week of recovery I go back to work, still grieving.

Rick, one of the bouncers who's always trying to hit on me, asks if I'd like to come back to his apartment for a nightcap and a backrub.

"I know you lost one of . . ." he touches his head. "Maybe I could help you feel better."

I stare at him so hard he's perfectly still for a moment. "You have no fucking clue," I say.

"You could tell me how you feel at my place," he says.

I slam an empty plastic pretzel bowl against the counter. It breaks in two. Rick steps back. "You have no fucking clue," I say again.

He doesn't bother me for the rest of the evening.

The snakes weigh my head down, literally and physically. Tonight they are heavy with confusion. Drunk people depress me further. I can't wait to leave the bar. My snakes drink beer out of near-empty glasses when I'm not looking. I'm toasted by the time I get off work, barely have it in me to walk home and flop on the couch. I'm mad at my snakes, prefer to medicate with chocolate, but they want booze. I go to the bathroom but can't throw up, peer at myself in the mirror, and freeze for a moment because I look like shit. The snakes loll around my head. My eyes are dark, sunken, drunk.

That's what makes me puke.

It's better that way. Gets all the toxins out of my system. I rinse my mouth with warm water. I have to get away from the bar. I can't let my snakes fall to temptation and develop some chemical dependency. They don't have my willpower. I need to give them a better life than bartending and book sorting, but that means quitting my jobs, going to school full-time.

That will be heavy financially. I worry it will be hard on my snakes, give them more headaches, but I'm so tired of all those long nights and the turn-to-stone cracks from drunk people. When I call Violet and tell her about the decision, she is pleased and worried.

"Just don't take on too much, dear," she says.

Too much debt. Too much stress. Too many dreams of the millions of ways my life will improve after I get a degree. I know nothing is guaranteed.

When I tell Katie about my decision, she says I'm crazy.

"Stick with what you've got," she says. "It's better than debt. You can sleep at night. I've given up on anything more, just need a paycheque to feed myself and my kid. The hell you know is better than the hell you don't."

She makes sense, speaks to my worries. She was the first in her family to go to college, to try and lift herself out of a blue-collar existence, but right now the important thing is paying bills. That's what it comes down to. Food on the table. Keeping the gas and electric going.

I'm trying to muster the courage to put in my two weeks' notice at both my jobs on the night I return to my Greek mythology class. My prof is fine for the first hour, but then he asks me if I think the Minotaur is connected to the Greeks conception of primal male desires. Everyone snickers.

"Sir," I say after class, "the only thing I know about Greek mythology is that I don't turn people into stone."

My prof nods and smiles. "It's very interesting how the stories get twisted," he says. "Perhaps we could discuss this over dinner sometime."

"Isn't that a little improper?" I say.

"It's not strange for exceptional students like you," he says.

"I don't think I'm exceptional," I say, "at least in the studenting part." I turn to load my books into my backpack. I bet he wants a trophy girlfriend to show off to all the other Greek scholars at the next conference. No one could best him by dating a siren.

"But you're really something," he says, putting his hand on the small of my back.

I don't tell my snakes to bite my prof, but I don't stop them. In that second when I let them attack, I firm my commitment to go to school full-time next semester. I wouldn't have let them bite him three weeks ago. I cared too much about my grade. About those three credits. But I can't do this stupid balancing act anymore. I have to make the jump. I don't know if I'll land in a soft place. I don't know if jumping is the best thing to do. But I'll have a lot of time to think about it while I'm in the air.

My snakes get my prof on the arm. They have very small teeth, so the wound is more of a pinch than a bite, but they have strong jaws.

"Aack," he screams.

I pivot.

He clutches his wrist. "Are they poisonous?"

"No," I say, "they're little garden snakes. You'll be fine."

"But you'd be immune to your own poison," he says.

"They're not poisonous," I say.

He runs out of the room, yelling for a doctor.

I roll my eyes, load my Greek mythology text into my backpack, and feel the caress of two of my snakes against my arm. I rub a finger over their heads. Sweet little guys.

My feet aren't as granite heavy as they were when I walked into the classroom tonight. That weight has been transformed into the weight of my backpack, the weight of books, the weight of things I need to learn. I hunch forward a bit while I'm walking, but at least I can move.

Seventeen Episodes in the Life of a Giant
(or, Ruminations on My Garbage Can)

Cellophane wrappers from two packages of shoelaces.

I'm twenty-seven years old, eight feet six inches tall, might be the world's third or fourth or fifth tallest woman but I don't care to know. My shoes are so big that a single lace won't do, so I have to tie two together. The laces always break because I pull too hard, so sometimes Mom ties them for me. I toss the wrappers in the trash on top of Mom's banana peel. She eats a banana every day at breakfast. I take out the garbage on Mondays just as the peels are beginning to stink.

After breakfast but before I go to work at the stationery store, I finish writing my will. There isn't much to it since I don't have much stuff—books and clothes and records because I fell in love with vinyl at a young age. Mom is worried anyway.

"I don't want you to think about things like that." She uses her stern voice, practising for the day ahead like she often does at eight in the morning. Mom teaches elementary art, spends her time plying children with crayons and markers and tempera paint.

I say, "I want to make sure everything is secure. I want to make sure it all goes to you."

"You don't need to," says my mother, "you'll be around a long time. At least if you stop thinking like this."

I keep writing. Giants usually go early, in their thirties or forties, from heart disease. I have the same circulation problems my father did, my hands and feet always feel cold, and I'm only five years younger than he was when he died. I have a physical twice every year and the doctor says I'm fine, but I never quite trust him.

I walk to the stationery store because it's only three blocks away and it's hard for me to fit in cars. Mom has a minivan, one with the front passenger seat removed so I can sit on the bench in the middle and fit my legs where the front seat would have been. It's still a bit awkward, and she has to help me out so I don't stumble. At the store I'm on my knees most of the day and direct customers from the register. Clerking on my knees hurts after a while, even with the foam pad I keep behind the counter, but I don't like standing up in the store. Some people still come in just to see me. Most try to be discrete, but teenagers snicker and ask why I don't play basketball. I am always very polite, very kind, even to rude people. I've won the employee-of-the-month award eight times in the past year and a half, which is a record though there are just four employees.

Around noon the guy who works at the rent-to-own place three doors down comes in for paperclips. He does this every day, says he needs them for the store, but they can't use that many. The rent-to-own guy is six feet tall. Around my age. He gives me a tiny smile when I hand him his change. Some days I think he's sweet. Some days I think he's creepy.

"Hi," I say, "how are you?"

"Fine," he says.

I make small talk so he has an opportunity to ask me out to lunch, but he never does. It's amusing to see his cheeks flush and his pupils widen. I think he's attracted to me more than curious, but it's hard to tell. No one has ever asked me on a date, though I am terribly kind.

Bakery bag, slightly damp with used coffee grounds, containing two-day-old French bread crumbs.

After work I stop at the bakery. Mothers stare. Kids point. I smile down at them and say hello, ask if they are having a nice day. The girl I have a crush on waits on me. I like the bakery, but come here often because of her. She's petite and in her early thirties. I ask for a baguette, watch her hands as she chooses one from the rack and slides it into a long paper sack. Her hands are small and I know she has good muscles from working with trays of cookies and cakes and rolls and bread. I want her to knead my shoulders.

"Thanks," I say when she gives me the bread. It's what I always say. Dumb. I'm too tired to converse. One problem with being a giant is bouts of weakness. It's hard for a large body to be strong all the time. Some nights Mom helps me take off my socks.

Empty bottle of acetaminophen (my mother believes in buying generic drugs).

I take painkillers every evening because my knees ache. The number of bottles in the trashcan is embarrassing, but I need at least four pills for them to have any effect. Mom says Dad was the same way. He was almost nine feet tall. My mother is five foot three. They met when he modeled for her college life drawing class. The instructor felt that having a larger-than-life model would somehow help his students see details.

BEARDED WOMEN

For a while my parents didn't think my father could conceive. It was a glandular issue. As my mom says, my father's member was not to scale with the rest of his body. But, if it had been properly sized, it wouldn't have been possible for the right parts to fit in the right places.

My father died when I was two, before my size was clear. In all his pictures he looks a little sad. Dad was the world's fourth or fifth or sixth tallest man—not good enough for record books, but good enough for ads. He did promotions for sports equipment and pants and breakfast cereals, squirrelled away money in stocks and bonds and savings accounts. Sometimes people drove by the house to take pictures of him doing normal things—weeding the garden or washing the car. Once he stood by the trashcan for half an hour posing for passes-by, a freakish and dutiful husband. The photographers paid ten dollars a shot. If anyone did that to me, I'd hit them. But Dad wanted to provide for my mother and me, knew his time was limited.

Empty chicken noodle soup can.

Mom and I have soup and bread for dinner (I hate cooking and she's too tired). Afterwards we work on my latest outfit, a lavender pantsuit. We make all of my clothes. Mom pins the fabric and I cut it as she worries about my social life.

"You should have a relationship," she says, but I know she doesn't want to marry again.

"Nobody would date an eight-and–a-half–foot-tall woman," I say. Wouldn't be worth it if I might die in five years. Besides, Mom is all the company I need. I haven't told her about the bakery girl I like or the rent-to-own guy who might like me. She'd just pester more.

Mom peers at me over the rims of her glasses. Though she is shorter than me it feels like she is bigger, takes up more space when we sit at the table or on the couch. I don't understand if it's a cruel trick of the mind or the eye that makes her shrink when I look at her.

I trim all the fabric to fit the pattern, plan to start sewing the following evening.

At four o'clock in the afternoon, my mother calls the store. Her voice wavers. My grandmother, her mother, had a stroke. She lives in a condo in Arizona. My mother will fly there tomorrow morning. I do not know my grandmother well, have seen her eight or nine times since I was ten. She sends me two hand-sewn blouses every Christmas.

I tell my boss what happened and she hugs me with frail arms. She's just over five feet tall, shorter than me even when I'm on my knees. No one can ever hug all of me.

Ten damp crumpled tissues.

My mother and I sit side by side on the couch. Her pupils are the size of saucers. In sorrow she is huge. Mom daubs her eyes and asks if I want someone to come and stay with me at the house. I shake my head. I'm an adult. Should be able to care for the house on my own. But I don't know if I can. I used to unload the dishwasher but broke too many plates, so now I'm responsible for taking out the trash. Mom is more confident about my abilities.

"You'll be fine." She nods. "Mr. Wilson is always home if you need help."

Mr. Wilson is seventy-something, has lived across the street from us since before I was born. He keeps to himself—knits, drinks black coffee, and smokes outside because that's what his wife made him do when she was alive.

"How long will you be gone?" I say. Mom shakes her head. I don't want her to leave. Selfish, but it's early May and she could be in Arizona all summer. I've never seriously thought about moving out of the house, finding a place of my own, that my mother might not be around to care for me. I worry no one else will love me enough to do all of the small constant things she does. Everyone understands little people need shorter counters and step stools and special pedals in cars, but they don't think about tall people, how sometimes I need help washing and dressing when I'm feeling weak. My father lived with his parents until he married my mother. I assumed I'd be like him, one of those ancient children.

Three empty paper packets of instant oatmeal.

Mom leaves at six in the morning. I wait to cry until she is gone. I make oatmeal for breakfast, though I'm not hungry. Mom doesn't like oatmeal, eats raisin bran, but she always throws away my empty oatmeal packets before I can. I almost forget to pitch the packets, leave them by the coffee maker expecting her hands to whisk them away. I dump most of my oatmeal down the garbage disposal.

I have problems with the buttons on my blouse. My grandmother should have sewn on larger ones. Because Mom isn't here to fasten them I wear a rayon shirt, one I can pull over my head. I walk to work and hope being around people will make me happier, or at least take my mind off my mother. It works for a while. I smile. I direct customers to envelopes and erasers. I am excruciatingly polite, trying for a ninth employee of the month award, another chance to have my name engraved on that little plaque in the break room. An obscure kind of immortality. The rent-to-own guy needs ballpoint pens. I decide he looks more cute than creepy, has possibilities.

"When are you going to ask me out for pizza?" I say. He stares at me. I smile. Sadness makes me say things I wouldn't normally, and I'm anticipating lonely dinners.

"Um," he says, "I didn't know you liked pizza."

"I do," I say. "Don't most people?"

His cheeks flush pink, then almost purple. "My boss needs the pens," he says.

It will be interesting to see if he comes back tomorrow.

At work I occupy myself with customer service, but afterwards I break down crying in the bakery. The bakery girl's fingers remind me of my mother's hands and how I am too dependent. Mothers gawk. Children stare. Three of my tears could fill a Dixie cup. The bakery girl comes out from behind the counter to pat my back. I want to tell the bakery girl I love her because her fingers are so delicate. Instead I say my grandmother had a stroke and my mother has gone to be with her. I tell her I am worried, let her assume it's out of concern for my grandmother and not my own self.

She tells me she's sorry.

I apologize for crying.

"It's okay," the bakery girl says. I want to ask her to go out, get coffee, but I don't.

I walk home and can't stay inside, pace around the block to tire my legs. I'm on my sixth lap when Mr. Wilson yells at me from his front porch.

"You doing some sort of marathon or what?" he says.

I walk to Mr. Wilson's porch, tell him about my grandmother and how Mom has gone to be with her. Mr. Wilson lights a cigarette, says I should call him if I have any problems. He gives me two pairs of hand-knitted socks every Christmas. His wife died eight years ago. She was around seventy, a sad but more expected age for dying than thirty-two.

Broken glass shards wrapped in three paper towels.

The glass is filled with water when I bump it off the kitchen counter and onto the floor. I should only use plastic cups and paper plates until Mom returns. My body is hard to control. This is not necessarily because of my size. I'm probably just a clumsy person. Mom says my father was quite graceful.

I bake a frozen pizza for dinner, eat in the living room because Mom insists we eat in the kitchen. I want to break habits. I turn the TV on for the company of voices. Every room in our home echoes. My parents bought the house because it was old and had high ceilings and doorways so my dad could be comfortable. I wonder what he would have said if he'd known I would become a giant. Maybe he would have felt bad about it, passing on the pains, but the one reason I like my size is because this is what I have of him.

Doodles of squares and triangles made while talking on the phone with my mother.

Mom calls every night and asks how I am doing.

I say I miss her company. I miss her sympathetic glances. I miss the way she'd rub my shoulders without asking.

"When will you be home?" I don't think I'm whining, just being honest and lonely.

Mom isn't sure how much my grandmother will recover—she can't speak or move her left hand, but she can feed herself. Mom says she might need to stay in Arizona for a while. She does not explain how long "a while" would be.

"I'm sorry," she says.

I want to cry, but I am an adult so I say I broke another pair of shoelaces this morning. We laugh. She says my father broke shoelaces all the time.

I think about my father when I'm alone, but I'm usually not alone much. I picture him, a nine-foot-tall ghost sitting in the plush recliner, watching me as I talk with my mother, nodding at our conversation. He's in the house like a lamp or a potted plant, so much a fixture that I don't think about it, would only notice if he were gone. The air would smell a little differently.

At work I start to think the rent-to-own guy is scared of me. He doesn't come in to the stationery store for three days. I feel bad because I was honestly hoping he was interested, thought I was kind, and wanted to ask me out for pizza. People say it's who you are on the inside that counts, but when you don't look like everyone else, most folks have a hell of a time getting past the outside. I've only ever gotten attention from creepy guys, ones who want to have eight-foot-tall kids.

In the evening I sit at the bakery near the front of the store, a space where they have small round tables clustered together with a scattering of chairs. Fitting on a chair is difficult, but I swing my legs to the side and pretend I'm five-foot-five. I eat day-old cookies and read the newspaper and glance over at the bakery girl. My mother's absence makes me avoid home because I'm worried something will happen and no one will be there to help. Better to be alone in public, to wait for the bakery girl to look over at me and smile.

Sometimes I don't answer the phone in the evening, don't want to speak to my mother because I'll start crying. When we talk, half the time the only thing I can say is, "When are you coming home?"

Tuft of hair cleaned from a brush.

I toss it in the little trashcan beside the sink while I draw water for my bath. I've been losing more hair since Mom's been gone. Maybe it's anxiety. Maybe it's age. My hair plugs the drain of the claw-foot ceramic tub. It's the one my dad used, but it can barely fit all of me. I'm sure I'm not getting all the shampoo out of my hair. Mom usually helps with that, dumps cups of water over my head until the suds are gone. When I get out I lose my balance, always fear this even though we have a plastic mat on the bottom of the tub. As I fall I imagine bashing my head against the back of the tub, cracking my skull, blood running rivulets into the water, but I land squarely on my tailbone, let out a yelp because there is no one to hear me. It hurts to fall from four and a half feet up. I sit in the tub for seven minutes while the water runs out. Sore, sore, so sore. When I get out I keep to a crouch, no higher than I have to be. My backside pains. I think about calling the hospital, hope I didn't fracture anything, but I don't want an ambulance to come because I fell on my rear. I grit my teeth and decide to wait until morning, assess the size of the bruise. I dry carefully, use my dad's thirty-year-old towels. They are threadbare. Mom sewed two towels together to make one large enough to dry all of him.

My father, filmy and sympathetic, sits on the easy chair in the living room. I ask how many times he fell like this. He shrugs because there were too many to count. When my mother calls, I almost tell her about my fall but stop just before I mention it. She couldn't do anything but feel guilty half a country away, and I've already told my dad. I wonder how big my father thought my mother was, if she ever swelled to seven or eight feet while he was still alive, or if she stayed five-foot-three. I wonder if my father's parents were like Mom, prone to growth, outsizing their normal bodies even if no one else could see it.

Mom collected my Dad's advertisements, glued them in scrapbooks. He's always with little kids to accentuate his height. Some of the kids look at him with wonder and others with slight fear, like he's a fairy tale giant. I hate fairy tales because giants are evil and stupid and eat people. I sympathize more with the giant than with Jack, go to sleep recalling his tumble off the beanstalk. It must have hurt.

I almost stay home from work the next morning—probably would if my mom were here—but I grit my teeth and walk. After a half block, it isn't bad.

Just before lunch, the rent-to-own guy comes to buy tape.

"Hello," he says, making eye contact for three seconds before peering down at the tape.

"Are you going to wait until I invite you out for pizza?" I say.

He looks up and gives me a small smile when I hand him his change. It's progress. Maybe a six-foot-tall guy won't be as cowed by me as a shorter one. We're the same height when I'm on my knees, which makes things almost normal. It's a decent kissing height. I blush after he leaves, usually don't think about kissing people other than cheek-kissing my mother before work.

Bakery bag with two-day-old peanut butter chocolate chip cookie crumbs.

I gain weight because I'm in love with the bakery girl. At least I think I'm in love with the bakery girl. She says hello when I walk to the counter and her eyes do not seem to widen at my size. She asks how my mother and grandmother are doing.

"They're okay," I say

"My grandmother had a stroke," she says.

"My grandmother is small," I say. "Frail." I worry she thinks my whole family is like me—gangly and huge.

"So was mine," she says. "Give your grandmother my best. I know how you feel."

Of course she doesn't, but I'm not going to correct her.

It's easy to love people who are kind to me, but I'm never sure how to interpret kindness. Maybe the bakery girl is just a nice person. Maybe I don't love her but her niceness, though I've always been in love with her delicacy. At the bakery I sit and eat a lot of bread so I can be around people. They have free jam and napkins on a small table in the corner. The jam comes in tiny rectangular tubs, plops on my bread in that perfect four-sided shape.

Crumpled grocery receipt for three frozen pizzas, two frozen chicken fingers meals, two teriyaki chicken meals, four cans of tomato soup, two chocolate bars with caramel.

I go to the store without a list. Mom always did the shopping. My trip is liberating and unhealthy. At home I bake a frozen pizza, sit on the couch, eat the whole thing though I had a lot of bread at the bakery. Mom would stop me, but I'm too hungry and have a lot of body to fill. A knock on the door. Mr. Wilson on the front step. He has his knitting needles, a bagful of yarn, and smells thickly of smoke.

"Thought I might come by and sit a spell," he says. He turns on the television, finds a channel with baseball. I take out the pantsuit that Mom and I started pinning before she left. Haven't worked on it since. I sit on the couch.

"You need a gentleman caller," Mr. Wilson says. "One who's not seventy-five. Here's a picture of my nephew." He takes his wallet out of his pocket. "A handsome boy. Thirty years old and no girlfriend. He does things with computers."

"I don't know how much longer I'm going to be around," I say, glancing at the tiny photo he shows me. It's hard to judge appearances based on a picture the size of my thumbprint.

"Shit," he says, "nobody knows when they're going to go. Just look at me here. I've been smoking a pack a day for sixty years and I'm still kicking."

I explain my heart problem. Mr. Wilson shakes his head. "You can't listen to everything doctors say. I never have."

Mr. Wilson excuses himself for a cigarette. My hands and feet feel no warmer after his pronouncement, but for a moment I consider the disturbing possibility I may outlive my father. I've figured on dying at the age of thirty-two since I was eighteen, so this is slightly upsetting, but I'm certain any plans I make will trigger the heart condition I know is waiting to erupt. I have never considered my body an ally. Mr. Wilson seems to think of his as a partner in crime.

Box of stale raisin bran.

My mother has been gone for a month and I hate raisin bran. I am learning to throw away my instant oatmeal packets so they do not collect by the coffee maker.

I haven't seen the rent-to-own guy for two days, but at noon he brings in a pizza box.

"I'm asking you out for pizza," he says. "I hope you like pepperoni."

We eat in the break room. My boss is happy to allow us that small courtesy. I think she worries about me.

The rent-to-own guy says his name is Dale. He wants to get a degree in accounting. He lives in an efficiency apartment above a record store, three doors from my bakery. He likes playing hockey and watching old comedies. Marx Brothers. Laurel and Hardy. Three Stooges.

I tell him I like sewing and do not skate because I have no balance.

"I bet you'd look amazing if you tried skating," he says.

"I look amazing enough already," I say. "And I bet I couldn't find skates to fit."

"Just glide in your shoes," he says without blushing.

I tell him I'll think about it, wonder if he wants to take me skating to see my slapstick crash on the ice, to make other people stare, but no one aside from my mother has ever bought me pizza, so I decide to interpret it as a mark of his sincerity.

Band-aid wrapper and two small pieces of waxy paper peeled off adhesive backing.

I cut myself while chopping tomatoes for a salad because I'm tired of pizza and want something fresh. I'm not used to paring knives. They're tiny and slippery in my hands. The cut is small but stings like hell because of the acid from the tomatoes. Still, I am pleased with my meek little salad and independent attempt to eat vegetables.

I tell my mother about the salad when she calls. She is proud of me. My grandmother has not yet regained feeling in her left hand. She probably won't. There is no one to care for her except my mother, because my grandmother doesn't trust nurses. Mom will be gone for a while longer. I take a deep breath and try to still my worries.

After telling her good-night, I walk three blocks downtown for the sake of walking. The bakery is closed. I scan the second-storey windows, most of them apartments, wonder where Dale lives and if he's looking out of his window and down at me.

Bakery bag with two-day-old lemon poppyseed and blueberry muffin crumbs.

I take a short lunch and get off work a half-hour early, go to buy day-old muffins and find the bakery girl is on break, sitting at the tables near the front of the store. I ask if I can sit with her for a moment. She nods. Getting into the chair is particularly awkward. I feel like I stretch across half the room. The bakery girl doesn't comment on my length, just asks about my grandmother. I watch her fingers as she tears the muffin in pieces.

"I'm a cashier at the stationery store on the next block," I say.

"I wondered if you worked around here," she says.

"You did?" I'm surprised she'd have thoughts of me other than the obvious why the hell is she so tall?

The bakery girl says she lives two blocks away in a duplex with her cat. She hates cooking, which is why she works in a bakery. Baked goods fringe benefits.

I tell her I made a salad the other night and it was a big accomplishment. She laughs. We are having an actual conversation. The bruise on my rear hurts like hell because the chair is so hard, but I am past caring. The bakery girl returns to work at five, says it was nice to talk with me. I float home. I do not tell my mother about the bakery girl. Don't want to get her hopes up.

Empty box of tissues, empty package of lozenges, three empty cans of chicken noodle soup, three empty cans of chicken and rice soup, empty box of soda crackers.

I get an awful cold, an achy head-throbbing cold, spend three days hobbling from the couch to the kitchen. On the third day, when the garbage is overflowing, I pull on a bathrobe (my father's old terrycloth) and haul the bag to the curb.

Mr. Wilson yells from across the street. "Thought you might be dead or something."

"Sick," I sniffle.

Mr. Wilson nods. Half an hour later he bangs on my front door, carries three boxes of tissues, a carton of orange juice, and a box of chamomile tea bags.

"I hate chamomile tea," he says. "But the wife gave it to me and it works."

Mr. Wilson offers to sit with me, but I tell him no. I am learning how to be alone and don't want him to catch my cold. (I don't say the smell of his cigarettes gets to me after a while.) I sit by the television and sip from the carton of orange juice, appreciate not having to worry about refilling a glass.

I'm ill for four more days, have several delirious one-sided conversations with my father. I tell him about the bakery girl and the rent-to-own guy, know he understands my uncertainty because he felt the same way when he met my mother. I know his colds were this bad since both of us have too much body to rid of the virus.

In most of the pictures I've seen my father is close to my age, but I can imagine twenty-some years added to his frame, imagine his hair greying and thinning, imagine us sitting side by side on the couch with heating pads on our knees after long days of commercial-making and paperclip-selling. After I've taken my cold medicine and am floating in that hazy space between wakefulness and sleep, I can feel his long thin fingers brush against my hands and face.

When Mr. Wilson deems I am well he brings me takeout, extra spicy Thai food. The curry is so hot I use half a box of tissues, but Mr. Wilson says the spices are cleaning out nasty things in my sinuses. I flush bright as a chilli pepper, but feel better afterwards. Less clogged. My father smiles from the armchair.

Cellophane wrappers from two packages of shoelaces.

Dale says that at the ice rink they don't care if you skate in your shoes. I buy new ones for the occasion. Mom is happy to hear I have a date. I wonder how my father courted her, what they talked about since she'd spent a semester's art class staring at him naked.

We arrive at the rink at seven o'clock on a Sunday morning because Dale says most people won't come until after ten. Ice makes me even less graceful than usual. Dale has chunky hockey-playing skates, whirls around the rink for twenty minutes while I tiptoe at the edge. He grabs my hand, tugs me away from the side, says he won't let me fall. I let go and slide toward him, peer down at my shoes. His hands hold mine, pull me gently. For about fifteen feet. I slip. Pitch forward because I don't want to land on my rear again. Careen on top of him. He did not realise my weight, curses as we both go down. Dale's knee twists in a painful way, although not one that requires medical attention. We hobble to his car. I am excruciatingly apologetic. So is he. This is because we both work in customer service.

I don't see Dale in the stationery store the next day, almost walk to the rent-to-own place to find him and apologize again. He was such a bright possibility. He bought me pizza. That night I mope and use a few tissues. He doesn't come to the store the day after that. I tell myself he was probably one of the creepy guys, repeat this idea for five days until I believe it.

"I'll call my nephew," Mr. Wilson says when I explain the incident with Dale. "He's a strong boy. Lifts weights. Could pick you up and cart you around town with one hand."

My mother gives me sympathy. "That's too bad," she says, "but not your fault."

I think on the other end of the line she's smiling. After a week I can smile, too. If Dale would hold a grudge just because I fell on him, the relationship wouldn't have worked. Beside me on the couch, my father shrugs. I know he waited twenty-seven years to find my mother.

Mr. Wilson says his nephew will visit soon and we'll go out for dinner.

Mom's absence isn't comfortable, but it's usual. Something I can accept if I break it into small increments. She will be gone another week. That idea is manageable. Larger periods of time are still difficult, so I don't think about them.

Bakery bag with two-day-old sugar cookie crumbs.

The bakery girl has a break at four-thirty. If I only take a half-hour for lunch, I can leave work early and have a muffin when she does. I learn the bakery girl likes crocheting and her cat is named Cinnamon. I tell her I like sewing. She compliments my new lavender pantsuit and says the colour goes well with my complexion. No one has ever said anything about my complexion before.

When I look away I know her arms and legs are growing. Her shoulders widen. Her back straightens until I am certain she is at least eight feet tall and our hands are the same size.

Ears

The second pair of ears are on the sides of my neck. They're a little smaller than my head ears and can't actually hear anything. All four of my ears are pierced, four holes each in the top ones, two holes each in the bottom. Most of the time I forget about the second pair, don't even notice them when I'm looking in the mirror. When I go out I wear turtlenecks and scarves because I'd rather not be stared at, but when I'm at work at the tattoo parlour I let them show. Customers tend to think they're some sort of self-imposed body modification.

I become a tattoo parlour mascot on the day my roommate Lee moves out to live with her asshole fiancé. We live on the bottom floor of three-storey house—Lee and her daughter share a bedroom, and my son shares a bedroom with me. Lee's fiancé has stayed the night at our place several times. Her daughter sleeps on the couch then, but usually ends up in bed cuddled next to me because Lee and the asshole fight so loudly. Even in my bedroom with the door closed you can hear the names he calls her. More than once I've told Lee that she and Prince Caustic have to keep it down. I don't want my son or her daughter to be hearing such things. Lee says the kids are asleep, but I know that's not true.

By the time Lee is packing her last few belongings I've known about the move for two weeks, but it's still a shock.

"You can't move in with that jerk," I say for the twentieth time while Lee loads her collection of stuffed animals into a milk crate. "He's abusive."

"He's small," she says. Burke is an inch shorter than Lee and maybe ten pounds lighter, but Lee's body is hunched in the morning after Burke's been yelling at her. "He always feels like people are challenging his manhood or something. I can't yell at Burke. It would hurt him too much."

"The bastard's not made of glass," I say.

"We're going to get counselling," she says. "He agreed."

My ex-boyfriend did, too, but I never managed to drag him within a mile of the counsellor's office. It took me six damn years to figure out he was a loser. He'd yell at me one minute and say he loved me the next. He claimed it was stress from his job and from us having a little kid that made him moody. I thought I'd marry him. He was Jacob's dad after all. Jake was three when we moved out. I had to do it while my ex was at work. We've been living with Lee ever since.

Lee is thirty-four and can barely read, convinces Jake or her daughter Izzy to help her understand her mail. I think she has some form of dyslexia and I'm not sure how she managed to graduate high school, but Lee is determined to a fault and won't get tested for a learning disability. She says she gets along well enough, but I know she's too embarrassed to admit to anything. That's why she's been working third shift at the auto parts factory for sixteen years. That's why she hates dating. It involves someone else finding out she can't read. Burke is Lee's first boyfriend since Izzy's dad left five years ago and moved to California. I'm pretty sure part of the reason they broke up was because she refused to get help and he refused to keep reading everything to her.

Burke is impossibly kind when it comes to helping Lee, reads her letters and books and magazines aloud, and follows under the print with his finger so she can pretend she's reading along. I don't understand these men we choose, how they can be so sweet about one thing, the thing that is most painful, but they're bastards about everything else. Lee and me, we both want to hold on to that drop of sweetness, but it nearly kills us in the process.

Izzy is clinging to her bed, refusing to leave.

"I want to stay here," she yells. "I won't go live in his stupid apartment. It smells funny. I hate Burke."

"Everything is going to be fine," says Lee, putting her hand over her daughter's fingers, probably in the hopes of easing them off the mattress. "You'll have your own bedroom and a new daddy."

"That jerk is not going to be my daddy," yells Izzy.

I'm tempted to stay and see how Lee resolves this dilemma, but Jacob and I have to get to the tattoo parlour. I work Tuesday through Saturday, eleven to five, take a dinner break and go back with Jake at six-thirty. We stay 'til nine-thirty on school nights, eleven on weekends. Lee waves good-bye to us and promises Izzy the moon if she'd only sit up.

At the tattoo parlour I work the register, do bookkeeping, sterilize equipment, and draw tattoos. My boss Zip is great at tracing pictures on skin and getting the colours right, but says he can't draw worth shit. Jacob climbs up on a red leather stool and sits still as a sphinx while Zip inks half a birch tree on some guy's back. Zip doesn't have a wife or kids and likes Jake, has already told me Jake can come to the tattoo parlour after school instead of going home to wait for me. I'd rather not let Jake be a latchkey kid, and I figure watching people get tattooed is just as educational as anything he could see on TV.

For months Zip has been asking me if he can use my face to advertise the tattoo parlour. He's a good guy and never pressured me about it, but he's mentioned the possibility from time to time. I've never been desperate enough to sell my picture before, but now I've got to figure out how to cover twice the usual rent plus make car payments and add to Jake's college fund. So with Lee and Izzy on the road to Burke's, I agree to be the store's mascot.

"You won't be a mascot," Zip says. He's finished the tree and is sponging ink and blood off the guy's back. The guy grits his teeth. Jake stares. "You'll be more like an emblem or insignia."

Of course this is just a nice way of saying mascot.

Zip says he'll get an artist to do a black-and-white drawing of me and give me an extra hundred dollars every month in royalties, plus fifty percent of the profits from the sale of any merchandise with my face on it.

"I get to choose who draws the new logo and paints it on the front window," I tell Zip, hoping that calling it a logo will make it seems less like it's my face. "You can use it on T-shirts and business cards. That's as far as I'll go." I have a certain pride in how I look, but don't want to be on a bumper sticker or book of matches or inked on someone's arm.

Zip snaps off his rubber gloves and scratches his nearly invisible blond goatee.

"What about bottle openers?" he says.

"No dice," I say.

"Story in the paper?" he says.

I shrug. "If they care to do one." I'm not figuring they will, but I've never been a good guesser.

Four weeks later Zip's photo is on page seven of the local paper. He's standing in front of the tattoo parlour beside my three-foot-high head, holding a T-shirt with the store logo on it. Me. I have to admit it came out rather nice—my black and white face looks cheerful, even attractive, and the four ears seem natural as wings on a butterfly.

Monday afternoon I'm standing in the driveway washing my car and not wearing a turtleneck or scarf, when the lady appears at my side. Or at least it seems like she appears. She probably just walks right up to me like any normal person but I don't hear her because I'm thinking about Lee and Izzy and how they moved out a month ago and I haven't heard from them in a couple weeks. The last time I spoke with Lee on the phone she said things were just fine and Izzy was getting used to the situation. I took that to mean she hadn't yet tried to kill Burke.

"Are you a harlot?" The lady beside me is plump, has short brown hair permed in loose curls, is wearing jeans and a pink T-shirt, and carrying a lawn chair. She is vaguely familiar, like I might have seen her at the grocery.

"I haven't had sex in six years," I say. Not since I left the ex and swore off men. I think Zip may have a thing for me but he's my boss and too nice a guy to try anything.

"You might be a sign of the apocalypse," says the lady. "Perhaps you should have been killed at birth."

I try to not take the last comment personally as she stands tiptoe and scrutinizes my forehead.

"Do you mind? I'm washing my car." I swat at her with the damp sponge and she steps back but doesn't leave.

"I've spoken with the angels," she says. "They said you may be a sign of the end."

"So?" I dip my sponge back in the bucket of suds. "They could have meant the end of jelly donuts or something."

"But the end is near," she says. "I knew it the moment I saw your picture in the paper."

"I'm thirty-one for God's sake," I say, "I have a kid. I'm not a harbinger of destruction."

The lady nods but sets up her lawn chair beside the sidewalk, takes a small pad of paper from her purse, and watches me with her head tilted slightly. I give her fifteen minutes of polite silence before I say anything else.

"How long are you going to sit there?" I ask.

"Until I get a sign," she says.

"I don't appreciate being stared at," I say.

The lady bites her lip. "This is nothing personal against you."

"Pardon me for feeling so goddamned insulted," I mutter and resume washing the dead bugs off my windshield. I remind myself I'm used to worse than this.

In elementary school at recess I stood by the chain link fence with three other outcasts. The smart girl insulted all the other kids in polysyllabic words. The fat boy had the best spitting range and accuracy of any kid in the fourth grade. The six-foot-tall girl was only teased from a distance because she had a great left hook. We moved after I finished eighth grade. When I started high school my mother bought me a lot of scarves and turtlenecks. She said there was nothing wrong with me but with the rest of the world. Around then I realised my parents probably just didn't have the money for surgery to get the ears off.

Jake's dad and I started going out during my senior year in high school. After three years of hiding the second ears under layers of cloth, I let him be the first person outside of my family to see them. He loved my ears, thought they were beautiful, said I should show them off in public. After a few beers he'd call me a lazy cunt and a good-for-nothing bitch, but even when drunk he never made any mean comments about my ears. I never understood how he managed to hold me up and destroy me at the same time.

The strange woman is still staking out our yard from her lawn chair when Jake gets home from school.

"Hello, Mrs. Simon," he says to her. He gives me a hug, goes inside.

I glance at the woman scratching notes on her pad, drop my sponge in the bucket, follow my son.

"You know that lady?" I say.

"Her son is in my class," says Jacob. "Isaiah." He tells me all the kids tease Isaiah because his mother stands on a corner between the school and post office downtown and tells everyone the world is going to end. She's been doing this since school started.

"Sometimes we sit across the street and watch," he says. "People driving by yell at her, but she doesn't shut up. Isaiah's mad at her because his dad divorced her a year ago after she went crazy. Now she lives in a yucky apartment and his dad sends her money every month and she doesn't do anything but yell at people. Isaiah has to stay with her every other week. He hates it."

But Jacob tells me odd things have happened. Mrs. Simon said a light would fall from the sky and the next day a streetlight cable broke and one of the lamps almost landed on a car windshield. She said it would be a time of monsters the day before Isaiah's dog had puppies, and the smallest one in the litter only had three legs. She said there would be an end to joy and a week later the bakery down the street from the school closed.

"The lady who worked there gave us free two-day-old cookies," says

Jacob. "Now we have to buy them from Shop Rite and they're not as good."

After listening to Jake I decide not to call the police about Mrs. Simon. At least not yet. You can't go through life with four ears and not have compassion for people who get mocked or called crazy, even if you think they might really be crazy.

Tuesday when Jake and I get home from the tattoo parlour for dinner, Mrs. Simon is already stationed on our lawn in her chair.

Jacob waves and says hello. She smiles at both of us. I try to smile back but it probably looks more like a grimace. We eat macaroni and cheese in the kitchen, and from my place at the table I can see her out our living room window. She doesn't do much other than take notes and look at her watch. There's extra macaroni and cheese and since I don't like it reheated I consider letting Jake take it out to her. In the end I put it down the garbage disposal. Mrs. Simon waves when we leave for the tattoo parlour. You could almost think she was a kindly neighbour sunning herself instead of a second-rate prophetess.

"Lady," I say, "I don't want to be mean, but you realise I could call the authorities and register a stalking complaint."

Mrs. Simon cocks her head. "But I'm not hurting you. I'm just taking notes."

"And I'm not calling the police," I say, scratching the ear on the right side of my neck. "Not yet. I just wanted to let you know."

Mrs. Simon looks down and scribbles more in her pad.

Jake crosses his arms once we're in the car. "She's really kind of nice," he says. "Just crazy."

I shake my head. I guess being stalked by nice crazy people is better than being stalked by mean crazy people, but stalking is stalking. It takes me a while to focus once I get back to the parlour. When I start playing around with a few tattoo sketches I feel a bit better.

Around eight in the evening two college-aged girls with multiple piercings in their ears bounce into the shop.

"You're the woman on the window," they bubble. "Can we get a picture?"

I blink at them a couple times, then glance over to Jake. He'll probably want to take swimming lessons at the Y once school lets out, and he's going to need new summer clothes. I look back at the girls and tell them it will cost two dollars. The girls whip out a little camera and Jake takes the photo since Zip is inking an apple onto some lady's ankle. The girls both hug me and tell me my ears are really cool. Then they buy shirts. It feels nice to be appreciated and yet rather disturbing, like I'm some sort of pop star.

Thirty shirts have sold in the past few days and Zip says he'll have to order more from the supplier. At least my slight celebrity is profitable. Zip is good to his word on my extra cash, gives me a hundred dollars plus another two hundred from the T-shirt sales. I treat Jacob to ice cream on the way home.

"I want a shirt with your picture on it, too," says Jake.

"No," I tell him.

"But a couple kids at school have them," he says. "And you're my mom. If anyone gets a shirt it should be me."

"You need to be wearing shirts with sports team names or something," I say. "Not me."

"But you're better than any stupid sports team," he says. "I want a shirt with you on it."

"We'll see," I say, which is what my mother said when she meant no.

Jake knows this and kicks lightly at the dashboard as he licks his ice cream.

Mrs. Simon reappears in her lawn chair on Wednesday afternoon, has her pad, a can of cola, and a sandwich in a plastic bag. She watches while Jake and I play Frisbee in the yard. Jake asks if she'd like to join us. She smiles and shakes her head no and scribbles more notes.

When we go inside to eat dinner, Jake says, "She made good cookies for Isaiah's birthday treat last month. We should ask her to bring some next time she comes." I decide it's not a bad idea, send Jake outside with his request. It's the least she can do since she keeps staring at me.

Wednesday night Izzy calls the tattoo parlour and asks if she can come back and live with me. She says things at Burke's are awful.

"Has he yelled at you?" I say.

"He yells at Mom and she defends him," says Izzy. "She says he's the only really understanding guy she's ever met. It's a load of shit."

"Is your mom home?" I say.

"She just left for work," says Izzy. "That's why I called you now."

"I need to talk to her about this," I say.

"You know she won't listen to you," says Izzy.

I bite my lip and say I'll call Lee tomorrow.

On Thursday I phone Lee on my lunch break, maybe not the best idea because I think I woke her up.

I say Izzy called me. "She's not happy."

"She's adjusting," says Lee.

"She says Burke still yells at you," I say. "I thought you guys were going to start counselling."

"We will when he can work it into his schedule," says Lee. "Everyone is adjusting now. Izzy is learning what it's like to have a dad again, and Burke is figuring out how he needs to act around kids. They'll be good for each other. He's helped me so much, you know. No other guy has ever done that. Izzy just needs to give him a chance. She'll be fine."

Lee hangs up the phone.

I think about calling her back but I don't. I know she's a stubborn woman, won't listen. And I hate telling others how to parent.

Thursday afternoon Jake and I find Mrs. Simon in her chair on our lawn with a paper plate on her lap filled with chocolate chip and sugar cookies. She hands me the plate cheerfully while telling me that my second set of ears look slightly pointed at the ends and that's probably a bad sign. I thank her for the cookies.

At work we have sold almost one hundred shirts. People are popping in and out of the store, wanting to get photos with me and paying five dollars for the privilege. The fuss is strange because I've been working at the parlour for a few years and nothing like this has happened. Zip says I was just keeping too low a profile and not to doubt the power of merchandizing.

The annoying part is when people take pictures of me without permission. Tonight I'm near the back of the shop sterilizing equipment and all of the sudden there's a flash like lightning and some college guy is hightailing it out of the store.

"Asshole," I yell and glance over to Zip who winces and looks at the floor. I glare at my black and white image on the tattoo parlour window. Before Jake and I leave, Zip gives me a large check for shirt royalties. It's money Jake and I need, so I don't press the issue further. I tell myself things will get better, that all the stupid publicity will die down and I'll still get my extra hundred a month.

Friday afternoon Mrs. Simon has moved closer to the house, is halfway between the sidewalk and the porch.

"Other people live here, too," I tell her. "They might have problems with you taking over our lawn."

"But I'm not hurting anything," says Mrs. Simon, knitting her eyebrows like sitting in the middle of our yard should be the most natural thing in the world.

"I don't care." I walk around her and grab the arms of her lawn chair, heaving back with my whole weight. I can't budge her. She's too heavy.

"That's it," I say, stomping around the chair to face her. "I'm calling the police."

"Mom," Jake says, "she gave us cookies."

"The cookies were very good," I say, "but this is an invasion of privacy. Mine and my son's. I could file a harassment charge and get you arrested without much trouble."

"I'll move," she says, "I'll move." Mrs. Simon stands up and touches the back of her chair, looks at me with sad eyes. "But don't you understand I'm trying to help people? I'm making them aware." She sounds genuinely hurt and I can't help but feel a little sad for her.

"You need to understand that I need my lawn," I say quietly.

Mrs. Simon turns and drags her chair back to the sidewalk. She doesn't look at me or Jake when we leave. Jake grumbles for a while about Mrs. Simon's cookies and our chances of getting more of them, but Zip gives him a sheet of temporary tattoos and my son invests the rest of the evening putting them all over his arms.

Jake spends Saturday afternoon with me at the tattoo parlour. When we get home for dinner at five, Mrs. Simon and Izzy are sitting on the front porch, chatting. Izzy has a suitcase.

"I can't stand it there," she says. "Last night I hit Burke when he yelled at Mom. He hit me back and Mom yelled at both of us to cut it out. I called him a bag of rat shit and he called me a little cunt. He grabbed my arms and shook me, then I gave him a shiner."

Izzy pushes up the sleeve of her T-shirt to reveal four dark oval blotches.

"Oh God." I slump against the porch railing. "Is your mom home? Does she know you're here?"

Izzy shakes her head. "She was taking a nap when I left."

I call Lee and tell her Izzy's at my place. I don't have time to ask her what the hell she's thinking living with a child abuser before she slams down the receiver. Ten minutes later Lee pulls into our driveway, erupts from the car with her hair uncombed and makeup smeared. Burke steps out of the passenger side, stands beside the car with his hands in his pockets. He's wearing dark glasses and is smaller than I remember, maybe five foot four. He glances down and toes the pavement. Just looking at him you wouldn't think he was a bastard who hit kids.

"You scared the shit out of me," Lee says. "I woke up and you weren't there. Get your ass in the car right now."

"Not until you break up with Burke," says Izzy. "He treats you like shit." Izzy glares over her mother's shoulder at the accountant. She's almost as big as Burke, and stockier.

"What the hell is this about Burke hitting Izzy?" I say.

"They slap each other like kids," Lee says. "It's not bad."

"It's a grown man hitting a twelve-year-old," I say.

"He didn't hit," says Lee, "he just grabbed her arms. Izzy shouldn't have been in the room, anyway. When Burke is mad he says things he doesn't mean."

Mrs. Simon squints at Lee and Burke in turn.

"I don't care," says Izzy. "He's not going to be my dad, and you're not going to be my mom if you marry him."

Lee grabs Izzy's wrist and tries to haul her off the porch, but Izzy hardly budges.

"Lee," I say, "let her stay the night if she wants."

Lee doesn't stop tugging. Mrs. Simon bounds up and grabs Izzy's other arm, pulls her toward the house.

"What the hell," says Lee.

"She doesn't want to go," says Mrs. Simon. "It's not a good place for her."

Lee stomps off the porch and back to the car. "One night," she calls to Izzy, "but you'll have to come home tomorrow."

Izzy clenches her jaw as her mother and the bastard drive away.

Jake and I are both hungry and there's not much time before I have to be back to work, so I microwave a couple of frozen pizzas. Izzy drags her suitcase inside the house and Mrs. Simon, good to her word, slinks back to the sidewalk. Even though I'm hesitant about it, I invite Mrs. Simon to eat with us because I'm happy she helped get Lee to leave. Mrs. Simon wanders around the kitchen while the pizzas are cooking, peers into cupboards and drawers. I wonder what the hell she could be looking for, if she thinks my silverware may give her clues about my true nature, but when she finds the plates in the cupboard she sets the table.

While Mrs. Simon is busy I think about calling child protective services, flip through the phone book until I find the number. I scribble it down on a notepad and stare at it for several seconds, but in the end I don't call. I can't. Izzy is safe now, and maybe this is the sort of wake-up call Lee needs to leave Burke on her own. Shouldn't it mean something to her that her daughter has run away? But I remember too well how hard it was to leave a guy I thought I loved, even though he treated me like shit. For six years I stayed with my boyfriend, despite his hard words. I told myself things would get better. I told myself Jake needed a dad. I finger the ear on the left side of my neck. My boyfriend really loved those ears. I miss that.

At dinner Mrs. Simon and I let the kids talk about school while we give each other sideways glances. I take Izzy and Jake to the parlour in the evening. Izzy brought half of her clothes and her school books, so she's set for a few days. In the car she tells us what Mrs. Simon told her as they sat together in our yard, how she started seeing little pinprick lights about a year and a half ago, started sensing things were going to happen before they did, started being struck with messages.

"The streetlight did fall down," says Jake. "It was cool. Glass everywhere, like an explosion."

That night I make up the couch bed for Izzy who frets over her mother.

"Maybe she won't come back," Izzy says. "Burke hates me. I hate him. I want to stay here for good."

"I don't know how much I can do since I'm not your mom," I tell Izzy. Unless I call child protective services. But Lee helped Jake and me when I left Jake's father, when we didn't really have anywhere to go. I don't want to see her prosecuted.

"Even Mrs. Simon makes more sense than Mom does," Izzy mutters.

I bite my lip.

I have Sunday and Monday off work. Because I can't stand the thought of watching Mrs. Simon in the front yard, I take the kids to the zoo after lunch. We have dinner out and go see a movie, get home at nine-thirty. There's a message from Lee on the answering machine. She says Izzy can stay with us for a couple of days, and I figure Lee is feeling guilty because deep down she knows Burke is an idiot. I also figure Burke wants a break from Izzy.

Monday the kids walk to school together. I go grocery shopping and to the laundromat, come home just before they get back. When they walk in the door, both of them are wearing plastic ears on the sides of their neck. Izzy's are pink and Jake's are green. They show me how they attach with little adhesive strips.

"We got them at the drugstore," says Izzy. "Everyone at school is wearing them now. They have all colours. Pink and blue and red and green."

"Oh Lord," I say. "Take them off."

"No," says Jake, touching his green ears with the tips of his fingers, pressing them against his neck. "They're cool. I like them. They're like yours."

"My ears are not toys," I say, stepping toward him. "Take them off."

"We paid a dollar for them," says Jake, clamping his hands over the green ears as if they're hearing some awful sound his other ears can't pick up.

"All the kids are wearing them," Izzy repeats.

"God," I say, leaning my head against the doorframe. The kids glare at me, their arms crossed, their ears bright. Dammit. I always said I'd be the sort of parent who wouldn't care about dyed hair, tattoos, or piercings. Even though I don't like the ears, I let the kids keep them on. They can be removed. And I've always tried to think of my own ears as something of an accessory. It would be funny if I weren't pissed, didn't have the urge to swipe Jake's ears off his neck when he walks past me in the kitchen.

Mrs. Simon and a little boy arrive at our house around four-thirty. I figure the boy is Isaiah. Jacob waves to him and they start playing Frisbee in the yard. Izzy talks with Mrs. Simon on the porch, keeps glancing at the driveway like her mother and Burke are going to materialize.

"You were right to leave that place," says Mrs. Simon to Izzy, but she looks at me and squints hard, like since I'm a sign of the second coming I should have the power to right things.

Sorry, lady, I think. I'm not as magical as I look.

Even if Lee hasn't left Burke yet, Izzy is safe and that's what matters for now.

Tuesday afternoon at the tattoo parlour, people with plastic ears filter through the store to get pictures with me. After the eighth or ninth photo it starts to get annoying. Part of me feels like I'm being appreciated. Part of me feels like I'm being mocked. Zip stares at the plastic ears and I tell him about the ones Izzy and Jake were wearing. Zip nods and rubs his hands together. I know he's going to make a few calls, find a plastic ear supplier. Izzy and Jake arrive at the parlour still wearing their extra ears. I don't think they took them off for bed last night.

When we arrive home for dinner, Mrs. Simon and Isaiah are on the porch. I give them a nod and troop inside. Izzy chats with Mrs. Simon. I hear them through the open window.

Mrs. Simon says, "That's how he's going to be known, as the kid whose mother tells the future. That's what I'm giving him. Maybe he'll have a gift, too."

I shake my head, keep my fingers crossed that Isaiah can just live down his mother's reputation. Everything she says sounds so earnest, I can't help but feel bad for her. Maybe she really thinks this is a good thing for Isaiah. But she doesn't hear the playground teasing. Or she ignores it well.

Back at the tattoo parlour Lee troops in around seven. Izzy locks herself in the restroom in back. Lee knocks on the door until her knuckles are red.

"Dammit," she says, "you need to come home. Things are going to get better. They are getting better. Burke and I are going to counselling next week."

"No, you're not," I say, leaning against the wall by the bathroom door.

"If that bastard yells at you again I'm going to punch him even harder," says Izzy.

"Counselling," says Lee, pounding on the door. "I'm going to make an appointment."

"That's bullshit," Izzy says. "You said you'd make an appointment last week and the asshole said no way in hell was he going."

Lee gives up after a half-hour, has to get to work. She's near hoarse and Zip is giving her dark looks, says she's going to scare away customers.

I watch her leave. On the way out she passes three people with plastic ears coming in.

By Thursday morning the ear trend is all over town. At the grocery store there are little kids, toddlers, with tiny ears on the sides of their necks. Even some of their mothers have two sets of ears. Elementary school kids running past the tattoo parlour window on their way home have two sets of ears. Half of our customers are wearing them, too. It's so pervasive that the ears start looking normal to me. Expected. When the kids and I get home, Isaiah and mother are in the front yard arguing about ears.

"I don't understand why I can't wear them," he says. His fists are clenched. Mrs. Simon is trying to pry his hands open and not having much success. Isaiah writhes out of her grasp, tucks his arms close to his chest, and pretty soon he's in a tight ball on our lawn. Mrs. Simon looks down at him, frowns and shakes her head.

When she sees me and the kids, she blushes.

"Isaiah," she says, "you need to stand up."

"No," he says, his voice muffled since he's in a tiny ball. "Not until you let me wear my ears. Not until you stop standing on the corner and yelling things and making the kids laugh. Not until you get a real job and move out of the stupid apartment. I hate you."

"We'll talk about this later," she says. "There are people here. Jake. Your friend."

Isaiah raises his head, sees Jake, uncurls from his ball and runs toward my son.

Mrs. Simon watches him, hands on hips, says, "I'm sorry about that" to me.

Mothers embarrass their kids. Kids embarrass their mothers. Such is life. I shrug. By the time I call the kids in for dinner, Jake has helped Isaiah attach the ears to the sides of his neck. Mrs. Simon mutters something about the devil under her breath but doesn't make him take the ears off.

Friday afternoon the middle-aged guy comes in with his camera and starts taking pictures of me. I stare at him for a moment. Most people realise their audacity and stop photographing me when I glare. Not this one. He snaps six photos then turns around. I think he's going to leave, but he starts taking picture of Jake sitting on his red stool.

"Hey," I say, "my kid is off limits." I march over to my son but the paunchy guy is still clicking away, gets a couple of pictures of me and Jake before I get between them.

"Quit it," I say, but the guy skirts to the side a bit, gets shots of us both before he puts down his camera. I'm trying to decide if I should lunge for the camera or not when he fishes in his jeans pocket and hands me a twenty, then tousles Jake's hair.

"Thanks," he says cheerfully.

Maybe if it were the 1920s and I were in a sideshow with fat ladies and bearded ladies and skeleton women, I would be fine with the fact he doesn't ask to take pictures, just gives me cash and figures that makes everything okay. Even now, maybe if I didn't have a kid I wouldn't mind weirdos like him as long as I was paid enough to be on display. But I do have a kid. I am a mother. And mothers do a lot of things because of their children that they wouldn't do otherwise. I left my boyfriend because I was worried about the effect it would have on Jake to hear his mother being called all those awful names. And now middle-aged men are patting my son's head like Jake is just another exhibit.

I lose it.

"You are not fucking touching my kid." I wrest the camera from his hand and grab his arm, grip it hard enough to make him wince and writhe and clutch at the air trying to escape.

"Lady," he yelps, "you're hurting me."

The middle-aged man is bigger than me, maybe six foot and two hundred pounds to my five foot four and one-twenty, so I'm not quite sure how I manage to haul him past Zip, four staring customers, and thirty feet of wall covered with tattoo flash pictures. Must be adrenalin.

I fling him out the door and throw the camera after him. It cracks against the sidewalk.

"To hell with it," I tell Zip. "This is it. No more shirts. No more logo."

Izzy and Jake and I take all the shirts and there's nothing Zip can do about it. Of course there are already lots of ears and shirts in circulation and I can't do a damn thing about it, but I can stop more from being sold. Kids and mothers and tattoo shop patrons will wear the ears for another week or two until everyone has them, until they look so normal they are old, and then everyone will move on to the next fad.

When we arrive home, Lee and Burke are standing beside Lee's car in the driveway. Mrs. Simon and Isaiah are at the edge of the driveway, maybe five paces away from them. Lee marches up to Izzy as soon as she gets out of the car, grabs her daughter's arm.

"Honey, you need to come home," says Lee, tugging.

"Not if you're going to put up with all the shit from that bastard," says Izzy.

"Don't talk to me like that," says Lee.

"He does," says Izzy, glaring at Burke. "Just learn to read already. It's not some big fucking secret that you can't."

"I love Burke," says Lee, but her throat catches.

"He gave me fucking bruises," says Izzy.

"A great storm will strike you down," Mrs. Simon says to Burke.

Burke fidgets.

"Your wealth will be consumed," Mrs. Simon says. "Your stone heart will be crushed."

Lee glances at Burke. Izzy glares at him. Lee tugs harder and Izzy's feet slip just a bit, a couple paces closer to the car. I wonder how long they will keep this up, who will win out, and I hope it's not Lee. Izzy should not be going back to Burke's, whether or not he's afraid of her. Mrs. Simon grabs Izzy's other arm and she and Lee are both tugging.

For a very brief moment I'm certain that my second pair of ears can hear the voices of angels. Maybe it is the brightness of the sun in my eyes but I see Lee with many ears on her neck and chest and arms, plastic ears that don't hear. I see her skin pocked with closed eyes. But as I say, the sun is bright and what I think I see only lasts a moment.

I take a deep breath because Lee is my friend. Because she is a mother. Because I want to believe she is trying to do what's right for her child. But she's not. I walk over to Lee and she smiles at me like she thinks I'm going to talk with Izzy and tell her to go back to Burke's.

"If you try to take her," I say, "I'm going to call child protective services."

Lee's eyes are huge. "God." She drops Izzy's arm. "You're my friend. You're supposed to support me on this."

I shake my head. Mrs. Simon lets go of Izzy's other arm. Izzy steps toward her and Isaiah and Jake, the plastic ears bright on the sides of their necks.

"Come on," Lee calls over her shoulder to Burke. "We have to get her home. She's our daughter. You said you'd help me do this." Burke toes the ground and doesn't move.

"Come on," she says again, but he is still. Lee looks from me to Izzy to Mrs. Simon to Burke. She drops to her knees on our lawn, her elbows on the grass, her head on the grass, her hair spread out like a dark halo against the green. She is shaking, crying, and when I squint I can see her trying to cover her many ears, her many eyes, with one pair of hands.

Combust

Mother is not happy about the wheelchair, though it has a motor and she admits she can't get along well on her own. She is a large woman, a strong woman. For thirty years she spent nine hours a day shaping loaves of bread, lifting trays of cookies and tins of muffins out of ovens, and wheeling carts of frosted layer cakes. She got bigger after she retired because her appetite didn't decrease with her activity level.

Mother is even less happy about going into the nursing home, especially since her mind is working well. She expresses her displeasure by flinging stuff across the room. Greeting cards. Plastic flowers. Cups of water. Whatever she can grab.

"I don't belong with geezers," she says, tossing a crocheted pincushion at the wall. "They don't know what the hell is going on."

I tried to make her room comfortable, hung all of her posters of France on the walls, but Mother invests her time cataloguing every possible slight and threatening to call lawyers.

"I said we'd have to put you in a care facility if you didn't find a home nurse you liked," I say when I visit. I work full time at the bank, couldn't care for her on my own and don't think I'd want to.

"The twits here don't know what they're doing," says Mother. "My lawyer will be calling me back tomorrow."

"Mother," I say, "you can't file a lawsuit because your peas were cold."

"You think I'm lying," she says. "You think living here is just peachy."

"I don't think it's as bad as you make it out to be," I say.

"The lawyer will be calling tomorrow," she says again.

I sigh. The home is okay. Everything looks clean. No patients are left drooling in the hallway. The nurses and orderlies are pleasant. I think they're regular angels for putting up with Mother.

"They're trying to starve me," she says. "If my ankles didn't feel like shit, I'd walk right out of here." The nurses are supposed to control her diet, reduce her food intake, but this hasn't worked. She doesn't want to listen to them talk about her blood sugar, and they don't want to put up with her threats to sue for elder abuse.

The only person she likes is her doctor, this young guy named Dale who has black dreadlocks, calls Mother "Miss Muffet," and says there's no way in hell she's getting two pieces of apple pie at dinner.

"We won't be able to budge you from your tuffet," he says.

"I'm going to starve," says Mother.

"Tell it to the spider," says Dale.

Mother smiles. You don't quell Mother, you spar with her and then she's happy. Mother has always been an angry person, but she's more upset with being in the home than with me for putting her there. It's my job to feel awful about that part.

I inherited my father's slight build, but I have my mother's temper, her tendency to erupt without warning. At first I thought I'd be able to avoid those explosions, but the best I can do is hide them. There are times when I have to throw things. Stomp around. At work after a terse discussion with my boss/co-worker/client I step into the ladies' room and lock the door so I can slam my shoe against the counter several times. More than once I've come out of the restroom and found a concerned-looking colleague. I just smile and say there was a problem with the toilet.

During my lunch break I call my sister. It's been a week since we last spoke. She and Mother have never gotten along. I was the firstborn, had four years experience with Mother before my sister came along, and I learned how to talk back. My sister wasn't a fighter, just crumpled. Mother didn't understand people who wouldn't argue. After high school graduation my sister moved as far away as she could, to Seattle. Mother has not forgiven her for the distance. My sister doesn't understand why Mother is so mad.

"I hate her," says my sister. "Tell her to stop calling me."

"Last night a nurse pulled me aside," I say. "They're sure Mother has had a few little heart attacks. Diabetics can get those and not feel pain because of nerve damage. When she goes it'll be sudden. You'll feel like crap if you don't call her. She wants to hear from you."

"So she can yell at me about how I don't love her," says my sister. "We've both become childless spinsters because of her. She turned us off to that whole marriage-and-kids thing."

"I'm not a spinster." I think you have to be at least sixty to be a real spinster, and I'm only forty-three.

"I'm a spinster," says my sister, "and it's because of Mom."

"She loves you," I say.

"She never loved me enough to figure out why I didn't love her. She never cared to figure out how I operate."

"Mother isn't a detail person," I say.

"I'm her kid," says my sister. "She should care how I operate."

"I know," I say.

I have been a mediator between my mother and sister for years and I'm not happy about it. After hanging up with my sister there's no time to go into the bathroom and hit something. I have to push that anger back down, return to work.

My first afternoon customer is a lady who wants to set up a certificate of deposit.

"I'm putting money aside for my kids to go to college," she says, an excuse to show me wallet-sized photographs of her daughters. One kid is in second grade and the other is four years old. About the same age difference as my sister and me.

I type up the paperwork for the certificate of deposit and feel the heat in my fingertips, the anger that's released after a good shoe-banging and a few expletives. I should excuse myself and go scream, but that wouldn't be professional. Just a few minutes and I can escape . . .

The lady tells me one of her daughters wants to be a ballerina. The other wants to be an astronaut.

I want to drag my sister from Seattle to see Mother. They're both good people. I love them very much. But they're too fucking obstinate to be nice to each other.

I feel a stab of pain in my left ankle, smell char and nylon, glance down and see fire sprouting from a patch of skin big as my palm. The flames are two inches high, red-orange at the tips and blue near my skin. I scream, roll out of my chair and on to the floor, and yell for my client to call 911.

In the hospital bed I sit cross-legged to examine the blister. It's small, maybe two inches in diameter, and looks like a burn someone would get from a splash of hot oil. I can't explain why it's not worse. The nylons are ruined. My ankle hurts like hell. I try not to cry.

A nurse takes a few more vials of blood. A doctor runs four interns through the room.

"This is the first case of spontaneous combustion our hospital has ever observed," she says.

The interns squint at me, Combusting Woman A, and scribble on notepads. They linger in the room for five minutes, check their watches, fiddle with their stethoscopes, and clip out the door when I'm no longer interesting.

I slam my empty plastic water glass against the bed so hard it cracks. I slam it again and again until it shatters and plastic shards fly across the room.

A nurse pokes his head in the room and asks what's wrong.

I tell him that aside from catching on fire, I'm just peachy.

I don't know how I'll explain this to my boss or to Mother. She'll blame Dad's genes. A nurse unhooks some of the tubes and lets me sit in a plastic chair in the shower. I feel a bit safer, though I don't think I'll combust again soon. I also feel drained, but that's been happening a lot. I get tired easily, need more sleep, more coffee, more makeup under my eyes in the morning.

I stay in the hospital while doctors conduct blood tests, bone marrow tests, hormone tests, kidney and liver function tests, and take endless urine specimens. I destroy three more glasses and a potted plant sent by my co-workers, and start igniting again when there's nothing more to smash (because the nurses said I went through my plastic glass quota). Each episode of combustion is correlated to a rise in my blood pressure and thoughts of Mother.

I call Mother from the hospital. She blames Dad like I knew she would.

"There was something wrong with him," she says.

"Mother," I say, "I don't care whose fault this is. I just want to stop igniting."

"All I'm saying is that you're not going to find the answer on my side of the family," she says. "Your father was the one who played with fire."

My dad was a welder who worked on farm equipment, grain silos and elevators and other big pieces of metal. He travelled all over the country, was good at what he did and made quite a bit of money doing it. When I was little Dad wasn't home much. The amount of time he stayed with my mom and sister and me shrank and shrank until he didn't come back.

"The lawyer called me today," says Mother. "We might have a case."

"Lovely," I say and feel that familiar burn sensation in my ankle. I don't have anything else I can break, and the nurses warned me about ripping the sheets. I guess they'd rather I set the bed aflame. I tell Mother I need to hang up. There's about twenty seconds of pain before a certain area catches fire, so I can grit my teeth and grab a damp towel. When the fire erupts it's like a release, a good ache even if it's an intense one.

After ten days the doctors can't find anything physically wrong with me, and send me home with a large tub of ointment.

Even after he left, my dad was faithful financially. He sent cashier's cheques to supplement Mother's income until my sister turned eighteen, then we never heard from him again. Mother put together reasonable outfits from Goodwill and brought home day-olds from the bakery every night. We feasted on cookies and brownies and muffins. I had my father's metabolism, nothing stuck to me, while Mother gained all the weight I should have had.

My sister was different, her digestive system was easily disturbed, but Mother didn't understand why she didn't eat like we did.

"You're too nervous," said Mother. "You need more meat on your bones." She made my sister sit at the kitchen table until she finished three blueberry muffins. Too much. My sister threw up. Mother thought she had an eating disorder.

"She's embarrassed by my size," said Mother. "She doesn't want to become this large."

"She's not embarrassed," I said. "She just can't eat like you."

My sister was terrified of Mother, though Mother didn't believe me when I tried to explain it to her.

"Why the hell should she be scared of me," said Mother. "I'm her mother for God's sake."

Dad would have understood my sister, but he left when she was three. Mother needed a sparring partner, a role my sister couldn't comprehend and my father couldn't fill. Sometimes I'm mad at him, but it's hard to sustain that anger because I know Mother is impossible.

I wear a bathrobe around the house, sleep in the bathroom on an air mattress covered with a fire-retardant blanket with a bucket of wet towels by my side. I hide all of my good dishes and glasses on a high shelf in my closet, use paper plates and cups instead. I catch fire every other day, don't know when I'll be able to return to work. I take wet towels in the car when I drive to the nursing home to see Mother. She looks much better than I feel, plump and pink-cheeked even though she's got a cough.

"You need to eat more," Mother tells me when the orderlies deliver her lunch. "You're too thin. Your body doesn't have enough food to burn. That's why you're catching fire."

"I thought it was because of Dad," I say.

"Him too," says Mother, "but you're also skinny."

She coughs hard. I sit up straight in my chair, but she waves her hand at me and shakes her head. Mother has developed a heavy cough—she calls it her heart cough—and it's the same one her sister and brother got before they died. After twenty seconds the spasms stop.

"That gets the bad stuff out of my system," says Mother and takes a large bite of mashed potato.

Three weeks after I start combusting, my sister sends a plane ticket to visit her in Seattle.

"You need time to relax," she says. "That job stresses you out too much."

"Mother is dying," I say. "That stresses me out too much."

"She's going to keep kicking for another ten years," says my sister. "That's how she is."

"Mother isn't immortal," I say.

"Thank God," mutters my sister.

"If you keep talking like that I won't come."

"I'll be nice," she sighs. "I want to see you. A vacation will do you good."

Mother isn't happy when she hears I'm going to visit my sister rather than my sister taking time off work to fly back to Ohio.

"Your sister hates me," says Mother.

"You and her don't see things the same way," I say.

"Which is why she hates me and never visits," says Mother.

"Have you called her?" I say.

"When I call she doesn't answer," says Mother.

"When I answer she yells at me for not visiting," says my sister later that evening. "I don't want to visit someone who's going to yell at me."

Nobody wants to be the first to be civil. My sister is passive-aggressive. Mother's just aggressive. Dad was like my sister. Quietly rebellious. He moved farther away rather than risk confrontation. I'm not sure why he married Mother, but she has a surety about her that he might have liked. Mother doesn't hesitate, was probably convinced they should be together, and made my dad believe the same thing.

I'm mad at him for leaving my sister with no one who was calm. She could have curled with Dad on the recliner chair while Mother and I fought. I don't understand why my dad thought that my sister and I would be able to deal with Mother if he couldn't handle her on his own. I don't understand why he stopped communicating with us after that last cheque.

I have to take a couple sedatives before the plane trip to Seattle, too worried my anxiety over catching fire will make me catch fire. I'm afraid the flight attendants will somehow divulge the risk I pose, not let me on the plane, but I get shoved into a seat along with everyone else. The trip passes in a haze. I feel floaty, not really in my body. The flight attendant has to shake my shoulder so I remember to get off.

I stumble into the airport and see my sister and am struck by how much she looks like Mother without the padding of weight. She is almost but not quite too thin. My sister grabs my shoulders and hugs me, but I can feel the hardness of her shoulder blades while Mother is all alarming softness.

"You look tired," she says. I tell her I'm just coming to. She clicks her tongue at me for taking the sedatives but I tell her it was that or spend the whole flight in terror of combusting.

Seattle is a pleasant change. The air is cooler and wetter than Ohio's. My sister thinks the chill will help with my temperament and the combustion. We spend the weekend chatting and watching movies and going out for brunch. She even pays for a massage, says I need it to get rid of stress.

I try to talk about Mother, but she doesn't want to hear it.

"The nurses are serious," I say after we get home from my massage.

"I don't care," says my sister. "I don't want to see her."

"She loves you," I say, "just not in a way that's easy for you to understand."

"What good is it then?"

"It's love," I say. "That has to count for something."

Pain in my ankle. Before I can run to the kitchen and grab a damp washcloth, I've ignited again. I burn for a couple moments while my sister sprints to the bathroom for an old towel. I stand up, get away from her couch so it doesn't burn, but the fabric that was near my leg has already charred. Fuck.

"You're not supposed to think about her," my sister says as I swaddle my leg in the towel. "She gets you worked up."

"You both get me worked up," I say.

She drives me to the ER. The burn is more serious than usual, will probably leave a blister. In the waiting room my sister isn't as mad over the couch as I thought she'd be.

"I'll pay for the damage," I say.

"No," she says. "It's part of the risk I accepted when I invited you to visit. I just wish you could get this stress out of your system."

"You and Mom are responsible for it," I say. "You won't even have a civil conversation over the phone."

"She can't have a civil conversation over the phone," says my sister.

"This is all her anger coming out of you."

"It's how she communicates," I say.

"Not with me she doesn't," says my sister.

"You should let me pay for the couch," I say again.

"No," she says. I think she feels a little guilty about the situation, realises that she and Mother play a role in my combustion, even if she doesn't want to admit it.

The nurse calls my name. My sister and I explain we were frying fish and the pan with the hot oil got knocked off the stove and splashed on my ankle. The doctor examines my wound while my sister folds her arms and grimaces. I'd tell her how much she looks like Mother, but she'd hit me.

I have spent the past thirty-nine years trying to explain to my mother and sister why they can't get along. Why can't I say screw it, let myself accept that even though people share genes, they might not be able to stand being in the same room for more than fifteen seconds. Maybe my sister is right and Mother would only yell if she visited. I know Mother would scream out of love, because she misses my sister, because she wishes my sister lived closer to home, but my sister would not interpret Mother's screams in that manner.

I know if I saw my father I would react to him the same way Mother would react to my sister. Scream at him out of love.

"Did you ever try to look for Dad?" I ask my sister as we drive home from the hospital.

"Once," she says.

"Are you mad at him?" I say.

"No," she says.

"Why not?" I say. "He left us."

"He left Mother."

"And us," I say. "He doesn't love us. Not enough to write. We don't know if he's alive."

"We'd remind him of her," she says. "Maybe he thought we'd be the same way. Maybe he thought we'd hate him."

"So you feel better with no parents at all," I say.

"We got duds. Not all people who are parents should have been parents."

Maybe she has a point. There are certain people Mother was not fit to mother, and my sister was one of them. At the same time, my parents are my parents and we owe each other something. Explanations if not love.

On Monday morning my sister has to go to work, tells me to relax and have a good time. I take a walk, go out for coffee because it's Seattle and I want to be around people without needing to talk to anyone. In the coffee shop I watch old men doing crosswords. I want to pick one who could be my father and be mad at him. I wonder how many of them could have stood up to Mother, stayed around longer than my dad, but maybe those wouldn't have been men she wanted to marry.

I sit down across from one of the old men. "My father left when I was seven," I say. "Can I be mad at you instead of him?"

He takes off his glasses. "And where will that get you?" he says.

"I keep wanting to explode," I say.

"You won't break anything, will you?" he says.

"No," I say, "I'm getting better about that." But if I don't break things, I ignite. I hope that being mad at a father substitute, someone I can see and touch, will help.

"Well," he says, "go ahead."

I look at him, so calm and willing, and I can't think of a damn thing to say.

"You can start whenever," he says.

"I don't know where to begin," I say.

"Did I hit your mother?" he says. "Did I yell at her?"

"No," I say, "it was the other way around. Usually I don't blame you for leaving, but sometimes I do. I blame you a lot." I feel my fingers getting hot, squeeze them tight against my palms. Anger builds behind my eyes, wanting to come out.

"I'm sorry I missed your birthdays," he says. "That's probably something you were mad about. Birthdays and Christmas."

"No," I say, "you sent money. It was okay."

"That was good of me," he says.

"Yes," I say. "I'm angry not for me, but for my sister. She needed you to be around and you weren't."

"I didn't realise that," he says. "I'm sorry."

"And you stopped sending money after my sister turned eighteen. We never heard from you again."

"How sad," he says.

"Why didn't you send a card?" I say. "You could have told us where you were."

He pauses.

"Maybe I was scared," he says.

"That's what my sister says," I say. When I'm talking I find it's easier to direct the heat into my hands. I grab my coffee mug, feel that anger seep into the black ceramic cup which gets a few degrees warmer.

"Has she forgiven me?" he says.

"You," I say, "but not Mother."

"And what do you think of your mother?" he says.

"She needs to be translated," I say. "Not everyone understands her."

"I know people like that." He nods. "When were you going to start yelling at me?"

"I don't know," I say. "It's more difficult than I thought it would be."

"Can I get you another coffee?" he says.

"You don't have to," I say.

"Refills aren't expensive," he says, tugging the cup from my fingers. "And I always hoped you'd grow up to be a coffee drinker."

When I call Mother that evening I don't tell my sister. She's just gotten home from work and her shoulders droop. Tired. Good. She flops on the couch and turns on the evening news, says we should go out for Chinese after she's had a chance to relax.

I dial Mother's number in the home, wait for the ring, for her to answer, then I flick on the speaker phone. I sit on my sister before she knows what's happening.

"Hello, Mother," I say.

"What the hell," says my sister, pushing my back. I don't budge. I'm not really heavy, but weigh enough to keep my sister stationary.

"Who's this?" says Mother.

"Me," I say. "Us. In Seattle." I'm holding a mug filled with cold water and a teabag. By the time we're done with this conversation, it should have steeped and be ready to drink.

My sister pounds my back with her small fists. "Get off me," she says.

"But then you'd leave the room," I say.

"Is that your sister?" says Mother.

"Yes," I say.

"Dammit," says my sister.

"That is no fucking way to speak to your mother," says Mother.

"I wasn't speaking to you," says my sister. "This is crazy."

"I'm not getting off until you say something nice," I say. "Something without swear words. That goes for both of you."

I feel my sister grimace at the back of my head. On the other end of the line Mother has lapsed into rare silence. Warmth surges into my hands and feet—not a burning heat, but a powerful one, like I could light candles with my fingers. Mother and my sister sigh in unison.

"Well," says my sister.

"Well," says Mother.

It's a start. I hold the mug a little more tightly. I can wait a little longer.

Three

You'd very much like the three-legged man. Your grandparents might have seen him when he was still performing in the sideshow, might have told you about his act in which he kicked a ball with his third leg, danced three-legged jigs, and stood on his third leg while reading suggestive limericks. He was really quite spectacular.

The three-legged man left the sideshow when he was thirty-nine and his daughter was fifteen. He liked performing, but it got tiresome and he wanted to do something else. Be a normal guy with a house and a kid. This is more difficult with three legs than with two, but the three-legged man did an admirable job of it, though he is not sure his daughter would agree. They moved to a reasonable town and bought a small home. The three-legged man planted annuals along the front walk, tomatoes in the backyard, and had a second career as a mail carrier for eighteen years.

The three-legged man's daughter graduated from high school and college and medical school. She was very intelligent. She became a radiologist, married a trombone-playing nurse, had a daughter, and divorced. The three-legged man and his daughter, who is now fifty-two, do not talk about the sideshow years. He invites her and his granddaughter for dinner every Sunday (although his granddaughter is young and busy and does not always come). Every other Sunday his daughter brings a bottle of wine. The three-legged man is a teetotaller. His daughter drinks the whole bottle (except when his granddaughter comes and has one glass). You would not know when his daughter is drunk because she is so neat. Never slurs. Never swaggers. Just swears a lot. The three-legged man's former wife also liked wine too much. Remember this for later.

You'd like the three-legged man's daughter. She smells slightly of honeysuckle, wears brightly coloured skirts, has a pleasant voice, and is good at explaining things to other people in a reassuring tone. If you happened to see her in the grocery store bread aisle and asked her advice on whole wheat versus seven-grain bread, she would explain to you reassuringly why one kind, probably the kind you wanted in the first place, was both healthier and tastier than the other. You can understand why it is good she went into the medical profession.

The three-legged man's friend Odelle is a good artist, but she is only known locally so you would not have heard of her. She is sixty-seven, nine years younger than the three-legged man, and accustomed to the idea of wrinkles, of the aging body. It was her idea to paint him in a series of different nude poses from classical art. Michelangelo's David. Rodin's pondering man from The Gates of Hell. She even painted him as an old man on the ceiling of the Sistine Chapel, reaching out to touch the hand of God. The three-legged man particularly likes that painting. You would, too. His daughter does not. Odelle's work is going to be shown in a local gallery. There will be hors d'oeuvres and an art critic from the local paper.

"That woman is going to make you the talk of the town," his

daughter says at Sunday dinner after finishing the bottle of wine.

"I hope so," says the three-legged man.

"I don't even know why I'm so fucking worried," says the three-legged man's daughter. "You'll be the embarrassed one. Not me."

"That's what I keep telling you," says the three-legged man. He tries not to grimace, shifts on his stool and taps his third leg on the floor like he does when he's anxious. The leg grows out of his spine and it's hard for him to sit in regular chairs.

"She can't paint worth shit," says his daughter. "The show will flop. No one will come."

"Time for you to cool off," says the three-legged man as he stands up.

"The ones who do come will gawk and point. A fucking sideshow. That's what you've always wanted. To be a goddamned freak." She often says this when drunk.

The three-legged man slides his hands under his daughter's arms, lifts her up like a big doll, and walks her down the hall to the bathroom. His third leg swings behind him like a tail. You would smile to see him if you did not know that his daughter was drunk, and you would not know that she is drunk because she is so neat, doesn't resist. The three-legged man sits his daughter on the closed toilet. She crosses her arms. Crosses her legs. Smirks because she knows she's upset him. The three-legged man closes the bathroom door and brings his stool from the kitchen to wait outside.

His daughter is too like her mother, holds the poison in, doesn't throw up. She spends her days interpreting X-rays and CAT scans and other images of the possibly ill at the hospital. There she is quiet. Technical. To the point. When the three-legged man sees his daughter's co-workers at the grocery store and bank, they comment on how intelligent his daughter is, how calm and focused. The three-legged man thanks them politely.

He knows every family harbours its own spectacle. The private ones are the worst.

You must understand that the three-legged man loved his wife, but had to send her out of the trailer when she was drunk. There wasn't anywhere to put her inside. Eventually she ran off with a human pincushion. Many in the sideshow had a weakness for liquor. The three-legged man raised his daughter alone from the time she was seven. He thought he did well enough, but when she was a teenager she spent time with the children of other performers, kids who drank as much as their parents. The sideshow was failing. Nobody had much money. Everyone wanted to forget that.

The three-legged man knows he was not strict enough with his daughter when they travelled with the sideshow, but he amended himself when they moved to town. He made sure his daughter obeyed curfew. He surreptitiously sniffed her words when she came home, searching for an odour of beer or mint meant to cover beer. He did not allow alcohol in the house. His daughter did well in college. He kept his fingers crossed.

The three-legged man fetches his sketchpad from the kitchen counter and returns to sit outside the bathroom door. He took up drawing after he retired from the postal service. He does not show his drawings to many people, but if you saw them you would think they were reasonably good, though the proportions are a bit off. He's been sketching Odelle from memory, drawing her like a tattooed woman, penciling mountains on her arms, rivers winding up her thighs, mesas across her abdomen, a waterfall to the side of her right breast. Her body becomes many landscapes. He draws for an hour that becomes two. Three. He listens for his daughter.

Since the three-legged man was a mail carrier for so many years and did his route on foot, he got to know everyone in town and everyone got to know him. The daily walk kept him fit, and the profession kept him social. He became a fixture. When the three-legged man goes to the barber, conversation is the same as when any other man gets his hair cut, although the three-legged man needs to sit on a stool because the barber's chair is not very comfortable. The three-legged man and the barber and any customers who happen to be waiting discuss the weather and how it is unseasonable, high school sports teams and how they are worse than average, the old days and how they were invariably better than now. The three-legged man knows these are normal things for crotchety old men to discuss, and he is pleased to do it. If you had grown up in town, when you saw the three-legged man on the street you would think of mail, not his third leg. The three-legged man feels conflicted about this. He likes that his third leg has become normal, part of who he is, but its oddness used to earn his living.

The three-legged man opens the bathroom door after six hours. His daughter sits on the closed toilet, reading a magazine. He keeps his art journals and copies of National Geographic Magazine on the counter. For dinner they eat simply—turkey and cheese sandwiches. The three-legged man reminds his daughter that Odelle's art show is Wednesday at seven.

"You should stop by," he says. "If only for a few hors d'oeuvres."

"All those people looking at you naked," she says.

"Most of the people in Renaissance paintings are naked," he says.

"They're also dead, not standing beside the canvas."

The three-legged man shrugs. In his daughter's mind he will always be embarrassing, with or without clothing. When they first moved to town, she made a point of walking three feet ahead of him wherever they went. You might say this is normal teenage behaviour, but even now the three-legged man's daughter cringes when they are together at a restaurant. She never drinks wine in restaurants or around friends, only in the company of family.

If you went to school with the three-legged man's granddaughter, you would not remember her. She was quiet, not a wonderful or poor student, and she tended to stand in the middle row when class pictures were taken. If asked to describe her, you would say nice, which is what you say when you can't think of anything else, because it doesn't really say anything. Her most memorable feature was that she had a three-legged man for a grandfather, the three-legged man who delivered your mail, but this would not be remarkable to you because you would have grown up with a three-legged man delivering the mail and you would have assumed that's what three-legged men did. The three-legged man's granddaughter was notable because she was good at art—not drawing but clay and sculpture, anything three-dimensional—but this would not be something you would recall now, so many years later.

The three-legged man's granddaughter works in a costume shop, does alterations and makes simple garments. The three-legged man is proud of her, but he knows his daughter is mad that his granddaughter did not go into medicine.

"We need more women in the field," she says. She blames the three-legged man for her daughter's love of costumes. He showed his granddaughter sideshow pictures and encouraged her to make hats and masks when he cared for her after school. The three-legged man's granddaughter says she is trying to convince her mother to come to the gallery show, but so far her efforts have proved fruitless.

The three-legged man and his daughter were each married for ten years. It took that long for the three-legged man's wife to run off with the human pincushion. It took that long for his son-in-law to tire of his daughter's twice-monthly bottles of wine. The three-legged man's son-in-law left his daughter on the night she said his trombone sounded like a sick donkey and she was going to sell it for scrap metal.

The three-legged man's son-in-law came to his house and asked to spend the night.

The three-legged man asked where his granddaughter was. He was worried, you see.

The three-legged man's son-in-law said he had tried to bring his daughter, but she wanted to stay with her mother.

The three-legged man let his son-in-law make a bed on the couch. He called his daughter's apartment and spoke with his granddaughter. She was seven, said her mother was sleeping, and refused the three-legged man's offer to come and get her. You may think the three-legged man should have insisted his granddaughter spend the night at his house. He would agree with you, as he had a difficult time sleeping that night.

After his daughter's divorce, the three-legged man cared for his granddaughter from three in the afternoon when she got out of school until seven at night when her mother picked her up. This was when the three-legged man gave his granddaughter construction paper and paper plates and markers and feathers and beads and glitter and lots of glue. She made hats and masks, went home sticky and sequined. His daughter rolled her eyes but kept silent.

The three-legged man's granddaughter lived with her mother until she was eighteen, but she spent holidays and every other weekend with her father. She has always known her mother needed more care than her father, which the three-legged man finds admirable. The three-legged man knows his daughter is a kind and generous person twenty-eight days every month. He and his granddaughter do not speak about the wine. They sit quietly and wait for something to change. Understand the three-legged man has learned there isn't anything else he can do.

The three-legged man invites Odelle to dinner once or twice a week because it is better than eating alone, and because she has painted lovely pictures of him and not asked for a penny in return. Odelle has slim fingers and arthritic knees, which means she must sit when she paints. She is not squeamish about nakedness and neither is the three-legged man. He thinks the wrinkles of age have made him more interesting to look at, like a partially burned candle. Odelle is not his girlfriend, although sometimes the three-legged man is wishful.

"Would you like to be a couple?" Odelle asks him the day before the gallery show while they eat beef stroganoff over noodles. Odelle is always straightforward.

"A couple of what?" says the three-legged man. The thought of romantic relationships both excites him and causes him to make bad jokes. You understand that sort of nervousness.

Odelle rolls her eyes. You understand that sort of exasperation.

"I'm sorry," he says, "I'm old."

"I know," she says.

"Are you offended?" he says.

"Not by your age," she says.

The three-legged man would like to have a girlfriend. The three-legged man is terrified at the prospect of having a girlfriend. Embracing new things makes him worried. Not embracing new things makes him feel stodgy.

"Can we just keep on like this?" he says.

Odelle nods. He cannot tell if she expected this response or if she is disappointed.

"Are you nervous about the show tomorrow?" she asks.

"My body has never made me nervous," he says.

"But the same can't be said for other people."

"Other people have never made me nervous," he says, thinking of his daughter who makes him not so much nervous as wistful.

The three-legged man has regrets. After his wife left, he told his daughter she would return. He was hopeful. He kept his daughter hopeful. She started to hate him for it, blamed her father for her mother's departure. She wasn't comfortable being the child of a three-legged man, but perhaps not many people could be.

Once when the three-legged man's daughter was drunk, she told him she'd been terrified her daughter would inherit a recessive gene, have three legs.

"Three fucking legs," she said.

Because his daughter was drunk, the three-legged man did not take a great deal of offense. He was a bit relieved and a bit dismayed that his granddaughter had two legs.

His granddaughter says, "I never thought having three legs would be a bad thing."

You may or may not agree, but remember that if you lived in the same town as the three-legged man, you would have grown up thinking three-legged men delivered the mail, so your thoughts on three-leggedness would have been closely related to your impressions of the postal service.

The three-legged man often sits on a stool in the living room in front of a full-length wall mirror. He draws himself, practises foreshortening on his legs. There are five sketchbooks on the three-legged man's coffee table. Drawings of him sitting and standing and walking, both front and side views. Drawings of Odelle as a fat lady, a sword swallower, and a tattooed woman. Drawings of his wife and daughter and granddaughter, always a three-quarters view. They have the same small nose and small ears and pronounced chin. The three-legged man last saw his wife when she was thirty-one, a year older than his granddaughter and twenty-one years younger than his daughter. In the drawings of his wife, she has aged to look more like his daughter.

The three-legged man's daughter stares at pictures of the insides of people all day—their bones and organs and muscles. She diagnoses images. Sees what makes people work. What has gone wrong. She is good at what she does. A very intelligent woman. All sorts of nurses and doctors have told him so. Understand the three-legged man is very proud of his daughter. She wants to help people.

His granddaughter says that on some nights when she was growing up, her mother came home and had three glasses of wine. Not the whole bottle. Maybe half.

"When I asked if something was wrong," says his granddaughter, "she shook her head and said she had a rough day at work."

Your mother or father probably told you the same thing on many occasions.

The three-legged man's granddaughter says her mother reads the obituaries every morning. Sometimes she follows under the text with her finger, mouths the words. After three cups of coffee she nods to herself and drives to the hospital.

At the gallery opening, Odelle wears a peach-coloured dress made of gauzy material that flows around her hips. The three-legged man wears a suit and tie. He has three suits and doesn't wear them often because he has to get them specially made. If you saw him in one of his suits you would think he looked very dapper. The three-legged man would say that he should look dapper because three-legged suits are not cheap.

The three-legged man's dentist and barber compliment the pictures, as do several retired mail carriers who only have two legs. If you saw the paintings you would agree—his third leg looks so normal, so natural, so expected, you could think all humans were tripod people. The three-legged man says he's glad he wasn't born in a time when doctors would have tried to take the leg off. He was saved by poor technology.

After the show, the three-legged man and his granddaughter and Odelle go out for coffee and cheesecake. Rich desserts are one of his weaknesses. He was pleased with the show but keeps glancing out the café window to see who is walking by.

On Sunday the three-legged man's daughter and granddaughter come for dinner. His daughter brings a bottle of wine. The three-legged man knows he should say something, but he doesn't. Understand that saying something would not change anything. They eat grilled chicken breast and discuss the costumes his granddaughter is making for *A Midsummer Night's Dream*.

The three-legged man's daughter sees his sketchbook lying on a corner of his desk, open to one of the pictures of Odelle. She is drawn like Eve, standing beside the tree of knowledge, ignoring the snake and the apple. The three-legged man thinks it is one of his best drawings. (You probably would, too, or you might prefer the one of Odelle as a tattooed woman.) His daughter picks up the sketchbook and stares at the picture. She takes a pen from the pocket of her jeans, uncaps it, and starts scribbling over the picture, a four-year-old's scrawl.

The three-legged man and his granddaughter gape. The three-legged man is not entirely sure what his daughter thinks of Odelle beyond normal dislike, but he has wondered if his daughter still thinks he should be married to her mother.

His granddaughter stands up, grabs his daughter's arms, wretches the sketchbook away, and holds his daughter's hands behind her back.

"Too tight," says his daughter.

"Good," says his granddaughter who is not usually a violent person.

The three-legged man stares for a moment, oddly pleased with his granddaughter's reaction. His notebook is on the floor, opened like a moth. The three-legged man walks around the table, picks it up, closes the pages, and lays the notebook beside his plate. He pries his granddaughter's hands from his daughter's wrists, hugs his granddaughter so her arms are pinned to her sides.

"Get out," says the three-legged man to his daughter.

She doesn't scream expletives, hangs back for a moment, perhaps waiting to see if he will shove her in the bathroom. He doesn't. She leaves. The three-legged man watches her from the kitchen, through the living room window glass. Her head is high, her posture perfect.

The night his wife left was a usual night. She was tipsy. He ordered her out of the trailer. You would have agreed it was reasonable that he do this. He figured she'd come back when she was sober. Instead she went and found the pincushion man. The three-legged man waited for a week for her to come back. Then he waited eight years. His wife was often a good and kind and generous woman. You would have liked her.

The three-legged man and his granddaughter sit in his living room. The three-legged man wonders what he would do if his wife came back now. He wonders if he would recognize her. He wonders if she would be at all remorseful.

Butterfly Women

The skin flaps ran the length of my body from my wrists to my ankles so I looked something like a flying squirrel. The flaps were loose and full, but if I lifted my arms more than a foot above my head I felt a pull at my side.

When I was little the doctors and my father wanted to cut the flaps off, but my mother didn't let them. She wanted to wait until I was older, let me decide.

My family went out to breakfast every Saturday at a diner three blocks from our house. Melba and Janice, the two waitresses, had brown puffs of hair, white aprons, too-red lipstick, doted on me and complimented the little pink caftans my mother made. When I was five years old I ordered a Belgian waffle for breakfast. My mother cut it and I reached for the maple syrup and knocked over a glass of orange juice with my flap. The juice flowed across the table onto my father's lap.

"Dammit," he yelled, standing up and letting the juice drip further down his pants. I cringed. I can't remember exactly what he said, something about my flaps getting in the way, making me clumsy. I couldn't finish the waffle.

My father divorced my mother a month later, left while I was asleep. Later my mother said my father would have left whether or not I had flaps. She explained that she and my father were the sort of people who could be together for a little while but not a long while. I have hazy memories of my parents yelling in the kitchen, my father saying he didn't want to have a bat for a daughter, my mother yelling back that she did not give birth to a bat but a butterfly. I liked thinking of myself as a butterfly. It made my flaps hurt less.

I started gliding when I was five years old. Jumping off the slide in my backyard was more exciting than sliding down it, and my fall was slowed if I spread out my arms, let the wind catch under my flaps. It took a few tries to figure out how to land, but once I got the hang of it, kept my legs flexible and bent my knees, it was pretty simple. I jumped off the slide ten times before my mother saw me from the kitchen window, ran out yelling that I had to stop or I'd break a bone. I pouted on the swing set for a while, then looked back at the kitchen window. No mother. I climbed up the slide and made six more jumps before she ran out screaming again.

My mother was the school principal, one of the first women in the area to have that job, though I didn't appreciate it until I was older. When kids at school teased me, called me flying squirrel girl, my mother said they were just jealous. I didn't feel any better. When I was in second grade, workmen were making repairs to the roof of the school and left a ladder leaning against the brick wall. I climbed up. The building wasn't high, just one storey, but some tattletale sprinted to the office to get my mother. She was standing on the ground surrounded by second graders when I spread my arms and jumped. I sailed down, landed without a bruise, but my mother kept me in the office for the afternoon and grounded me at home for a month.

Mom was there when I fell off my bike and bruised my flaps. She was there when I got chicken pox, made me lie still while she coated the flaps with calamine lotion. For a week I was miserable and itchy because there were as many bumps on my flaps as the rest of my body. Oatmeal baths didn't help. My mother put mittens on my hands so I couldn't scratch the flaps.

When I cried that my flaps hurt because I raised my arm too high, stretched the skin, my mother pulled me beside her on the couch, gave me a tissue and a cookie.

"You're beautiful," she said. "I've never created anything quite as lovely as you."

I chewed my cookie and stopped crying for a little bit, stopped asking my mother if I could get the flaps taken off. I liked that I could soar off the back of the slide, even though my mother threatened to take away my allowance if I kept doing it.

My father sent gifts at my birthday and Christmas until I was eleven years old. Then the presents stopped. He had moved across the country to Oregon, had another family, another wife, another set of kids. Kids without flaps.

"Boring," said my mother. She let me draw on my flaps with nontoxic markers so I could look even more like a butterfly. "See how pretty they can be?" my mother said.

I nodded but wished I could wear normal jeans and shorts like other kids, not just the caftans my mother sewed.

I started sitting on the roof when I was twelve years old, in junior high. I got home before my mother, who was usually at school until five. Our house was two storeys high. The roof sloped gently so I had to be cautious, but it was easy to go out through my bedroom window and hang my legs over the edge of the roof, over the gutter. I faced the backyard and a field of clover and Queen Anne's lace, often lost track of time and was still sitting there when my mother got home.

"No desserts for a week if you don't go back through the window," she yelled. Or no allowance. Or no TV. I jumped anyway. My mother gasped. I knew she was afraid I'd fall by accident, not be able to spread out my arms. I didn't understand why she wanted me to keep the flaps, told me to have pride in them, but never let me do fun things.

When I began having periods, I had to start wearing underwear. My mother bought extra-extra-extra-large satin panties, helped me put them on and pull my extra skin over the waistband. Skin bunched against my body, drooped like angel wings or dead flower petals.

"I want to get the flaps cut off," I said to my mother while standing naked in the bathroom, save a pair of pink panties designed for old women who weighed three hundred pounds.

"Honey," my mother said and hugged me tight, "just try this for a while. Soon I'll show you how to wear tampons."

I gritted my teeth. I had to wait until my period was over before I could resume flying, before the flaps were worth the hurt.

When I was in tenth grade my mother was diagnosed with diabetes. She had always been a large woman, rounded and imposing, but she shuddered in the doctor's office when the nurse explained how she'd need to give herself finger sticks every morning to test her blood sugar level. My mother and I sipped diet soda in the hospital cafeteria. I patted her arm and felt the pull on my flap.

"It will be okay," I said, "you just have to be more careful now."

"Careful not to lose toes," said my mother, glancing down at her feet. "Careful not to have a heart attack."

"Don't talk like that," I said. "You'll stay healthy."

"I thought I was," said my mother. "I want a sweet roll."

"You can't have one. You know that."

"This isn't going to be a good life," she said.

"They make sugar free everything now," I said. "All kinds of sweets."

"Not a good life," said my mother, shaking her head.

In high school I dated boys who read sci-fi and fantasy novels and were entranced by my flaps. When we went to my house after school I showed them how I could fly. A couple of them wanted to jump off the roof with me. I told them they were crazy, but the boys were insistent. Two of them broke their ankles and I had to call an ambulance.

"You always have to show off," my mother muttered as she sat beside me in the emergency room. "Boys will date land-bound girls, too."

"I tell them not to jump," I said. "Boys never listen."

My mother sighed. "Stress like this makes me want chocolate."

I gave her a couple of the sugar-free chocolate buttons I kept in my purse.

"Not as good as the real thing," she said.

"What was your blood sugar this morning?" I said.

"I'm still alive and kicking," she said.

I knew she cheated sometimes, ate sweets and took extra insulin.

"I worry about you," I muttered.

My mother put her hand on my knee and grimaced.

"You can't keep injuring your boyfriends," she said. "The guy you marry will be in a full body cast by the wedding."

No boys liked me enough to date me more than a month, but I didn't tell my mom that. I had a reputation as being hazardous. Sometimes I kind of liked it. Other times it was annoying. Not much different than the flaps.

I went to college to get a degree in education and become a first grade teacher. Much of children's literature was based on fantasy, things that were special and out of the ordinary, so when I explained to my students that I was a butterfly woman, the kids smiled and nodded. They liked the big colourful caftans I wore, the way that fabric flowed around my body.

I got the first tattoo on my flap when I was twenty-three. A Renaissance angel with a sword under my left elbow. My mother cheerfully paid for half of the cost. I think she hoped I'd quit flying once I'd found another use for my flaps.

I bought a house in the country, only one storey high so it wasn't as good for flying, but on breezy days I could jump from the roof and float several feet before touching the ground. I added more small tattoos—hummingbirds, cardinals, a griffon, a phoenix, and a gargoyle with tiny wings.

I was by myself a lot in the evenings, but I didn't mind the quiet after being around little kids all day. I dated a few guys, mostly teachers and librarians, but no one who I wanted to marry. My mother kept asking if I had a special friend.

"Not many guys know what to make of me," I said.

"You're lovely," she said. "Anyone can see that."

I didn't feel like explaining the full dating logistics because she was my mother. The extra skin made sex problematic—I had to be on top, and my partner had to watch his elbows and knees. Part of me was afraid of having children. I worried they would have flaps, too. I couldn't explain the fear to my mother, since she thought the flaps were great. At least that's what she told me.

My teacher friends admired the flaps, but it was hard for anyone to understand what it was like to live with them every day. Sometimes I dreamed of myself without flaps. I saw them hanging in my living room like two big canvases, covered with tattoos of winged dragons and seraphim and parrots. I dreamed myself wearing normal clothes, having normal sex, shelving high books without that constant pull on my arms. I woke up after the terrible dream-realisation that I was grounded.

When I visited home I showed my mother the latest tattoos. I added a peacock by my right ankle, a lovebird by my left, and a Pegasus next to my right wrist. My mother fingered the tattoos carefully, smiled and nodded, said I had good taste.

"You've made your skin so beautiful," she said.

"The flaps decide a lot of things for me," I said, grazing the peacock with my fingertips.

My mother chose to ignore this comment.

She drove to the store to buy groceries for dinner. I went out my old bedroom window to sit on the roof, smell cut grass and clover. The field behind the house was purple with them. I thought about my father, wondered what he was doing, if he ever thought of me and felt sorry. My mother said the flaps weren't the reason he left, but I didn't believe her. Since he divorced my mother when I was five, I found myself trapped in self-centred childhood logic. Of course I was to blame for the divorce. Of course it was my fault.

I felt the wind catch under my flaps, the slight ballooning of skin. My attitude about my flaps changed from day to day. Sometimes they were the most fun things in the world. Sometimes I hated them. But even then I knew that if I got them cut off it would be an impulsive act, one I didn't let myself consider too hard.

My mother came home before I expected her, marched outside with her hands on her hips. For a moment she looked exactly like she did when I was twelve.

"Hey you," my mother yelled. "That's dangerous. Go back through the window."

"Mama," I called down, "I'm fine. I've done this a million times."

"And scared me every time," said my mother. "Someday you're going to land wrong on your ankle and then you won't be fine."

"I'm careful," I yelled.

"That's what Auntie Bernice said before she got pregnant with Doug," said my mother.

I jumped, spread my arms, and spent five midair seconds watching my mother gape. I landed a little hard and twisted my ankle, walked back inside without wincing but took a glass of ice water to my room while my mother read in the living room. I dumped the water in the upstairs bathroom sink and put the ice in a washcloth to make a cold pack for my ankle.

At dinner my mother asked how my ankle was doing.

"They're both fine," I said.

"Uh-huh," said my mother, smiling slightly.

That night she checked her blood sugar and frowned at the reading on the meter.

"Too high?" I said.

"I'm fine," said my mother.

She had a folder crammed with pamphlets about the effects of diabetes, ways the body could deteriorate. She could lose her sight to retinopathy. Lose her feet to poor circulation. Have tiny heart attacks she might not feel because of nerve damage in her chest. My mother didn't like having to be careful about what she ate, railed about her numerous medications.

"I'm obeying the rules because I want to be alive to see my grandchildren," she muttered.

I didn't know if I wanted to have children, especially because I had thirty new ones in my classroom every year. When I got home I only wanted to speak with another adult, if I talked to anyone at all. But it was easier to nod at my mother's comment than say anything in response. I wanted her to stay healthy.

When my mother turned sixty-six she retired from being an elementary school principal and moved to an assisted living facility because of her diabetes. The disease aged her too quickly. Her doctor whispered to me that she hadn't been checking her blood sugar carefully. She was getting neuropathy and sometimes her hands and feet felt numb, made her afraid of falling.

After the move my mother and I sat in her new kitchen, drank coffee and ate whole wheat crackers.

"I was getting lonely anyway," she said. "This is better."

"I want to get the flaps taken off," I said, mostly because I wanted to see her reaction.

"I'll write you out of the will," she said. My mother took another sip of coffee. For a moment I thought she was joking. Then I wasn't sure.

Six months later my mother called to say she might be developing retinopathy of diabetes in her left eye, losing her sight.

"I'll need to have surgery," said my mother.

"Oh Lord," I said.

"It's not a big deal," she said. "Fairly routine. That's what the doctor told me."

"Make sure the rest of you stays healthy."

"I wish my body would cooperate," said my mother.

"I'll visit this weekend," I said.

I couldn't concentrate at school. What if my mother couldn't see me anymore? She refused to admit she had the disease, ignored the diabetes so it was killing her faster. What if she'd already had a couple of little heart attacks that she wasn't able to feel? What if she had a big one?

I told my students a story about a butterfly woman who worked in a sideshow. Her act was to jump from ladder to ladder fifteen feet up, leap to the next as the first came crashing down. She didn't have flaps of skin, just an airy costume and a lot of balance. I said the sideshow butterfly woman was magic, and children should never try to jump off a ladder. My students asked if I was magic, too. I told them no.

That evening before I left for my mother's apartment, my period started. I grumbled and yanked on a pair of baggy underwear that confined my flaps and made it difficult to drive because of the pull on my arms. When my mother reached out to hug me, I wrapped my flaps around her body so tight the skin hurt more.

We drank tea in the kitchen. She discussed the dining room set and the good china and how much they should be worth because they were antiques.

"You might want to keep them and see if they gain value after I'm gone," said my mother. "Or you could sell them if you need the money."

"Are you dying?" I said.

"These are things we'll have to discuss eventually."

"I can't keep the flaps after you go."

"Don't be silly," said my mother. "It shouldn't matter if I'm here or not. They're yours. Now the pitcher and basin set on the dresser over there is at least one hundred and fifty years old so it should be worth a fair amount of money."

"This is all you're really going to leave me," I said, grabbing the edge of my left flap and shaking it. "Wings. You wanted me to keep the flaps and you've never wanted me to fly. What the hell am I supposed to do with them?"

"They're beautiful," my mother yelled back. "I want you to keep them. But I don't want you to get hurt because of them. And I don't want you to lose them when I'm gone."

I stood up so fast my chair fell back on the floor. I stomped down the hall to the bathroom but tripped on a throw rug and twisted my ankle which was already temperamental from too many hard landings. The fall pulled hard at my flaps, stretched them, and I was sure the skin was torn. I sat on the floor and cried until my head stopped hurting.

I peered into my sleeves. No blood. I padded back to the kitchen, limping slightly. My mother sat at the table, pinching the skin between her fingers, pulling it tight.

Markings

Breakfast with my sister is a disaster. She wants to make muffins, but I have to crack the eggs and measure spices and hold the bowl while she stirs. She can only use her right hand since the stroke, and the work I can do versus the work she can do leaves her frowning. I'm wearing a short-sleeved shirt so my tattoos show, which further annoys her. She doesn't like being reminded of them. When my sister spreads jam on her muffin, the knife slips and falls onto her white pants. I help her change. She grumps around afterwards, but there's not much either of us can do.

I need to get out of the house and suggest a walk to the park. My sister slumps on the couch and crosses her arms.

"Once you get outside you'll feel better," I say as I sit beside her and ready her socks and shoes. "Now give me your foot."

She refuses to move, so I bend down and grab her ankle and rest it on my lap. I tug her sock over her toes, then slide on her shoe. She knows my fingers ache in the morning, but she's decided that if I'm going to torture her, she's going to torture me back.

"I'm not trying upset you," I say, though she'd accuse me of that if she could talk. I can see it in her eyes and hear it in the voice she used to have.

"I know what you're saying so you don't have to look at me so loud," I say as I pull the second sock over her foot.

My sister grimaces. She thinks I'm making fun, but I'm being honest. All her gestures come with words. Sometimes we talk through raised eyebrows, finger-points, and nods.

I think about saying something to her about assisted living facilities. There's a nice one on the other end of town. I called them yesterday to inquire about rates, but I don't want her to accuse me of making threats. In the past week, putting my sister in an assisted living facility has become more of a serious consideration. I hate to say that I'm getting too old for this, but I am.

Once her feet have been properly attired, I drag my sister out the door to the park.

"The sun will do us both good," I say.

My sister glances back and forth as we walk the two blocks. She doesn't like being with me in public places because of my short-sleeved shirts and short skirts.

"Really," I mutter. "What good are those lovely pictures if they're hidden?"

On my right arm is Aphrodite. There's a snake curling around my left arm, ending on an apple at my wrist. A female angel wields a sword on my right leg, and on my left leg Eve demurely covers her intimate areas with her hands. I like that my tattoos have been distorted by cellulite—Eve and the angel have gained weight and wrinkled along with me. They are meant to be seen. I am meant to be seen. And I am old enough not to care what other people think.

At the park my sister eases down on a bench. It's been a year since her stroke. When she was released from the hospital I moved in to care for her. She didn't want to go to a facility. Too expensive, she wrote on the pad of paper that had become her mouth. She wanted to stay in her apartment. But I know that all day long she thinks intelligent things that she can't say. It drives her crazy. She was a teacher after all, is used to giving instructions and being obeyed.

While I am sympathetic, I get frustrated with her moods. If she had an assisted living apartment, she'd have her own bed, her own space, and wear a little alert device with a button she could press if she needed help. The nurses and other residents would probably be more patient with her than me. But my sister doesn't want to move. The process is more complicated since she has her wits about her. It's easier to put family members in a home when they don't know what's going on.

A fat woman puffing by on a morning jog stares at us.

I smile and wave. My sister glances over to me and bites her lip.

When we were children we lived above our mother's tattoo shop. Mother wore skirts that covered her ankles and blouses with sleeves to the wrist, but everyone in town knew that her skin, save her hands and feet and face, sang with colour. Mother tattooed soldiers from a nearby military base during the day, but at night women came wrapped in shawls and darkness. They wanted roses on the small of their backs, said their husbands found the markings erotic.

When we walked to the bank or grocery store my sister strode several paces ahead of us, pretending she wasn't related. Later, when she was in high school, we couldn't get her to accompany us on any outing. She said she had to stay home to study. Even then she was planning her escape. Mother must have known. But she also knew we were always being watched. That was why she walked with the light grace of a dancer, and made sure my sister and I were angels in public. If we acted out she'd spank us so hard we couldn't sit down all evening.

In the tattoo shop I sat beside Mother as she drew designs on arms and legs and backs with a template. She stretched the skin tight and switched on the tattooing machine, sponged away ink and blood as she worked. My sister curled herself tight as a cat in a living room chair and shut out the din of the tattoo needle. She went to college. I studied tattooing with Mother. She started inking my skin when I was fifteen, and I continued working on myself when I was old enough to learn the art.

After she'd moved out of Mother's apartment, my sister turned and walked in the other direction when she saw Mother and me on the street. Mother was demure, didn't say anything about my sister's rebuffs, but at home while listening to her usual radio programs she kept a handkerchief at the ready. I hated to see her mourn the person my sister had become, but she'd always worried about appearances.

"They're not staring at you," I whisper to her in the park.

My sister looks normally old. There's nothing odd about her at first glance, though she spends long minutes in front of the bathroom mirror, turning her head this way and that, trying to push wrinkles off her face with her good hand. Sitting beside me makes her even less conspicuous. She doesn't believe me when I say this, and slides to the other side of the bench. I shrug and chat with passers-by, particularly the older gentlemen. Wilson pauses to say hello.

"You're looking fresh as spring daisies," he says to us.

I thank him. My sister looks away.

Wilson and I talk about his dog and his grandchildren and the pleasant weather.

"We need to get coffee together," he says. "Make a date of it."

I say that would be lovely. My sister hunches lower on the bench. Wilson tips his ball cap and wishes us both a good day.

"Who else is going to flirt with old men except for waitresses who want bigger tips?" I mutter to my sister after Wilson leaves. "They deserve a good flirt with no strings attached."

My sister never believed in flirting. When she could talk, she said it was disingenuous.

"I'm not going to bring someone home," I say. "We're just playing."

My sister sighs and crosses her good arm over the limp one. She once dated a man for two years before she discovered he was married, so she's very concerned about who's genuine and who's not. While I understand that, I won't deny myself an enjoyable experience because of silly fears. I've had men friends, shared a bed with a few of them, and wouldn't mind doing it again, but my sister would never agree to such a thing in our apartment. I try to be considerate of her needs, though she doesn't appreciate how my life changed when I moved in with her. No more boyfriends. No more nights with guests. No more casual chatter over meals.

My sister glances from side to side and then down at her stomach.

"What's the matter?" I say. I have learned to be keen to her movements. "Hungry? You didn't have much breakfast."

She glances sideways at me, shrugs.

"I'll get us some ice cream," I say as I stand and stretch.

As I walk to a vendor the tattooed snake twists lazily around my arm and Eve's hips jiggle. I love my whole body except for my hands. They're wrinkled and knobbed and never stop aching. Sometimes I want to be a starfish, chop off my fingers and grow new ones. I forgot to take my pain medication after the muffin debacle because my sister was weeping.

When I come back with the ice cream cones, my sister holds out her good hand but looks nervous, like she wishes she hadn't admitted she was hungry. She has a hard time keeping up with ice cream drips, gets one down the front of her lavender blouse and starts sniffling.

"Don't worry," I say, daubing her with a napkin and tucking another one into her collar.

She cringes, hates bibs, but it's the best way to catch the ice cream drips.

I eat my ice cream and enjoy the sun for a few minutes.

My sister tugs on my arm. She's dropped her ice cream on the sidewalk (intentionally) and wants to leave.

"Honey," I say, "we cleaned the ice cream off your blouse."

She tugs my arm again.

"We haven't even been here twenty minutes," I say. "I'm not ready to leave. Relax. Close your eyes. Breathe the air. Feel the sun."

She whimpers, stands up and pulls my arm again. She wants to say how embarrassed she is. I wrest free of her grasp and stand beside her.

"Sit." I push down on her shoulder. She never wants to be in the park very long. It's irritating. "I'm sick of making allowances for you. For once we're going to stay when I want to."

My sister pouts. She's gotten very good at that in the past year. In desperate moments I wish she'd have another stroke. It wouldn't be a great shame if she lost her capacity for pride. Being old embarrasses her. Old people embarrass her.

I finish my ice cream. My sister is stone still. Fuming. I don't want to treat her like she's seven, but she acts that age when she doesn't get her way. I resent that she resents me. It's not easy to care for someone who does not want care. I worry that if I put her in assisted living she'll despise me, but if I don't put her in assisted living we'll hate each other even more.

"I'm sorry I got mad at you," I say.

She stares at her right arm, the lifeless one.

I sigh but notice Stuart doing the daily crossword and glancing at us from two benches over. We see often him at the park in the morning. He lives in the retirement complex nearby. He's a kind man, sometimes brings us coffee or a pastry from the bakery. We have shared details. I know his wife had a stroke five years ago and died of a second stroke two years ago. He knows I operated my mother's tattoo shop for decades but sold it seven years ago.

"Sorry," says Stuart when he sees me looking at him. "I didn't mean to interrupt."

I make room for Stuart on the bench and wave him over. At the moment I'd like the company of someone who isn't my sister. Someone who isn't terribly cross. Someone who, and I'm ashamed to admit this, can talk.

My sister stiffens, grabs my arm with her good hand and tries to pull me away from Stuart like I'm three years old. Sometimes we fight over who gets to protect who.

"You look nice today," says Stuart to my sister.

My sister tries to smile. She hates being singled out as much as she hates my flirting. I think she sees the same coquette in me that she saw in Mother, who tended to flirt with her unmarried male clients. I don't pretend to know what happened in Mother's bedroom after we were asleep, but I don't doubt she had company from time to time. I see nothing wrong with that, since I've done likewise.

My sister usually hated my mother in silences, but there was one time they argued at dinner and my sister yelled, "You don't even know who our father is."

Mother set down her fork and blotted her lips with a napkin.

"Do you want his address?" she said quietly.

"You have it?" my sister squeaked.

Mother nodded.

"Why didn't you tell us?" my sister said.

"You never asked," said Mother.

"I want it," said my sister. "Of course I want it."

I watched Mother copy words from a small leather-bound book onto a piece of paper. A name and a street address, I imagine. Possibly someone in town. Mother had impeccable handwriting. She could have been a calligrapher.

My sister folded the paper and slipped it in her pocket. Mother asked if I wanted the address, too. I said I'd think about it, but knew my answer would be no. If this man was too embarrassed to visit us, why should I care about him? I imagined he might be watching Mother and my sister and me from street corners, monitoring our progress to the grocery store, but I assumed he had his own wife and children and was less ashamed of them.

I never asked my sister if she spoke with the man, but she wanted the paper and the opportunity. I doubt her pride would have let her chat with our father and divulge what she knew. There are many questions I keep silent when I'm around her.

I help Stuart with the crossword, correct a couple answers that don't fit the grid. We chat about my mother's tattoo shop. He says he'd like to see it someday, and perhaps take us out to lunch afterwards. I nod and say that would be fun. I don't tell him that sometimes I find it difficult to visit the storefront, but that's because I can't work a needle like I used to.

"You should see this," says Stuart. He begins to unbutton his shirt, showing off his wrinkled chest. My sister puts her hand over her mouth, but Stuart keeps unbuttoning until he can slide the fabric off his shoulders and reveal the tattoo of a falcon on his arm and one of a raven on his back. Their wings droop, preparing to land on some invisible perch. I appreciate the pictures as well as the other marks on Stuart's body, patches of light and dark and scarred skin. After a certain age everyone is a novel.

Stuart buttons his shirt and we resume chatting about how it's nearly lunchtime. He asks if we would like to join him for a sandwich. Our hands inch closer on the bench. When our fingers graze, I feel a little surge in my chest. Surprising, almost, how the sensation doesn't change. Stuart cradles my hand in his and rubs his thumb over my fingers.

My sister screams.

Stuart and I stare at her.

"What on earth is the matter?" I say. "Why can't you have a pleasant morning at the park like a normal person?"

"Is she right in the head?" Stuart whispers.

"I don't know," I say, not caring that my sister can hear me. "Goodness knows what's working in her mind and what isn't."

That shuts my sister up. She gives me a good stare, stands up, and starts walking out of the park. Stuart and I watch her for a moment.

"Should she leave on her own?" he says.

"No," I sigh. "I need to go after her."

"It was pleasant chatting with you," he says, squeezing my hand. His touch makes my fingers hurt, but I don't care. I catch up with my sister at the stoplight.

"You are perfectly awful," I yell.

She grins at me, malicious, then begins to cross when the light changes. I almost don't go after her, but Mother would never forgive me. As I trail my sister, I remember how, when we were little and played games of pretend, she was good fairy and made me be the evil one. She got to decide because she was older, but I liked my role more than she wanted me to.

In the middle of the street I grab my sister's fingers and try to pull her back, but she yanks her hand from my grasp. We reach the sidewalk and I take her hand again. She screams like I was trying to kidnap her. Passers-by stare. She keeps screaming. I know they are not looking at me or the pictures on my body. They're thinking, *Batty old woman*. I ache for my sister and her wordlessness. Family should care for family. That's what Mother said. That's why I cared for Mother until she was on so many medications that neither of us could keep them straight and she needed to go into a home.

I let go of my sister's hand, turn around, and walk back to the curb. Stuart should still be at the park. I'll explain everything to him. He'll understand. We can go for lunch together. My sister can unlock the apartment door with her good hand. She could live alone, in her own small place, if there were nurses close by to assist her. I have known this for a while. I almost peer over my shoulder to see if she changed her mind and is following me back to the park, but I don't care to look.

To Fill

Iris is folding clothes and watching television when she finds the donut-eating competition and the petite Asian woman eating donut after sugar-glazed donut. She tears them to pieces, crams them in her cheeks, chews with ferocity. Her name flashes in small white letters across the bottom of the screen. Denise Yin. The announcers whisper as if at a golf tournament. Denise is ahead by eight donuts. The men beside her are gargantuan, shovel donuts in their mouths with singular focus, but Denise beats them all. Forty-five donuts in seven minutes and she doesn't even look ill.

On the couch Iris clutches the unfolded socks, holds them close to her mouth. She can almost taste the sweet crumbs.

The burly men on television, fingers and mouths shiny with donut glaze, gaze at Denise with worshipful eyes. She might as well be a goddess, standing with arms raised above her head, the crowd cheering as if she has indeed proven herself immortal. The commentator announces Denise has broken the world record for donut eating, and that she also holds the record for eating hardboiled eggs and burritos.

Iris glares at the socks as if wishing them to be donuts. Denise can't weigh more than a hundred twenty pounds. How can she eat so much? Iris ponders this while making soap in the afternoon, cinnamon-scented bars, recalling how the tiny woman smiled so wide it looked like she could eat the world.

Iris runs the soap-making business out of her kitchen, has her own little embossed label and business cards, Nature's Suds. She makes a batch of soap every day, has five bookshelves in the laundry room and living room where the bars cure for a month. Before wrapping the soaps she tests them with pH paper, has to make sure they aren't too caustic, won't burn skin. She sells to boutiques and gift shops as far as Toledo, an hour away.

In college Iris majored in art, spent her days with oil pastels, dry pastels, and conté crayons, rubbed her fingers raw against flat expanses of paper. It was where she met Flynn who was brown-haired and practical and thin as a paintbrush. He studied statistics, wanted to sell insurance. By the time they graduated everything was planned—the wedding, the house, the eventual children. Iris would stay at home, sell her drawings. Flynn would open his office in a space next to a Chinese restaurant and Iris would bring him lunch each day so they could eat together. Iris thought it was perfect until a year and ten art fairs had passed with few sales, not even enough to buy more pastels and pencils and paper. Flynn said it was fine, he was making enough for them both. Iris moped for two months, wanted to pull her own financial weight, so she started making soap to sell. She had learned from her grandmother, a woman of thrift who made her own wrapping paper, bought everything in bulk, and distrusted chemicals meant to cleanse her skin. Iris found soaps were easier to sell than abstract drawings, and in six months she'd earned enough to cover soap supplies and art supplies and then some.

She has been married to Flynn for five years and hardly ever draws, feels a certain futility in picking up a pastel if no one appreciates and buys her work. But people buy soap. Iris tries to be satisfied with that, even if her profits are a few bare dollars compared to what Flynn earns.

At dinner she tells Flynn about the donut-eating contest.

"Denise ate donut after donut," Iris says. "She could have eaten ten more in two minutes flat. All these big guys were just staring at her. It was amazing."

"That's repulsive." Flynn scrunches his nose and twirls pasta around his fork. "Why would anyone want to do that? It sounds like contestants would be dropping left and right from heart attacks."

"She seemed to be okay," Iris says.

"That's the sort of person who needs her head examined," says Flynn. "And good health insurance."

Iris wants him to be impressed, but he starts talking about his latest clients, their insurance policies.

"How are soap sales?" he asks.

"Not bad," she sighs because she is never sure how to read him when it comes to her business. Sometimes he seems sincere, encourages her to expand, other times his tone is so light she doesn't think he takes her seriously.

"One shop ordered twenty lavender soaps today," Iris says. "But you should have been home to see the contest, those big men. None of them had even cleared thirty donuts while Denise had eaten forty-five."

"Good spaghetti," says Flynn.

"Thanks," Iris says because sometimes he is like this, impenetrable.

That night Iris dreams of Denise, of standing beside her at the end of a long table. They cram chocolate donuts into their mouths, laughing between bites, while Flynn and four big men stand at the opposite end of the table, nibbling and gawking. Such beauty in this forbidden gluttony. When Iris wakes she is refreshed, drooling on her pillow. Something in their stunned expressions invigorated her. Iris imagines her breath still smells of chocolate.

They had been married three years when Iris missed her period. She waited five weeks to tell Flynn, just to be sure. He was so happy, hugged her tight around her hips. She could already feel her body expanding, was a little surprised because babies were still something of theory, something that happened to other people. Iris was okay with the idea of pregnancy, walked around the house for a couple of days cradling a ten-pound bag of potatoes because she believed in practice. They called her parents, told a few friends, were hugged and taken to brunch.

During the sixth week, a Sunday morning, she found a red stain in her underwear. Flynn called her parents, called the friends, spoke in a soft voice while Iris sat on the edge of the toilet and looked at her underwear soaking in the sink, cold water to remove the blood.

"At least we didn't tell more people," he said, holding her shoulders tight and sniffling into her sleeve. Iris nodded, felt more empty than she expected, but she wasn't sure if she wanted to be a mother yet. It was harder six months later. She skipped another period, made a quiet announcement to Flynn, found a spot of blood in her underwear the following week. They cried for a night and he asked if she wanted to try again soon or wait a while. Iris shook her head, not sure how to explain what she felt. He was mourning the lost babies, but she was mourning something else, the idea of babies, the lack of control, how she should have been able to keep it, that small gathering of cells, hold it inside her body for nine months.

Several weeks after watching the donut competition, Iris sees the flier at the grocery store. Five of the world's top eaters are challenging novices in a benefit tour to raise money for the hungry. Denise is pictured among them. The tour is stopping in Columbus, two hours away. It costs a dollar and two cans of food to get in, and five dollars to match stomachs with the eaters.

Iris wears a skirt and short-sleeved blouse, her good black flats, and leaves a note for Flynn saying she is going to Columbus for business. On the front seat of her car are two cans of soup and a box of Nature's Suds soaps. She is nervous, has not tried to sell her soap this far away or in cities as large as Columbus. Iris wants to expand her business but fears store owners will tell her no. Yet going to see Denise makes Iris excited, somehow bolder. She straightens her blouse and skirt before walking into the first store with the box of soap and a pile of business cards.

The owner agrees to a consignment deal in minutes.

"Very pretty," she says, nodding at the lavender and orange-cinnamon soaps.

Iris manages to arrive at the competition a half-hour early. It is in a dim bar that smells faintly of beer and pine cleanser, has wooden floors. Iris sits in the first row and taps her shoes.

When the eaters emerge from a back room, the audience cheers. Iris spies Denise beside a slim Asian fellow and three large white men. There is a call for contestants to participate in the cupcake-eating challenge. Nine men ante up, take their places at the long table before platefuls of cupcakes. Iris is intent on Denise, must be staring because Denise returns her gaze, winks. Iris blushes. She wants to sit beside that woman, that power, but hadn't considered competing. Still she is hungry, didn't eat breakfast or lunch, too nervous. The smell of chocolate cupcakes makes her feel emptier, a hole that flows down to her feet. Iris is opening her purse and paying five dollars before she can stop herself, sitting down in the last chair between two men with doughy elbows.

She breathes deeply while a judge explains the rules, how regurgitators will be disqualified. Iris feels her hands sparking with the drive to consume, to fill herself. She can't count the number of cupcakes on her plate before the whistle blows, the contest begins. Iris finds if she opens her mouth wide enough she can cram a whole cupcake inside. She chews with an unknown fervour, not even tasting the chocolate, just focusing on the next cupcake in her hand. The contestants each have a glass of milk, and the men beside Iris take delicate sips, but she can't waste time even though her throat feels thick and sticky. She forces cupcake after cupcake, barely counting because the number is less important than the next mouthful. The first few are easy, then the smell of chocolate becomes tiring, her cheeks full, her tongue gummy. The man beside her spits cupcake into his hand and is disqualified. Iris keeps going, tearing, chewing. The timer rings and Iris rests her wrists against the table, hands coated with chocolate crumbs, mouth stuffed with a final sweetness before she swallows. She expects to be sick, but is filled with an odd sense of accomplishment like she has just run a marathon, a satisfaction in her stomach and head.

The tally is announced—she ate eighteen cupcakes, came in sixth overall but first among the novice eaters. Iris wipes her fingers on a damp cloth, looks up to find Denise standing in front of her, hand extended. When Denise speaks she has a soft southern twang.

"I'm Denise," she says.

"I want to learn to do what you do," Iris says, then blushes because she sounds pathetic.

Denise grins.

"Keep at it," she says. "There aren't too many people who think this is a serious sport, and certainly not a sport for women. The best way to get better is to go to competitions on a regular basis."

"That's it?" says Iris. "What if I can't get to many competitions? I don't know how my husband will feel."

"That's why I'm single." Denise rolls her eyes. "It's hard to find people who understand this sort of thing. A lot of us marry within the circuit. Easier that way."

"Oh." Iris feels herself emptying again. She had hoped for a whiff of support.

Denise tilts her head.

"I don't coach too many people," she says, "but you seem to have talent."

Denise says the secret is to expand the stomach slowly, that thin people can expand it more, to the skin, since it isn't ringed by fat. She says to start water training, drink six cups at a time and increase it by a cup per day until she can drink a gallon at one sitting. Some people train with cabbage, eat ten pounds twice a week, but perhaps she could start with four.

"Be careful to take it slow," says Denise. "It's dangerous if you go too fast. You can cause internal bleeding. Go on a diet before competitions to lose a few pounds so you can gain it back. And exercise, build up muscle."

Denise shakes Iris's hand, wishes her luck. When Iris goes to the ladies' room she is almost giddy, but in the stall she feels a hot rise in her throat, turns quickly, and all eighteen cupcakes go neatly into the toilet. She glares at them, angry at her body. Her cheeks flush. How could she not exercise this small control over herself? Iris kicks the toilet until her feet hurt, and still she keeps kicking.

She gets home late, eight o'clock, orders a small pizza for Flynn and a large salad for herself. Iris magnets Denise's picture to the fridge and tells Flynn about the soap sales. With a dull hope she tries to explain the cupcake-eating contest she happened to find.

"For charity," Iris says because maybe he will think better of it. "I ate eighteen cupcakes in five minutes." She wants to focus on that small victory.

"Why would you want to do that?" says Flynn. "Didn't you get ill?"

"You get disqualified if you get ill," Iris says. "I met Denise, the lady I saw eating donuts on television."

"At least you sold more soap," he said. "That's good."

"I want to go into training," Iris says. "Training for eating."

"That's stupid," says Flynn. "Dangerous. You're busy enough. I thought you wanted to expand into more stores."

"I do," Iris says. "But I want this too."

"Crazy." He shoves a piece of pizza into his mouth. "You shouldn't do it. You have your soap. Your art. It's wasteful. People don't need to consume that much."

This is what she expected, but still Iris feels disappointed in Flynn. He chews his pizza like a disinterested cow. That night she goes to bed with visions of cabbage dancing in her head.

After breakfast Iris jogs two miles, drinks six cups of water, and feels only slightly ill. She makes soap, measures oils into her stainless steel pot—coconut, olive, and sunflower—mixes the lye with water in a plastic bowl and adds it to the oils. Then it is a matter of stirring until the mixture turns creamy and cloudy, saponifies. She adds the other ingredients, oatmeal and honey and dried milk powder, then pours the liquid into a tray lined with waxed paper and sets it on one of the bookshelves in her laundry room to harden. Iris loves the process of soap, the combining of textures and colours and perfumes, seeing what happens when she uses cinnamon oil for scent, ground coffee as an exfoliant, and beet juice to dye the bars. It is like magic, she thinks, taking something caustic and making it cleansing.

Iris buys a four-pound head of cabbage, shreds and cooks it tender-crisp in a tiny bit of butter, adds a sprinkling of dill and fennel seed, and eats it all in ten minutes. The last cup is most difficult. She burps tiny cabbage burps all afternoon but feels happy. The next day she drinks seven cups of water, eats another head of cabbage after lunch, and makes cocoa-scented soap with grated chocolate and instant coffee for colour. She buys ingredients for stir-fry and two more heads of cabbage.

"Why so much cabbage," Flynn asks when he peers in the fridge.

"I wanted cabbage soup or some stuffed cabbage rolls," she says. Iris uses a lot of vegetables and a little chicken in the stir-fry, gives herself an extra-large helping.

"Your appetite's back." Flynn smiles. "You ate so little at lunch, I was worried."

"Oh," she said. "I'm fine. I've started jogging in the morning."

When she met Flynn, Iris liked the idea of insurance agents, people who wanted to protect others from disaster. She liked that he was the traditional sort who always paid for dinner, opened doors, bought little gifts for her. He liked that she was an artist and told her that his mother did watercolours. When he brought some to show her, Iris thought the paintings were a little dumb, just flowers. She liked abstract work, pictures not meant to represent things but emotions, the intangible. Iris nodded and smiled at his mother's paintings because he was supportive of her own art, happy to sell insurance while she worked with pastels and booked herself in art fairs. Yet Flynn was not broken as Iris when her art didn't sell. She knew they were not depending on it for income, but she thought she would do okay, could help a little financially.

Even though Flynn wanted children, Iris wavered on the idea of motherhood. She did not tell him, figured when it happened she would adjust to it, be happy. Everyone said you felt differently when the child was yours. And Iris liked the idea of babies, of being able to produce a life like a tiny masterpiece.

After training for two weeks Iris can drink eleven cups of water, eat six pounds of cabbage in eight and a half minutes, and she jogs three miles a day. She has lost three pounds. Denise said she wasn't supposed to train with food, just cabbage and water because they were low-calorie. Iris buys two boxes of donuts anyway, arranges them on a platter on the kitchen table because she wants to try it once. She sets her digital egg timer for six minutes, hopes she won't need that much.

The first five donuts are easy, Iris rips them in half and stuffs her cheeks, swallowing larger portions than she should, not chewing thoroughly. She feels the food slide down behind her breastbone like she's eating golf balls. Her fingers squish donut pieces flat, she tucks them between her lips, cannot spit them out though she feels sick. At five minutes forty seconds she shoves in the last donut piece and swallows her mouth empty. The timer beeps triumphantly. Iris is pleased. It is a matter of endurance, one-mindedness. All afternoon she walks a sugary cloud of pride, even with her stomach ache.

When Flynn comes home she is making meatloaf for his dinner and a spinach salad for herself since she isn't hungry. He sees the donut boxes in the garbage can, asks why so many. Iris says she had the ladies over for morning coffee.

"Where are all the dirty cups?" he says, a hand on her waist.

"I washed them already," she says, wiping her fingers on a towel.

"Did you throw up the donuts?" he says.

"No," Iris says, "that's against the rules." She realises her mistake, covers her mouth.

"Why do you want to do this?" he says.

"Because I can," she says.

"You'll get sick," says Flynn, slapping his palm against her hip. "This is unhealthy. It can't be good if we want to have children. I don't want you to do this."

"Training like this every now and then won't hurt," she says. "I have to practise."

His lips purse pink as grapefruit. She kisses him and starts making her salad. Flynn says very little for the rest of the evening, even when she tells him two gift shops have increased their orders for soap. Iris is playful from the sugar, drags him to bed early and wraps her legs around his waist, her muscles already stronger because of jogging. It is rare for Iris to take initiative in lovemaking, but she feels herself glow. As they pulse against each other she thinks of how she overcame the creeping weariness of food that came with the twentieth donut, the twenty-first. A beautiful pink pleasure runs through her. She wants him to feel that, too. Flynn wheezes into climax and lies panting for a full four minutes afterward. Iris thinks it is the best sex they've had in their eight-year relationship, smiles to herself as she imagines the remnants of donut stickiness on her fingers. She licks her lips and can almost understand why, in competition, some people stretch their stomachs until they bleed.

When Iris finds Denise's picture off the fridge and in the kitchen trash she grimaces, wipes it off, and tapes it inside her medicine cabinet where she keeps makeup and perfumes. She secrets cabbage cores in the garbage can, covers them with old newspaper. She doesn't tell Flynn about her first competition in Cleveland, two months after she starts training. Instead she says she is going to market her soaps to new stores.

"I'm glad you're putting energy into expanding the business," he says, then turns back to the evening paper. Iris stands beside him for a moment, waiting to see if he'll say more. He doesn't. She goes to the laundry room and cuts bars of patchouli soap to take to Cleveland.

Iris arrives at the pizzeria a half-hour before competition begins. The goal is to eat a large plain cheese pie fast as you are able. Proceeds from the ten-dollar entry fee go to local food banks. She wears a pink sweatsuit with the sleeves pushed up, taps her foot while watching large men and a few slim ones take their place at the long table. Fifteen contestants in all. She is in the middle, glances up and down the row of males. They wrinkle their noses collectively at her and smirk. The officiator and owner of the pizzeria, a man with calm brown whiskers and a pillow gut, reads the rules of competition, how the winner's mouth has to be clear of food for the time to be official. A grand line of servers emerges from the kitchen. Each wears a red shirt, a white waist apron, and bears a large cheese pizza. They place the pies in front of the contestants with a singular thud, the pizzas still sizzling from the oven when the officiator blows the whistle. The contestants start tearing crusts, stuffing their mouths, chewing with the wrath of gladiators.

Iris rolls her first slice like a taco but the cheese still burns the roof of her mouth as she swallows in gulps that hurt going down. She tears pieces off the next slice, crams her mouth, sandwiches the third and fourth slices together and rips into them at the same time. Iris sweats with the heat of the pizza and starts to feel nauseous from the grease, but is only half done. Chew and chew and chew. She thinks of triathletes, how the body must go numb, into a rhythm, pushing and not pushing because it just needs to win, to finish. She ignores protests from her stomach on the seventh slice, forcing hunks of pizza into her gaping mouth that seems to grow wider with every bite.

On her last piece Iris hears a winner being declared, but ten seconds later, her final swallow, she is ready to burst and realises she has no way of alerting the judge. She waves her arms, a mad flash like flagging down a plane, looking for someone to grab. The pizzeria owner runs to Iris faster than she expected, has her open her mouth while he peers inside. He claps his hand on her shoulder, says, Five minutes five seconds, second place.

Iris is so excited she fears it will come up. She thinks no, no, it can't, pushes the pizza down with a sip of cola, two swallows then three. A painful moment of uncertainty. Her stomach sags, convinced. Iris has never eaten an entire pizza before, hadn't realised it would be like this, such uncomfortable pleasure, but all of her training worked. It is satisfying, her head and stomach both full in a way almost sickening. The other contestants gaze at her queasily.

She accepts her hundred-dollar bill and smiles for the photographer. Her picture will be in the Cleveland Plain Dealer, a paper Flynn doesn't read. In the bathroom she changes into a white blouse and navy skirt, stops at a drugstore for antacids before driving to the gift shops. Two of five agree to sell her soap on a consignment basis. Iris is home by six, in time to make dinner. Flynn gives her a little hug, squints at her plate of steamed broccoli.

For two days she is full but still forces herself to drink water, eat cabbage.

"Are you okay?" Flynn says at breakfast, his concerned fingers grazing her hand.

"Yes," she says. Iris jogs six miles after he leaves, drinks a gallon of water, and manages to nibble at some lemon chicken at lunch to prove to him that she is fine.

Iris researches food that can be used in soap making, which ones can be added for colour, scent, texture, and therapeutic value—poppy seeds, cloves, mint, powdered tea, paprika, cornmeal, orange peel, cucumber, strawberry, red cabbage, ground coffee, and honey. She experiments, mixes, sniffs, calls her new product line Soaps Gourmet. The gift shops love them. Iris buys more trays in which to pour liquid soap, rims the living room and dining room with bookshelves where she can let the trays of soap cure. She orders more business cards, a Nature's Suds return address stamp, and feels a little less dependent. Yet the way Flynn says that's great when she talks about the business makes it clear he has the real job, and she has a hobby.

But now there is her training, her eating. Iris isn't sure what to make of this odd talent. When she jogs in the morning the breeze is like a breath on her shoulders. When she drinks her gallon of water, eats her four pounds of cabbage, she knows she is improving. The tiny digital egg timer numbers blink her happiness. Iris had pictured herself as a wife, part-time businesswoman, and eventual mother, but now she has something besides that, another piece. It has shifted her plans. She can decide not to have children. She can keep expanding her business. If she trains hard enough, someday she will be able to eat forty cupcakes at one sitting. But worry pricks the back of her mind. This is not quite fair to Flynn. Not what he bargained for. These thoughts do not prevent her from sneaking cabbage.

When Iris loses her period again she does not tell Flynn. After four weeks she takes a pregnancy test. Negative. The gynaecologist asks if she has started exercising more, gone on a special diet. Iris quietly explains the water and cabbage and running, surprised she is almost embarrassed. She has lost a few pounds, but not too much. The gynaecologist says this is common in marathon runners. Women eating low fat, low calorie diets and training intensively can lose their periods. She suggests a bit more food, a bit less exercise, and things should be fine.

On the drive home, pride courses through Iris's arms and legs. She is training like a marathon runner. In truth she does not miss her period. That night she swivels naked in front of the full-length bathroom mirror. Even though her hips have slimmed she isn't too thin, just athletic.

Iris takes weekend eating jaunts—cheesecake in Chicago, Jell-O in Cincinnati, corn dogs in Indianapolis. Always she brings soap and finds a couple gift shops willing to sell Nature's Suds.

"I miss you," says Flynn as they lay together in bed. "You've been preoccupied lately."

"The business is going well," she says. "Don't you want it to?"

"I don't want you to get in over your head," he says.

Iris closes her eyes and grimaces. She is tired but happy, makes two batches of soap each day, is selling in fifteen stores, and has been in seven competitions over the past three months. But she knows Flynn likes security, stability, wants her around the house. When the marriage began, that was where Iris figured she would be. She feels slightly neglectful, turns to Flynn and smoothes her hand across his thigh, eases his jockey shorts down to his knees. He has been folding his own laundry and swept the house from top to bottom. She wants to reward him, pacify him, even if she isn't in the mood.

Flynn moans softly as Iris thinks about the flier she picked up at the competition in Chicago—an almond banket eating contest in Holland, Michigan, for the Tulip Time Festival. Holland is reasonably close, five hours' drive. Iris tucked the flier in her desk drawer where Flynn wouldn't look. As he pants she smiles at him, imagining the thrill of that victory even though she isn't sure what an almond banket is.

The day before the contest, Iris tells Flynn she is going on a two-day soap tour to get her business established in Michigan.

"When will you stop expanding?" he says. "Isn't your distribution wide enough?"

"Just a few more stores," she says. Iris leaves at eight in the morning for shops in Ann Arbor, Lansing, Kalamazoo, and Grand Rapids where she stays overnight. In her hotel room she drinks a pitcher of water in two minutes, forty seconds.

Holland is a quaint city, rather pretty but overflowing with Dutch kitsch. Wooden shoes. Windmills. Tulips on everything—plates and socks and pocketknives and matchbooks and beer steins and commemorative spoons. Iris wanders past the clogging demonstrations, the blue-skirted women, and lets her stomach growl until the contest at two in the afternoon. She pays the entry fee and ascends the stairs to the platform stage, eyes the almond bankets, each a foot long and a couple inches wide, golden puff pastry logs with marzipan in the centre. About twenty people are seated at the long table, mostly men but a scattering of women. Iris thinks she recognizes a couple faces from the pizza and cheesecake contests. She sits next to a cheery middle-aged lady who's wearing a T-shirt with a tulip embroidered on the pocket.

"I just love banket," says the lady, cracking her knuckles. "It's a deal to get two for eight dollars."

"I've never tried it," Iris says and smiles. The lady is sweet but not a competitor.

"Lot of big guys here," says the lady, nodding.

"Yup," Iris agrees. And she knows she can take them all.

The whistle blows, the crowd starts yelling, Iris grabs the first banket and bites in. Crisp, not as easy as cheesecake but not as difficult as pizza. She holds the pastry in one hand and breaks off pieces with the other, stuffs her mouth and imagines Denise in the audience cheering her on. The last half of the last banket is trying—her mouth poked by crisp pastry, Iris thinks she can taste blood beneath the butter and almond paste. She feels the usual sick rise in her stomach, pushes the urge down. Control. Iris keeps eating, filling herself until she stuffs the last banket corner in her mouth, glances side to side. Everyone else has at least half a banket to go, and the lady sitting beside her is three quarters done with her first banket. She throws it on her plate and hugs Iris's shoulders tightly.

"That was marvellous, dear," she says, kissing Iris on the cheek with red painted lips.

Bulky Dutchmen shake Iris's hand and gaze at her flat stomach, murmur congratulations while gripping half-eaten bankets like relay sticks. The judge, a slight toothpick woman in a white blouse and skirt, hands Iris a burlap bag of one hundred assorted tulip bulbs, a five hundred dollar cheque, and a first place plaque with two tiny white wooden shoes at the top, red tulips painted on the toes. Iris is crowded by contestants who want to touch her thin fingers. One man asks if he'd seen her picture in the Plain Dealer. A matronly woman drags her paunched husband across the stage to greet Iris.

"We remember you from the cheesecake contest," they say. "That was something."

Iris smiles, surprised how comfortable she feels among these complete strangers. They are fellow eaters, thick-fingered and amicable, realise the need to stick together because no one else understands them, or, even worse, thinks they are pigs. But it is about survival, something primal. Those who can eat the most live. Those who can't die. Gluttons have staying power.

Three reporters at the bottom of the stage cluster at her feet, ask if she does any special training. Iris shakes her head, says it's all in the mind, determination. She cradles her plaque, waves to the crowd, feels the tap on her shoe.

Flynn.

He is easily shoved aside by a cluster of photographers from the Grand Rapids Free Press, Holland Sentinel, Kalamazoo Gazette and Muskegon Chronicle who jostle for her picture. Iris poses with her plaque balanced on her hip. She tells them the correct spelling of her name twice, and explains Nature's Suds and how Michiganders can find the soaps in fine gift shops. Iris feels Flynn grimace from twenty feet away, but her stomach and head are too full for it to make any difference.

She descends the stage steps and toes to him light as a dancer, ignoring his bricklike stance, shoulders square, arms crossed.

"You lied." He looks ready to snatch her plaque and smash it on the ground.

"How did you find out about this?" she says, her tone low and hard.

"Doesn't matter," he says.

"You looked though my desk." Bastard. She thumps away from him, swinging her bag of bulbs, heading to the parking lot at the other end of the festival grounds.

"No worse than you." He tugs her sleeve.

"I sold all the soap yesterday," she says, still marching ahead. "Five more shops."

"Congratu-fucking-lations," he says.

Iris swirls so fast Flynn knocks into her, almost loses his balance. He steadies himself on her shoulders, but she shakes his hands off.

"What is your problem with this?" she says.

"It's taking over," he says. "It's not what we planned."

She turns back around, starts jogging to the parking lot. He pants to keep up.

"You have to fold your own laundry a couple times a month," she says. "Big fucking deal."

"It's more than that," he says. "A baby. We want to get pregnant."

"Screw you," she says and breaks into a run. He grabs for her hand but she pulls it away. Iris doesn't stop until she reaches her car. She settles her winnings inside and leans against the open door to wait for Flynn and his insurance agent paunch. He arrives sweating.

"Follow me back," she says. Iris slips inside the car and ignores the shapes his mouth makes in protest.

They stop for gas in Fowlerville.

"I don't understand this," Flynn says across the gas pump. "You're different than before."

"I'm happy," Iris says and thinks of Denise, free and single, how she said many people married within the competitive eating circuit.

"Can't you see that eating that much is disgusting?" says Flynn. "It's harmful to your body. To us. I don't want you to do it."

Iris slides her hands down her own hips, feels the nice edges of bone. She has dropped one clothing size, mastered the banket, and feels healthier than she has in years. Of course she is different.

In ways it is nice he finally knows. She doesn't have to hide the cabbage or her water-drinking and can hang the wooden shoe plaque on their bedroom wall and look at it each morning before getting up to make coffee and toast and sometimes eggs. She feels terribly alive. Flynn looks like he isn't sleeping enough, has constant half moons under his eyes, shakes his head no when she asks if something is wrong. Iris makes three batches of soap every day to keep up with orders and goes to two eating events a month. Boston for baked beans, Louisville for moon pies, Mackinaw Island for fudge, and Oak Harbor for walleye (a charity event they ask her to do for a local food pantry; it doesn't really count since they pit her against the mayor and police chief and fire chief, but they give her a cute little trophy with a golden walleye on top). Often she places, not first but enough to cover gas and hotel. Her only accident is in Memphis. Fried peanut butter and banana sandwiches. Too thick and greasy. She can't keep them down.

She sees many of the same people at eating events, semi-professional regurgitators with full-time jobs—cab driving, hairdressing, carpet installation, and a former pro football player. Most are rotund but exercise regularly, drag around caravans of cheerily plump wives and children. Iris has light dinners with other contestants and their family hordes. They exchange stories before she drives back to her hotel, calls Flynn and tells him when she'll be back the next day. He never says much, just a quiet okay. She feels slight remorse, but his insurance business is going well, her soap business is going well, the house is well-kept, and she still brings him lunch.

Over Thai peanut noodles Flynn asks if Iris can make a fancy dinner on Friday. A prospective client is starting a screen printing venture, and needs business insurance, property insurance, and health insurance for ten employees.

"I want to have him and his wife over to meet you and discuss the policies," says Flynn.

Iris winds a noodle around her fork.

"This weekend is bad," she says. "I have the ice cream eating contest in Philly. Why not next week?"

"He has to make the decision by Monday," says Flynn, noodles drooping from his fork. "It's coming down to the wire, his business opens in a few days. I want him to see our home and my lovely wife and have a lovely meal cooked by my lovely wife."

"Why couldn't you eat out? Restaurants make better food than me." Iris narrows her eyes. Flynn usually goes somewhere ritzy to wine and dine prospective clients, none of this "lovely wife" stuff. He knows about the ice cream contest, she scrawled it on the calendar at home.

"I need you here," he says, putting down his fork and reaching for her hand. "I want your help."

"I was going to leave Friday at four." Iris lets him take her hand but leaves it limp.

"Can't you just skip one?" Flynn rubs her fingers.

"First prize," she says, "two plane tickets to anywhere in the United States and a thousand dollars."

"There's a lot of money at stake here," Flynn says. "You have to help me." He lets go of her hand, stabs fruitlessly at his noodles. Iris doesn't say anything.

"You'll make dinner?" Flynn says.

"Yes," she says.

Flynn smiles. "Thank you."

Iris makes lasagne on Friday morning, prepares garlic cheese bread, wraps both in foil and slides them in the fridge with heating instructions taped to the top. Flynn will have to romance the prospective clients in his lovely house without his lovely wife. She tells herself she is not a bad person, just has other agendas. Iris leaves for Philadelphia at three, following her afternoon cabbage. She is at her hotel by eight, drinks a pitcher of water, and does not call Flynn for fear he will disturb her concentration.

The competition is in a massive ice cream parlour built to look like the old-fashioned sort—waxed wooden floors, chrome fixtures, a counter with twirling stools, high school students standing sticky-handed and bored in the background. Round tables have been shoved into four long rows. Iris arrives an hour and a half early since sitting in the hotel makes her nervous. After she receives the red number five to pin to her T-shirt, she paces back and forth. She does not know what Flynn will say when she returns home. Iris tries not to think of his attempted sabotage; it makes her face hot. She smells the parlour odours of sugar and vanilla, gazes at the floor, comforting lines of honey-coloured wood. Glancing up, Iris sees contestants mobbing to pay the seven dollar entry fee, spectators gathering behind yellow caution tape, camera flash bulbs flickering prematurely. A man the size of a refrigerator who sports a goatee gives her a slight wave. She recognizes him, waves back. Bill, a cab driver in Tampa who holds the record for butter eating, seven sticks in five minutes. Iris respects his stamina, remembers him as a furnace of heat. He radiates it like a small dark sun.

Too soon the whistle blows, a signal for the contestants to arrange themselves behind the tables as half-gallon ice cream tubs are rolled out on large steel carts. Vanilla ice cream. The goal, to eat as much as they can in twelve minutes. Iris lifts her metal soup spoon, tests its weight as one would test a hammer. The whistle blows again and she plunges through her first tub. It is slightly melted, slides down smooth, but halfway through Iris senses the chill in her fingers, up her spine, the slight pain of cold trauma. Her mouth is freezing, her toes start to stiffen. She finishes the first tub, shoves it aside to grab the second, can barely feel herself swallow, thinks of ice cream hypothermia, her mouth too cold to melt it, but the ice cream keeps slipping down her throat as she shovels thick gobs. She cannot understand how or why her fingers keep moving though her brain is numb. This is worse than cheesecake or pizza or banket, worse than fried peanut butter and banana. Her thoughts slow, her stomach no longer able to tell how full it is, she thinks her body should be frozen, immobile, but somehow the spoon is moving, she empties the second gallon tub and goes to the third, tries to ignore the hoots and camera flashes. It is twelve minutes of trying to consume Antarctica.

When the whistle blows again Iris sags, can feel sharp points of cold in her throat. The four judges amble around the parlour, tallying buckets. She ate almost one and a half gallons, left a few gobs at the bottom. In a sparse five minutes the judges declare she has won second place, behind Bill who finished one and one half gallons exactly. Iris smiles a cold smile to herself. Not bad. One of the judges is shaking Bill's hand when his cheeks bloat. He makes a sound like panic. Everything erupts. The crowd gasps repulsion and takes pictures.

Iris swallows deeply, averts her eyes, covers her ears to the cheers and gags of the audience. She tries not to listen while pale Bill contests the ruling, argues he is the rightful winner since he kept the ice cream down for seven minutes. The judges say no, it had to stay down for the awards ceremony and pictures and hour of official clamour following the contest to be legitimate. Iris sits in a corner, sips sugar free hot chocolate provided by the ice cream parlour and concentrates on warming herself from the inside out. She ignores the chemical cleansing ammonia that ice cream shop workers are using on the floor. Bill loses his battle but Iris thinks he looks too ill to fight. She feels rather like a fraud when the judge grasps her sticky fingers, presents the certificate with the gold embossed lettering, but she accepts the prize. Various strangers come to shake her hand. Bill huddles against a far wall with a Styrofoam cup. Eventually she toes over to him.

"I'm sorry," Iris says. Her stomach churns; she has to think stay down, stay down.

"It's not your fault," Bill says, gazing at his knees without extending a hand. "We've all seen very experienced, professional people lose like this. No shame in it. Part of the sport."

Iris nods, unsure what else to say, so she leaves him, drifts back to the crowd of congratulations.

When Iris arrives home at eight Saturday night, Flynn is watching television, a Chinese cooking show. He hates to cook.

"He wondered where my wife was." Flynn changes the channel to another cooking show. "I said you were away on business. I burned the damn lasagne."

"I won the contest," Iris says. "We're going to Charleston." She pictures the sidewalks, the Spanish moss hanging from trees. It is where they honeymooned.

"You are," he says. "I'm staying here."

"You're coming," she says.

"You're out to ruin my business."

She says, "You didn't get a contract from the screen printing business?"

Flynn grimaces. "Whether I did or not isn't the point."

"You're going," Iris says. "A week away, just a week. You got the damn customer."

"I didn't think you cared about that," Flynn says. "You don't care about us. You don't care about having a baby."

"I made your fucking lasagne and garlic bread," she says.

He says, "But you didn't stay, I wanted you to stay."

"I was away on business," Iris says.

The hotel is painted the colour of salt, has palm-green accents around the windows, a long Southern porch with rocking chairs. Her room is decorated pink as the inside of a cotton candy cone and faces the beach. Iris walks Rainbow Row and buys a woven basket at the indoor market. Through a telescope on the docks she gazes at Fort Sumner as it sits stoically in the water.

The morning of her third day, Iris is recognized by a family as she walks on the beach.

"Hey," says a man the size of a loveseat, "you're the ice cream woman. I saw you on TV. You're even tinier in person. How do you do it?"

The loveseat man is married to a woman slim as two chopsticks. Their three children—a toddler, a middle-schooler, a teenager—are rounded with comfortable fat. The father hands the oldest his camera.

"Can we get a picture?" he says, scooting his family into position. Iris settles herself in the centre. The flash nearly blinds her. The father and mother and the two younger kids hug her in a mob like she is a long-lost cousin.

"Terrific," says the father. Iris watches the five happily waddle across the sand, up the path to the hotel. She is the ice cream woman. Iris tilts her head and thinks how much the loveseat man resembles those on the eating circuit, amicable fellows with paunches soft as cream cheese. She tries to imagine herself marrying a man like that, tries to find something attractive in his girth. Softness, perhaps. Acceptance. Sand pulls gently at her feet as she continues down the beach. When Iris squints she thinks the dunes could be piles of brown sugar. Cinnamon ice cream. Oatmeal. Mounds and mounds with no end. The breeze across her shoulders is slight and free, bears the lonely breakfast smell of cold coffee and toast.

Skin

It's called ichthyosis, but all that matters is that my skin is scaly and the scales flake off. My face and hands and feet look normal, but my arms and legs and torso get red and itchy, shed little pieces of skin like wilted petals. They're soft, feathery almost, but very, very annoying. Jenna, one of my daughters, has the condition, too. Today she calls me from school to say she's sick. Again. It happens when the other kids are teasing her. She knows I can't leave work and I tell her to stay in the infirmary until it's time to go home. I leave the jewellery store at five, hear more about the day when I pick the girls up from the babysitter's.

"Em's trying to sell my skin flakes on the playground," says Jenna. She sits beside me in the front passenger seat. Em is behind her. "She's saying they're magic."

Em's two years younger, fourth grade, and has my ex-husband Isaac's smooth skin. Jenna wears long pants and long-sleeved shirts to school most days, but Em has made sure that everyone in the elementary knows exactly what Jenna's arms look like.

"Your sister is not a sideshow," I say to Em.

"I'll give her part of the money," says Em. "Nobody's bought any skin yet. I'll have to work harder tomorrow."

I swear she's going to be in marketing someday.

"It's her skin and it's not magic and you can't sell it," I say. "That's disgusting."

"It's all over our bedroom," Em says. "I might as well do something with it."

Jenna mutters, "Use it as damn confetti."

"She swore," says Em. "No dessert."

"And no dessert for you for trying to sell pieces of your sister," I say.

"Hey," says Em. "New rule. No fair."

I check the rearview quick to make sure no one is behind me, then turn into the next empty driveway and shift into park.

"Listen, kiddo," I say, turning around, "there are some things that don't need a rule made about them ahead of time. This is one. If you try it again, you'll be asking for worse things than no dessert."

Em pouts and Jenna smirks and I back out of the anonymous driveway and feel a headache coming on. When we arrive home, Em stomps into the house. Jenna and I follow her, but both of us go to the kitchen sink, roll up our sleeves, and dust off the skin scales that have loosened. Everyone's skin flakes like this, just in pieces so small that most people don't realise it. Jenna's and mine wear off too slowly, so it thickens and looks kind of like alligator hide.

"So you got another stomach ache at school," I say.

"Some of the kids are nice," says Jenna, "but some of them are assholes."

"Jenna," I say.

"I've already lost dessert." She shrugs. "And they are assholes. My friends don't mind my skin. But the rest of them . . ." Jenna pauses, glances over to me. "They say I stink. And sometimes I do. On hot days. And after gym class."

"I know," I say quietly. Our skin doesn't let sweat escape, which is sometimes a bigger problem than itchiness and irritation. We take baths in the morning and evening because bacteria get trapped under our skin and causes us to smell less-than-pleasant. In the summer we have to take extra care since the sweat can't evaporate and cool us. When Jenna was little, two years old, Isaac let her be out in the sun too long and she got overheated. We had to take her to the ER. I never forgave him for that, especially because I was pregnant with Em at the time and didn't need more stress. I'm not superstitious, but sometimes I wonder if that aggravation is responsible for Em's temperament.

I give Jenna a couple cookies. Little ones.

"One more?" she says. I sigh but oblige. It's hard to say no to her. Especially after days like this. Jenna smiles, knows not to tell Em, but a minute later my younger daughter flings herself into the kitchen.

"Jenna's eating something," Em says. "And you told us no desserts."

"I gave her one cookie," I say, "because she had a difficult afternoon."

"She didn't even have to be in class," says Em.

"I'm sure she would have rather been there than in the infirmary."

"Why can't I get a cookie, too?" asks Em.

"You're trying to make her miserable," I say.

"I'm trying to make some money."

"You'll get to eat at dinner."

"Not fair," says Em. I walk past her to the refrigerator and find the chicken legs while Em huffs out of the kitchen. I am the mother of the bully and the mother of the bullied and I don't always do the best job of negotiating it, but what am I supposed to do when my own child reminds me so much of kids who teased me when I was younger?

My sister and brother and father and I all had ichthyosis. My brother was the oldest, I was in the middle, and my sister was the baby, so we had safety in numbers. My brother was an outgoing guy, the sort everyone liked, so while we did get teased, no one tried to gang up on us. Later he became an accountant and my sister went into architecture. Neither wanted to have kids. Both were worried when I got pregnant because there was a fifty-fifty chance I would pass on the condition. Ours wasn't a bad childhood, but it wasn't an easy one, and they didn't want me to give that experience to someone else.

Having a child entails an odd sort of narcissism. You decide that you're attractive enough and a good enough person to create more of yourself. Sometimes I think I'd do it again. Sometimes I think I wouldn't. One of my high school friends adopted because she's diabetic and didn't want to pass on the condition. But when I got pregnant with Jenna I was twenty-four and figured I should be able to have a baby, same as any other woman. After she was born with ichthyosis I didn't plan on having another kid, figured the risk of having a smooth-skinned baby was too great. I didn't want to breed rivalries. Understand that I love Em, I wouldn't choose not to have had her, but the second pregnancy was a surprise.

Tonight when I tuck the girls in bed I see Jenna's arms are a little red, inflamed.

"How are you feeling?" I ask.

"No worse than usual," she grumbles, glancing up at me with hard eyes. I don't regret giving her three cookies. I worry Jenna hates me because of her skin. Worry there is nothing I will ever be able to do to make it up to her. I have to try in small ways.

In the jewellery store I'm a gemologist, spend most of my day in a small room examining cut stones. Della owns the store, hired me to do appraisals and help her when she makes gem purchases, be sure that sellers have what they say they have. You can't just take their word for it. Sometimes they try to give us lesser quality or even synthetic stones, but Della says they'd do it a lot more often if she didn't have a gemologist.

I keep a loupe in my pocket for the initial examination, to spot obvious fakes. Faux diamonds, for instance, have facets that are rolled a little, without the crisp, sharp edge that a real diamond would have, and they're too clear inside, don't have inclusions like carbon flecks or small cracks. In the back room I have a small laboratory for closer inspections. Everything fits on a tabletop—the coloured diamond grading set, electronic scales, refractometer, dichroscope, spectroscope, and ultraviolet cabinet. Sometimes Della calls me out into the store to do an on-the-spot appraisal with my loupe, give an estimate of what a stone is worth or if it's genuine, but I don't like fast appraisals because they involve too much guesswork. I hate being rushed, prefer the quiet of my lab and having time to prepare longer reports on specific gems. Those involve pictures and diagrams, describe the stone in terms of its colour and clarity, its measurement in millimetres, the dimensions of its cut and crown height, and any damage or chips that may affect the value.

I love working with stones because of the lovely precision to the art, the weighing and measuring and calibrating. Sometimes I get a few skin flakes on the table when the cuffs on my sleeves aren't tight enough, but I tend to lose myself in my work and my body becomes immaterial, an afterthought. That focus helps me survive on days when I'm terrifically itchy and uncomfortable.

At the store I try not to think about my girls, but sometimes can't stop myself from wondering if Jenna will get sick again or what Em is telling the other kids on the playground. Em is shy around adults, but not peers. Jenna is the opposite, good with older people, but hesitant with those her own age. I understand her wariness. Even a few adults cringe when they see my skin, but they're not as rude or as hurtful as children can be.

Two days after Em's business fiasco, Jenna says her skin is dry and tight and it hurts to move. Her arms seem especially red, but I hate to let the girls miss school, and Em makes a big stink whenever Jenna does.

"Can't you try going to class in the morning?" I say to Jenna while I'm brushing my hair.

She sits mournfully on the toilet. "Mom," she says, "it's really bad."

"You could take a tube of lotion," I say.

"You know how it feels when it hurts a lot," she says.

"And sometimes I just go into work anyway," I say. "Because it's my job."

Jenna closes her eyes. "It really hurts," she says.

And so I let her stay home. I've taken off work a couple days in the past year because of pain, because sometimes it's best to sit in a cool bathtub for a few hours. Jenna has periods when her skin is worse—drier and thicker—than mine has ever been.

While she draws water for her bath and dumps oatmeal and salt in the water, Em paces and rants and demands to know why she can't stay home, too.

"She's making it up like she always makes it up when she says she's sick," says Em. "She gets out of everything."

"This is how it's going to be, kiddo," I say, handing her a bagel for breakfast because we're running late. "You have to get to school now. We can talk more later."

Em pouts during the drive, doesn't tell me good-bye when she gets out of the car.

At work I feel lousy. My skin is particularly itchy, probably because I was in a hurry this morning and didn't put on enough lotion.

Just before I go on lunch break, I get a call from the elementary principal telling me that Em has been caught on the playground trying to sell Jenna's skin. She managed to get quarters off three kids, but several other students told the teacher. Em's going to spend the rest of the day in the office doing homework.

"You love her more than you love me," Em says that evening when I pick her up from the sitter. It's the accusation all siblings make. What my brother and sister and I wailed to our parents from time to time.

"I don't," I say. Which is what all parents say. What my parents said. But I worry sometimes. I don't love one child more than the other. But Jenna has to learn how negotiate her body and she needs help to do it. I feel more for her than I do for Em. Is it favouritism or just empathy?

In the passenger seat, Em starts crying.

"You give her cookies," she says. "You let her stay up later. You let her stay home from school."

"She's older," I say, "and today she was hurting."

"You punish me more," she says.

"I don't love your sister more than I love you," I say, almost yelling it. The sound reflects back from the windshield and fills the car. Em cringes. Funny how the more helpless people feel, the louder they get.

"I don't love her more," I say quietly. "But I know she was in pain today because I have those same pains. And I punish her like I punish you when she does something that's not nice."

Em stops crying but doesn't say anything else. When we get home, Jenna is still in the bathtub, says she's been in and out of the water all day. She towels herself off and we go to my bedroom so I can apply lotion. It's best to do when our skin is still a little wet. I smooth it over her back and neck, places she can't reach.

"I want some lotion, too," says Em, wandering into the bedroom and sitting down beside me. I put some on her shoulders and her arms, but her skin is so smooth already, she doesn't need it. After I spend a minute rubbing her back, I peer back at Jenna whose skin looks even worse to me than it did before.

"I want some more," Em says when I return to lotioning Jenna.

"Jenna needs it around her neck," I say.

"If you'd rather have skin like this, be my guest," says Jenna.

Em thuds out of the room. At dinner she chews slowly, stares down at her plate, shrugs when I ask her about the history project that's due next week.

"Honey," I say, "you don't need lotion. Your skin is smooth enough."

"Brat," mutters Jenna.

"Hey," I say and narrow my eyes at my older daughter.

"Feeling like this doesn't put me in a good mood," says Jenna.

By the end of the meal, both girls are scowling at me. After dinner Jenna sits on the couch in her bathrobe, starts doing the homework papers her teacher sent home with Em. I load the dishwasher. Em plods to the girls' bedroom. I know I need time alone with her, think maybe next weekend Jenna could spend the afternoon with a friend and Em and I could be together, maybe see a movie or go to the park and get ice cream. I walk to the girls' room, hoping the promise will cheer her up.

When I brush through the door I find Em sitting in the middle of the floor, surrounded by a dozen or so of Jenna's shirts and a ruler. She's cut all the sleeves three inches down from the shoulder, scattered the pieces around her. I gape. Em smirks at me, measures down another sleeve before she hacks it in two.

"Goddammit," I yell.

Twenty seconds later Jenna scrambles from the living room, starts crying when she sees Em surrounded by sleeves. "How am I going to go to school when everyone can see my arms?"

"You don't want to go anyway," says Em.

"That's it," I say. I grab Em's arm and haul her up off the floor. She tries to wrest free but I'm holding tight. Em doesn't flinch. She's done what she wanted to do. Upset me. Jenna drops to her knees, gathers up her shirts and the sleeves. Any sympathy I felt for Em has drained through my hands and feet. The sleeves will have to be sewn back on Jenna's shirts, and I'll need to buy her several new ones because the seam will look funny.

"Grounded," I say. "No television or desserts for two weeks." Em keeps squirming. I don't know how else to punish this. Grounding alone isn't adequate. I can make her pay for a couple new shirts, deduct money from her allowance, but there's no way to make Em understand how it feels, the itching, the embarrassment, the need to be constantly covered.

I snatch the scissors up off the floor, walk to Em's dresser with my daughter still in tow, yank open a drawer and grab a long-sleeved lavender shirt. One of her favourites. I sit down on the floor near the still-crying Jenna, make Em sit beside me, and hand her the scissors and shirt.

"Okay," I say, "cut it up."

Em stares at me, then down to the shirt.

"I'm not going to do it," I say. "We're going to sit here until you do."

When she makes the first cut it's fast, on the bottom hem. She snips up to the neckline like she doesn't even care. She takes off the sleeves, cuts them at the shoulder, then lengthwise into two pieces. When Em cuts down the back of the shirt, from the neck to the bottom hem, she's not going as rapidly.

"Twelve pieces of fabric," I say. "At least." I want something that can't be stitched back together.

Em cuts at a slower and slower pace as the shirt is reduced to dustrags. It was a gift from me for her ninth birthday, a shirt she wore to school almost every week. It looked nice on her. I tell myself Em's growing, would have been too big to wear it in another half year. By the time Em has cut the shirt into eleven pieces, she's like Jenna, near tears.

"One more," I say, laying a larger fabric piece in her lap.

"I'm sorry," she wails, but I know it's not because of remorse.

"Keep going," I say.

It takes her five minutes to make the cut. Em's hands move like the scissors weigh ten pounds. She stands. The shirt pieces fall from her lap. Em flops on her bed and curls her body tight while I gather her sister's shirts and sleeves, pad out of the room.

"You should have made her cut up more than one," Jenna says when I find her in the living room. "Or let me cut up one of her shirts."

"One is enough," I say. "Especially since she had to do it."

"But she cut up fourteen of mine," says Jenna.

"And I'll sew them back together," I say, "or buy you new ones. Probably both."

"It still isn't fair," says Jenna, peering down at her arms then at mine.

"No." I sit beside her, go slack against the back of the couch.

"Can I have some ice cream?" she says.

"Sure," I say because I can't lift my hands to stop her, or to do much of anything else. Unfairness is the way of the world. But how do you tell that to a twelve-year-old? Maybe you don't. You just give them ice cream.

That night I sleep deeply, get up at ten in the morning and am greeted by a silent house. The girls have gotten themselves cereal for breakfast and are in different rooms—Em in the living room and Jenna in their bedroom, both reading. Jenna says good morning, tells me that the lotion we put on last night helped and her skin is feeling better. Em doesn't say anything. I figure it's best to let her pout.

On Saturdays I work a short day, noon until four, and trust the girls to care for themselves for a few hours. They know the number for the jewellery store and the neighbours are around if they need anything. Today I am wary to leave them, but I tell myself that after a night of rest we're all feeling better. Or at least less hostile.

At work I don't do much, just sit in my lab, brush the few skin flakes from my worktable, and stare at the tiny diamonds I use to grade colour. So small and even and perfectly cut.

When I arrive home, Em runs up to the car and hugs my legs as soon as I get out.

"Jenna locked me out of house," she wails. Em says it happened when she went outside to get the mail, and she's spent the past hour on the swing set. Jenna knows Em is terrified to speak with the neighbours, even though they've known her since she was born. I sit down with Em on the front step, pat her back before telling her to wait a moment longer while I go talk to Jenna.

"She left me alone," Em says, wiping her eyes with the back of her hand. "Is she gonna get punished?"

"Yes," I say quietly.

My older daughter is sitting on the couch wearing shorts and a T-shirt, her arms and legs flecked with white. She's watching television.

"How angry are you?" Jenna says.

"I don't know yet," I say.

Jenna says Em got mad at her because she wouldn't let Em watch TV. "I said she couldn't since she was grounded, then she went into the kitchen and got a pie plate and started burning skin flakes in it. It smelled awful. I yelled at her and told her to stop. She didn't. So I grabbed the matches from her. When she went outside I locked the door. I didn't want to put up with her shit."

"Jenna," I sigh.

"The pie plate's still there."

I take three steps to the kitchen door and see it on the table, an aluminum tin with neat piles of small white flecks and tiny charred bits inside. Tweezers and a magnifying glass are on the table beside the pie plate. I imagine Em burning the skin with scientific care. The scent of char is thick in the house. Amazing how such tiny pieces can create such a stench.

Jenna is watching some cartoon with little purple space aliens trying to take over a city. They keep getting run over by busses and shaken by dogs. It's kind of dumb. Jenna giggles.

"Finish the show," I say. "But after that, grounded like your sister. Same rules apply."

Jenna nods like she hadn't expected anything different. Sometimes you do what you have to do to get a moment of control. It's not hard to notice how the house is quieter with Em outside. Occasionally, very occasionally, I wonder if she wishes she had ichthyosis, too. I need to collect my younger daughter, but for a moment I stand in the kitchen doorway, looking at the burned skin bits, savouring silence.

Holes
(or, Annotated Scrapbook, Sections Slightly Charred)

Photo #1 (from personal archives): *Most of my face. All of my nose but only my right eye. Too much of my hair. The new perm makes me look like a poodle.*

Photo #2 (from personal archives): *My right hand with the quarter-inch hole in the center, between the bones of my ring and middle fingers.*

Photo #3 (from personal archives): *My left hand, a mirror image of the right.*

It's my first new camera in years. I have to test it out so I'm taking pictures of myself, the stuff in my apartment, and my hands. I had the holes made in them ten years ago. I was sure I'd earn more than two hundred a week travelling as The Fountain Woman.

Newspaper photograph dated 15 March: *The place where our trailer stood. Blackened cement block foundation, some of the charred metal shell, a few spindly trees in the background. Caption: "Local family meets with devastation."*

I decided to get the holes made the year after my folk's trailer caught fire, or rather exploded, because of a leak in the propane tank. Least that's what the propane company said. They claimed it was a hardware problem, but I think it was because someone forgot to seal the tank properly when they'd delivered propane earlier in the afternoon. After the explosion there was little we could do to prove that, because there was nothing left. The trailer was gone. Or, more precisely, in little pieces scattered over a quarter-mile radius.

We moved into a new trailer two and a half blocks from the old one. Smoke-stained kitchen utensils, clothing, and photo album pages came back to us over a period of months. Every other day we'd get a pair of socks or a sweater, a couple of butter knives, and a few sooty pictures. We washed the clothes, scoured the dishes and silverware, and I spent evenings going over the pictures with a kneadable eraser from the art supply store, trying to get off more soot.

Polaroid snapshot taken by my mother of my father sitting on the brown corduroy living room couch that we got from the Salvation Army (the cushions smelled faintly of sour apples). He wears a red sweatshirt and sweatpants, eats a powdered sugar donut, and has white flecks trailing down the front of his shirt.

Three weeks after the first trailer blew up and two weeks after we'd moved into the new one, my father went crazy. He refused to eat anything but donuts and orange drink, stopped talking in the mornings, didn't say much in the evenings, and refused to go to the paperclip and thumbtack factory with my mother. They'd met there, both worked in quality control.

"Please," said my mother to my father every morning while I ate cornflakes. "You have to get dressed."

My father smiled at my mother's request like she'd complimented his hair, and turned back to the morning news programs. I don't think he watched the shows as much as he stared at the moving mouths, the business suits, and the cheery expressions of the anchor people. Something about them, their orderly happiness, calmed him.

At the factory my mother opened every hundred and fiftieth box of clips or tacks and counted the number to make sure the machines were accurate. Often she came home with band-aids on her thumbs. My father made sure the thumbtacks had points and the paperclips were bent correctly. He liked the exactness of his job, the scales he used to be certain the right amount of metal was being used in each paperclip and tack.

My mother took the Polaroid picture hoping that if my father saw himself he'd come to his senses. He nodded at the photo and took another bite of his donut.

I was eighteen and had already decided to save my family by getting holes in my hands.

Grainy black-and-white novelty postcard of my grandfather, charred slightly in the lower left corner. He is young, maybe twenty-five, wears a short-sleeved white shirt and long black pants. He sits in a wooden chair, his hands tight against the chair arms, as blurry streams of water shoot up through the holes in his palms. White lettering under his picture: "The Fantastic Human Fountain."

There are two different stories about how my grandfather got the holes in his hands, but both of them involve him horsing around with a cousin while drinking bootleg whiskey and staking tomatoes in the garden. In one story the cousin pounded a metal stake through my grandfather's hand on a dare. In the other they were fencing and my grandfather fell down, tried to use the stake to support himself. The stake went between two bones in his hand in just the right place, left a hole the surgeon kept open with a surgical stainless steel tube. Legend has it my grandfather was still kind of drunk when he told the surgeon to do this, but he was also remembering the carnival that had been through town two months earlier, and perhaps already dreaming up his act as The Human Fountain.

My grandfather had a somewhat reputable surgeon make the matching hole in his right hand and insert another stainless steel tube. The wooden chair, his only prop, had hoses running up through the arms. Grandpa made good money on the circuit but left after ten years and returned to farming. He died in a combine accident when my dad was twenty-seven, five years before I was born.

"Sideshow life was probably safer than life on a farm," my dad often said when I was young. "I think he wished he would have stayed there."

"Craziness," said my mother and shook her head. "It wouldn't have been the place to raise a family."

My father shrugged. I think he would've preferred life in a sideshow to life working in a factory, but he was never one to say what was on his mind. This might account for the fact that, rather than say anything about the trailer exploding, he decided it would be easier to go crazy.

Polaroid snapshot of used beige Ford station wagon with brown Naugahyde seats and pink plastic beads hanging from rearview mirror. Sleeping bag, tent, two grocery bags of snacks, one pot, a cooking spoon, two gallons of water, and camp stove are not entirely visible but all piled in back seat.

When I decided to get the holes made I was thinking of the lost trailer, thinking of fountains, thinking of water, even though water wouldn't have helped the trailer explosion. I bought the station wagon cheap, planned to travel and be the second human fountain in our family, have appearances at tattoo parlours and carnivals, and send money home to my folks in Ohio. This way they wouldn't have to feed me, and I figured they could use the extra cash, what with my dad going crazy and all. I didn't tell my mother about my plan to get the holes, just said that I would be on the road for the summer, working in a funnel cake booth at county fairs.

"I don't like the thought of you running all over like that," she said. "It's not safe." She unloaded a bag of groceries, including boxes of donuts for my dad.

"I want to save for college," I said. A black lie, but one that would pacify her.

"College," she said, setting the sixth box of donuts on the table. She and my father had wanted me to take classes at the local community college in the fall, but when the trailer exploded, their extra money went with it.

"Maybe graphic design or something," I told her because she always said I was good at art. I hated drawing, even if I wasn't bad at it. I felt worse for my parents than I did for myself about the college money. They loved me. I wanted to help them.

"In September," she said and nodded. Her words were blessing enough for me to leave, even though I planned to be travelling in the fall. I knew I was not a college sort of person, but my mother never believed this. I figured since she gave birth to me, it was her right to pretend I was who she wanted me to be, and my duty not to object too loudly while going my own way.

BEARDED WOMEN

Colour photograph from ten-year-old newspaper advertisement. Cream-coloured brick building with sign over the front door: Piercings and Tattoos. Heavy burgundy curtains frame the windows on either side of the door.

I took pictures of my grandfather to the piercing salon, photos of him and my father when Dad was ten, holding a hose up to Grandpa's hand and shooting a stream of water through. The fellow who owned the salon was Indian, claimed to be a fakir who had pierced the hands and feet of other fakirs. He didn't have holes in his own hands, but there were black-and-white pictures all over the walls, photos of him with swords and nails sticking out of his arms. His face was wrinkled enough to make him about seventy-five, but his hands looked young, free of raised veins and knobbed knuckles usually associated with age. The fakir nodded at the pictures of my grandfather, said the operation would be free if I'd agree to be on display while I healed.

"Been a long time since I performed one of these," he told me. "They went out of style some years ago. If you were to sit in the window for a few days, be on display, I'd consider the bill paid in full."

I don't remember the operation, just that when I came to my hands hurt and were swathed in bandages. The pain was less than I expected, but I spent three days in a haze, drinking some sort of black tea through a straw from a flowered china cup. The fakir was a pleasant gentleman and a good cook who fed me curried rice and lentils and told me not to move my hands too much or too quickly. In the end I had to believe that he was a real fakir, or a real something-or-other, because on the third day when the bandages came off so he could show me how to turn and clean the metal posts, there was almost no swelling or redness. He'd inserted quarter-inch stainless steel tubes between the bones of my ring and middle fingers. I had to turn them around once each day, a full turn, and clean them with alcohol. After a week my hands were nearly healed. I don't think the body does that normally. The fakir gave me pink plastic plugs to keep in the holes when I wanted them to be less noticeable.

Polaroid of me and a seventy-year-old tattooed lady standing outside a tattoo parlour in Memphis, taken right after she told me I should have been born fifty years earlier. The rest of the pictures from this trip were lost when someone swiped my camera.

I drove through Cleveland and worked a few days at a fair just outside of Akron, spent time in Philadelphia and Louisville at tattoo parlours, then went down to Orlando and New Orleans. At first I was the Human Fountain and shot water through the holes, usually with a hose, but that bored people quickly. I thought up other little tricks, like putting a straw through my hand and drinking out of a glass, or fitting a pen or pencil through and writing my name. A few times I smoked a cigarette through the hole, but quit that one after I got burned. I spent most of my time in small towns along the way, got gigs at county fairs and in tattoo parlours. The owners usually gave me food and a place to sleep as long as I'd hang out and answer questions asked by customers.

I called my mom every week from a pay phone, told her where I was, and that the funnel cake booth was doing well. She sounded tired but pleased to hear from me, never mentioned my dad unless I asked.

"He's doing well enough," she said, which I figured to mean that he was still alive and watching television and eating donuts.

I liked travelling, but there were snags. The station wagon's front windshield began leaking during a rainstorm in Texas and the back windshield was quick to follow. The back seat smelled musty for the rest of the trip, no matter how much baking soda I poured on it. I ate a lot of peanut butter and jelly sandwiches and spent too much time sleeping in my car or on the couches of people who seemed nice. I know it was a miracle I wasn't raped. I made enough money to get by, but nothing to send home. There wasn't enough work for a young woman who wanted to sell the sight of her body as opposed to her body itself.

Christmas card photograph taken by me of my mother and father sitting side by side on the couch. Dad and Mom wear red sweat suits and Santa hats. Dad eats a donut and looks off to one side while Mom sits on his lap and smiles too broadly.

By the time I came home in the beginning of October, I had my health, my leaking car, two shoeboxes full of pencils and postcards and pins I'd picked up along the way, and two nice clean holes in my hands. With the plugs in, the holes weren't that noticeable. If I'd only been worried about myself I wouldn't have felt bad about returning with no money, but I was ashamed I hadn't managed to save anything for my parents. I'd prepared a lie for my mother about the holes being the result of some horrific funnel cake grease accident, how I'd needed the money I saved to pay for the medical bills, but when she saw the holes she just sighed.

"At least you're home safe," she said. I guess she didn't have the energy to fret too much as there were other things to worry about. Dad was still living on the couch in the new trailer. Mom was working twelve hours a day to pay for the trailer and Dad's medical bills.

I got a waitressing job at a diner and moved in with a friend who was studying to be a dental hygienist.

"I should have a place of my own since I'm an adult," I told my mother.

"You could still stay with us," she said with a slight smile.

"It's kind of small," I said. She nodded. I think we both knew I didn't want to see my dad every day. Or smell him. Sunday dinner was difficult enough, with Mom trying to coax Dad to the table for twenty minutes before she gave up and ate cold pot roast with me.

"I think he's getting better," she told me every Sunday. There was nothing else to say.

I got a job at a doll factory when I got tired of the diner, of being on my feet, of truckers eyeing my ass, and of freaking them out when I took the pink plastic plug out of my left hand and poured their coffee refills through the hole in a careful, thin stream.

Polaroid of funeral flowers sent by my father's sister in Akron. Arrangement consists of white roses and white lilies and white daisies, looks washed-out and spooky. My aunt wanted me to take a picture of the arrangement to send back to her so she could be sure the florist had done a good job, sent what she ordered, and not gone cheap on her.

Eighteen months after I ended my career as a human fountain and six months after I started working in the factory, my dad passed away. I don't know if there is a medical name for what happened to him, but somehow he moved backwards, lost coordination and bowel control and speaking skills, started drooling and had to wear diapers. He was fifty-three years old and helpless as an infant. The coroner said it was heart failure. It just stopped beating.

I took a week off work to help Mom out. She spent most of the time sitting at the kitchen table and unbending paperclips, making the wires into straight lines. I cooked for her, tidied the trailer, washed the floors, and sponged the couch with vinegar and baking soda to rid it of the smell of my father (more exactly, the smell of his waste products). Mom didn't want me to clean the sofa, came and sat on it when she realised what I was doing. After that I cleaned around her. It seemed like the best way I could help.

I didn't know what to say to my mother, sometimes just sat beside her on the vinegar-and-baking-soda couch and slipped unbent paperclips through the metal tubes in my hands.

"Do you think you might want to move closer to me?" I asked her. Since I'd started working at the doll factory I'd gotten an apartment of my own. It was a bit noisy at times, but I liked it better than my parents' trailer. The brick building felt sturdy.

My mother watched me playing with her paperclips and shook her head. We'd both tried to help my father, to save him, and we'd failed. She kept working at her factory. I kept working at mine.

That's the way it's been for the past eight years.

Black-and-white photocopy picture of me tying a doll's hair back with a big grey bow. Picture is on the front of a booklet given to new factory employees about company policies and safety hazards. (The grey bow would be pink if they spent more for colour copies.) I am smiling because my co-worker Gerry who took the photo just told a raunchy joke.

The plastic dolls arrive in boxes, one hundred sixteen to the box. The pink dresses and green dresses and lavender dresses come in bags, fifty to a bag, assorted colours. The bows we tie ourselves out of quarter-inch ribbon. The paint for the dolls' eyes comes in two-ounce jars with a label that says the paint fumes have been shown to cause cancer in California. Apparently they don't cause cancer anywhere else.

Sometimes I work at the station where we dress the dolls and tie back their hair. Sometimes I work at the station where we tie little bows and glue them on the dresses, one on each puffy sleeve and one at the waist. There is nothing on the glue bottle about glue fumes causing cancer in any of the fifty states, but it smells like it does. Sometimes I work at the station where we paint the dolls' eyes blue and nails pink so the box can say Hand-Crafted and Assembled in the U.S.A.

No matter what station I'm at, sometimes in the middle of my shift I sit for a moment with a partially finished doll in my hands and see that her fingers are curled in the same way my fingers want to curl at the end of a workday. The plastic that forms their bodies is not unlike the plastic plugs I use in my hands. After ten seconds of reflection, Judith the supervisor yells at me that this is not a tea party and I should get back to work.

By slowly increasing the size of the metal tubes in my hands over the past ten years, I've been able to enlarge the holes from a quarter-inch to three-quarters of an inch. The larger diameter means more water could shoot through the holes.

"I don't understand why you want to make the holes bigger," my mother says.

"Because I can," I say. "Why have quarter-inch holes in your hands when you can have three-quarter inch holes in your hands? It sounds more impressive." I don't tell her I'd still like to go on the road.

Photo #4 (from personal archives): *My living room/kitchen area. Posters of San Francisco and Chicago and New Orleans on the walls, blue secondhand couch under posters, twelve-inch television between couch and kitchen table. Two dolls, awards from work, sit on the television. They have blonde hair and pink dresses with merit patches sewn on them. My boss is a cheapskate.*

Mom drives over to my apartment for dinner once a week, brings bread and a vegetable, and I make some sort of main course. She still lives an hour away, alone in the same trailer she bought after the first one exploded.

"How is work?" she says right after she steps inside.

"Fine," I say, hugging her. "Did you go to that recipe swap meeting?"

"Didn't have anything worth taking," she says. "Not in the mood for cooking, anyway. Gwen who lives next door to me, her daughter works at the auto plant, but she's going to school at night. Becoming an accountant."

"That's good," I say. "You really should try that recipe club again. Or maybe a garden club." She never seems sad when I see her, but she never seemed sad when my dad was going crazy. It's hard to know what I can believe.

"No space for flowers," she says. "You've got a head for numbers. Night school isn't that expensive. You could afford some classes."

"I'll think about it. I worry about you getting lonely. You're not involved in anything social. When's the last time you went out for coffee with someone? Or on a date?"

"I'm fine," she sighs.

We spend the first few minutes of every conversation trying to convert each other. I worry that my mother is lonely and depressed and turning into a hermit. My mother is upset because she hoped I wouldn't end up working in a factory like her and my father. She thinks I could have done something better than tying bows. Maybe designed the dolls or the dresses for the dolls or the boxes that the dolls are sold in or drawn an ad to market the dolls. She thinks what I'm doing is insignificant. Maybe she also thinks what she does is insignificant, but that doesn't seem to matter as much.

I don't mind the factory, and I don't figure that after a few thousand dollars and four years of college classes that I'd find something I liked a lot more. Planning an advertising campaign to market the dolls doesn't seem more exciting to me than painting their eyes, and if I weren't painting their eyes, someone else would be.

Mom peers at the dolls on my television for the umpteenth time, shakes her head.

"I like the job," I tell her. "It's relaxing sometimes. Nice people work there. We chat."

"You chat," she says and cuts a wax bean into tiny pieces.

"What's wrong with chatting?" I say. "We're helping the time pass."

She shrugs.

My mother worries that I am not special. Or at least less special that she would have liked. She doesn't see the holes as anything important. As me trying to help the family. But maybe that's just because it didn't work.

Black-and-white picture of my father with his arms crossed, leaning against his Maverick (Mom says it was blue) and smirking. He wears jeans and a white T-shirt. The picture was taken shortly after my parents were married. The right corner is burnt and the whole image greyed with smoke.

My mother spends most of her free time restoring photos of my father, going over them with a kneadable eraser, trying to get off more of the soot. She's arranged the pictures in new albums and is writing down snatches of memory, what she recalls of my father, on index cards and sliding them into plastic sleeves beside the pictures. She brings out her albums after dinner, totes them over every week to show me her progress on the soot removal, though it's been ten years since the explosion and I don't think any more of the damage can be erased.

"I think they're looking better," she says. "Brighter."

"Sure," I say. "It's nice what you're doing."

Half of a black-and-white picture of my grandfather in a grey newsboy's cap and white shirt and dark pants. His palms are up, showing off the holes in his hands. The left side of the picture is black with char.

I don't think my mother knows I have twenty photos of my grandfather, taken from the box of pictures under her bed. She never paid much attention to the pictures of Grandpa unless Dad was in them. Some of the photos are burned badly, damage beyond soot, but I've made copies and cut out the dark spaces, am trying to draw what was there before the fire. On the nights when I don't go out with the ladies from the factory, I'm at home working on the pictures of my grandfather, restoring his arms and legs. I know he must have had wanderlust sometimes, moments when he was riding on the combine and looked across the field at cars driving by and wanted to be in motion, on the road.

I'm starting to map out a route, to find contacts along the way, more tattoo parlours and piercing studios that would sponsor me as a momentary celebrity. I have four thousand dollars saved up for the tour. A real one this time.

Photo # 5 (from personal archives): *Picture of me and my mother. She holds one side of the camera with her left hand and I hold the other side with my right. Our faces are big and close together.*

I try to smile like my father smiled. Wide. Uninhibited. The smile he had during those last few months when he was living on the brown corduroy couch and eating donuts. He looked happy like a six-year-old would look happy. He didn't want to be fifty-three any more. He wanted to be six a second time. Maybe he didn't think there was anything else for him to do. But what else was there for my mother to do but try and convince him to be fifty-three?

She leaves college brochures on the kitchen table while I'm in the bathroom, ones for me to find when she's gone for the evening. I slip telephone numbers into her purse, widows who live in my apartment building and meet to play rummy on Thursdays. We do this and are both content for another week.

In the picture you cannot see the band-aids on her fingers. You cannot see the holes in mine.

Things I've Been Meaning to Tell You

You don't remember me. I was small, quiet, the kid who wore plain T-shirts and ball caps and got lost in the fourth row of band; the kid who wasn't liked or hated but just there. But you remember her because she had the beard and the guts to grow it out even though she was the last person anyone expected to do that. She was so damn girly, wore dresses and makeup and was a baton twirler for God's sake, people liked her, but that was when her cheeks were smooth, before everything happened.

You have to remember how she was gone from school for a week, not that we thought about it at the time, but when she came back she walked to her locker like nothing was wrong, like no one was staring at this beard that was strawberry blonde like the rest of her hair. We were fifteen years old and her beard was better than any guy in our class had grown so far. I had dinky fuzz over my upper lip like a dying caterpillar, and I know your attempts weren't much better. But she had a beard and a ponytail and a fuzzy pink sweater and really, what the hell?

That was when everyone was dyeing their hair, getting piercings and temporary tattoos, trying to be different in all the usual ways. Part of me wanted to be rebellious, but if I'd gotten my ears pierced Mom wouldn't have blinked. She was a pop culture college professor, spent her days lecturing on trends, and saw me thrashing in the sea of fads. When I came home with a temporary tattoo of a spider on my bicep she said she liked it. No one at school noticed. Everyone stared at the girl with the beard.

Her grin was the same after the beard—she never smiled, she grinned—and I noticed that because the baton twirlers practised at the same time as the marching band, all of us on the football field. I was in the brass section, hefted my tuba while I watched her routines. Everyone had said she'd be on Homecoming Court, and for a while I didn't think the beard would stop that. She still sparkled like light on a newly polished tuba. But kids started whispering about her, wondering what had happened, if she'd had some weird cosmetic surgery, if she was turning into a guy.

She sat beside me in algebra—you were in that class, too—and she never got a problem wrong. Algebra was my worst subject and I wondered if the beard made her smart like a professor. (My mom was smart though she didn't have a beard. My dad had a beard but he was out of our house by then.) I wanted to ask her to help me with my homework, but I couldn't open my mouth wide enough to release the question. Science was the only thing I was good at, especially biology because that didn't need many numbers. I wished she weren't so intelligent because I could have offered to help her with the homework on flower parts and worm parts and frog parts. In ways she felt older than me, older than all of us, even though in algebra I heard you and the other guys talking when she went up to the board to solve yet another problem. Why doesn't she shave and look normal? She was so pretty before.

I should have turned around, I should have said something to you, but I was too quiet and small and it seemed like she could take care of herself. The beard didn't make her less beautiful, it was just something to get used to, a new way of thinking about a girl's face. She made me remember when we learned about the Egyptians and how the female pharaohs wore false beards as a symbol of power and wisdom.

She lived two blocks from my house and I followed her home every day. Sometimes she turned around to wave hello. I grimaced under the weight of my tuba and couldn't smile back. Once she asked if I needed help but I shook my head, didn't want to seem weak.

I know it was you, you and your friends, who rode up on your bikes and taunted her. You called her Bigfoot and said she'd never get married, and she said she wouldn't marry an asshole like you, and you called her a hairy bitch. I gasped. She threw stones at you and I know it must have hurt because she had good aim. I stood motionless and mute, a statue with a tuba, though I imagined myself running to help her.

You rode away, but she was panting and smiling. I walked up to her after she'd won the battle. There was nothing I could do but say, "I like your beard. I can't grow one."

"There's no trick to it," she said. "Just don't shave."

"It itches," I said.

"It only does that for a little while," she said. "Grit your teeth and resist the razor."

"The beard looks good on you," I said. It was as close as I could come to telling her she was beautiful.

Two weeks later at the football game, kids from the other band teased her behind the bleachers, called her she-man and she called them a bunch of brainless fuckers and a flute player gave her a shove and she cracked the girl over the head with her baton. She was out for that game and three games afterwards. I was in awe. Not long after that the rumours started—she was going out with a linebacker, she was going out with a point guard, she was going out with one of the guys who played defence—she had ten or twelve or fourteen boyfriends and had turned into one of those girls, the sort who was easy in the back seat of cars. But no guys bragged about her at lunchtime or after school, no one said he'd done it with her in his bedroom when his parents weren't home, so all her boyfriends remained faceless.

I talked with her after school on our walks home, but not about her boyfriends.

"I'm sorry you were suspended from the twirlers," I said.

"I have to stick up for myself," she said.

"Female pharaohs had beards to show they were wise," I told her. "But their beards were fake. They weren't as nice as yours."

"Thank you," she said.

She smiled at me. I lived on that smile until I heard she was going out with you. I didn't believe it at first because you were cruel. (I still want to know what you said to smooth over those hard words.) On the football field she twirled and shone, and by then I had learned what I could do alone in my room, face down on my bed with a couple of pillows. It was a new definition of magic, that tightness and release, and I thought of her.

I mentioned you to her only once.

"I thought he was mean to you," I said.

"He apologized," she said. "He's pretty nice when he wants to be."

"You shouldn't go out with someone who isn't nice," I said, but then wished I hadn't. It sounded like something a dad or a first grade teacher would say.

But she smiled and told me I was sweet, that I shouldn't worry.

I blushed. "I didn't mean you couldn't take care of yourself," I said.

"I'm just fine," she said. I don't know what we talked about after that, but it wasn't you.

I had to protect her from you and your insincerity. I knew you hadn't changed, but I didn't know how to warn her. There were too many cafeteria rumours about you and her in the stadium bleachers. I figured you had spread them, which is why I almost cried when she was on your arm at Homecoming. You probably don't remember the colour of her dress, a cherry blossom pink that set off her hair in the darkened gym. You had your hand on the small of her back and I left to pace outside for a while, then trudge home like the other dateless people who went to dances pretending we didn't care we were alone.

I feigned happiness to my mother, said I'd had a great time, but it was a cruel lie repeated by all of us who saw the people we wanted to dance with embraced by someone else. Nothing is like the passion of fifteen-year-olds who have read Romeo and Juliet for the first time in English and can imagine drinking poison for the one we love. It is the moment in our lives when that story makes the most logical sense.

I don't know if you saw the article in the newspaper four days later, a blurb on page two about the fifteen-year-old kid who lay down in the middle of the street with a tuba at seven-thirty Monday morning, two days after Homecoming. They couldn't use my real name because I was a minor, and in the end I was glad. I wasn't sure about death, but nothing made sense in life. I wanted to cry for help but didn't know the words to use, and Mom didn't keep enough prescription drugs around the house. I often suspected that I was invisible, so I reclined at the corner of Madison and Pine for a chance to be seen.

I had the fantasy that everyone has when they want to brush

death, dreamed she'd be driving along and find me in the street, but I was hauled to my feet by a woman who stopped her minivan three yards from me and my tuba, a woman who had two dangerously quiet toddlers in the back seat. Even those little kids knew I needed help. It was in their eyes. They understood my pain, had thoughts they could not say because they did not know the words. We looked at each other and sympathized as their mother drove me to the hospital. I was not injured, just a little chilled from the pavement because it had taken a while for someone to find me. The doctors said I was fine, just a head case, so my mother sent me to a shrink. I didn't mention the bearded girl to her, though I explained how I often assumed I was invisible.

A few kids looked at me strangely at school, perhaps suspecting I was the fifteen-year-old in the road with the tuba, but they didn't care one way or the other; the most they could muster for me was idle curiosity. Even after Homecoming, no one talked against you, but she was still a target. I heard the lunchtime jeers. You didn't try to protect her from being called a skank and a cunt and a whore. That was another reason why I cursed you on my walk home, another reason why I knew you didn't care for her. Why didn't you stop those taunts? I couldn't eat because the names filled my head with angry pressure. I knew I would explode with love, which is why I took off my shirt.

You must have heard the story, how I was so calm when I laid the shirt on the table, unzipped my jeans, and let them puddle around my feet. I stepped out of my shoes and stood in the middle of the cafeteria with only my socks and underwear, everyone staring. I sat down and resumed eating. I could use my skinny body to protect her for a moment, to silence the cruelty. That was my dream. I was almost as naked as David holding that sling after defeating Goliath, though my act landed me and my pile of clothes in the principal's office.

My mother came in and explained to the principal that I was a head case and seeking therapy. Because I was a quiet kid and this was my first notable action, he was happy to let me go without even a detention.

"What was that about?" my mother said on the way home, wondering if I was indeed a head case or if she should attribute my behaviour to some undiscovered trend.

"My head hurts," I said, which was true.

I saw the bearded girl on the afternoon following my disrobing, but couldn't explain that it had been for her.

"Are you okay?" she said.

"I think so," I said. Part of me was caught in the fantasy of saving her. I would have paraded around school every day in my underwear if only I could have replaced her as the spectacle. But my pitifully normal body wasn't worth attention, even when exposed.

We moved in December of that year, me and Mom when she got a job at a different college and I had to follow. I don't expect you to remember that, but I came back to town last year, my job brought me here, and the other day I recognized your name in the paper. I wanted to congratulate you on your marriage though I see your beloved is not her, so I wondered if you knew where she'd gone after graduation. I want to find her, ask if she shaved or if she's still growing out that strawberry blonde beard. I have twenty years' worth of things to say, now that I know the words.

Mothers

The week after my mom and aunt die it's surreal, but life is like that after people you love pass away. I drive to work at the archive and nobody knows what to say. My boss gives me a plate of peanut butter cookies and smiles carefully like she's afraid her face will break. The five people in my department sent a card and flowers to the funeral home, and now I don't mind awkwardness, how everyone scoots around me. I'm ready for silence because there's been too much talking at the hospital and visitation and memorial service and I'm sick of hearing people tell me they're sorry for the deaths like it was their fault. It wasn't.

I'm happy to scan pages from one-hundred-fifty-year-old books in peace. It's a good and bad time to have a mindless job. I don't want to think about anything. All I need is a couple minutes of blessed blankness, but my mind drifts back to my mom and auntie.

They were conjoined twins, had two sets of legs and arms and hearts and lungs, but they shared kidneys and a liver and intestines. So many organs were connected that when they were born their parents decided not to separate them. That operation was more difficult fifty-six years ago, would have been easier now, but Mom had a weak heart so my aunt's heart helped keep both of them alive. If my grandparents had made a different decision, Mom might not have lived.

But her heart stopped them in the end. Maybe they suspected it would happen, though it's not something Mom and Auntie would have talked about with anyone but each other.

Their doctor made the suggestion, the horrible suggestion, to separate them because it was her job to say awful things. I'd assumed my mother could be taken off to save my aunt, but even their surgeon said there was only a fifty-fifty chance it would work.

"We won't do it," Auntie said at our weekly Friday night dinner. "Absolutely not. We live together and we'll die together."

I don't know why I kept stuffing baked ziti into my mouth. I should have stopped. I should have insisted that kind of surgery wasn't the only option, even though it was.

"We should consider it," Mom said, waving her fork at my aunt.

"Consider killing you off." Auntie took another spoonful of pasta from the baking dish and didn't look at my mother.

"It's me or both of us," said Mom.

"It's both of us," said my aunt.

My dad and uncle and I looked at each other because it didn't seem like the conversation was happening. My brother wasn't there to share our confusion, but we were used to that. He lives in town, but we don't see him more than once a month.

"You should think about this more," said my uncle.

"Listen, buddy," said my aunt, "I've been thinking about it for fifty-six years. This is the way it's going to be."

My aunt and uncle divorced twenty-three years ago, when I was ten, but he still comes over for dinner twice a month. My aunt called him "buddy" instead of "cutie" like she used to, but I knew she cared for him because she couldn't meet his gaze for the rest of the meal.

Mom and Auntie couldn't decide what to study in college so they became bank tellers while waiting from some other profession to pique their interest, but they liked the bank so well they stayed there for thirty-six years. They were extroverted and cheerful, never gave a dishonest smile, and loved flirting with customers. That's how Mom found Dad. She waited until my aunt and uncle got engaged before everyone tied the knot.

My brother and I came from Mom's uterus, but our blood flowed through her and our auntie. Sometimes they were both mothers, but other times Mom was a little more maternal. She didn't want us riding bikes in the street. She made us wash our hands for thirty seconds before eating. Auntie said Mom might as well make us walk around with bike helmets and a can of Lysol. I don't know if I loved my mother more, but there was a connection I couldn't explain. When she cocked her head in a certain way, I could read her mind. That's how I knew there were things she told my aunt and no one else. I told myself that was normal, they were twins, but I felt like I was missing out on something. She was my mom, but we couldn't have secrets, we couldn't share little mother-daughter things. There wasn't anything she told me that Auntie didn't already know.

I have my own apartment, but since Mom and Auntie died a week and a half ago I've been staying at my old house with Dad. So has my uncle. Friends and neighbours have stopped coming by, so all we have are wilting flowers and leftover casserole.

After dinner my uncle and dad sit on the couch and try to read the paper but end up crying. Their tears threaten to flood the house, and it's a pretty big one when you consider all four bedrooms. My uncle wipes his eyes on his sleeve and gets out gin and tonic water to make us drinks. I have a couple but stay sober enough so he can lean against me on the couch. My uncle is a small man, only five foot four, so he's not difficult to support.

"I wanted to get back with her and now I can't," he says. "I'm ready to shoot myself."

I rock him back and forth, back and forth, until he stops crying. Then I stand, pull him to his feet, and walk him to my old bedroom. I take off his shoes and socks, pull back the covers, and tuck him in. He's had enough booze to give him a dreamless sleep. I pad to the bathroom where I've always kept a toothbrush. When I glance at myself in the mirror I see the shimmer of both their faces—Mom's small nose and pointed chin, Auntie's hazel eyes and full mouth.

I sleep in my aunt and uncle's old bedroom because I don't want my uncle to wake up on a mattress saturated with memory, though it hasn't gotten much use since he and my aunt divorced. Mom and Auntie slept in the same bed with Dad every night after that, but I can still feel the mattress divot made by my aunt and uncle and mom's bodies. I'm engulfed by their absence. The hugeness of loss. That's when I let myself cry.

Mom was more traditional than my aunt, which is why she was nervous about me being unmarried at thirty-three.

"You've had decent boyfriends," she said. "Weren't any of them keepers?"

But Auntie said I was doing the right thing by playing the field.

"You need to wait until you're really sure," she said.

I'm still not sure how sure is "really sure." My aunt said I'd know when it happened, so I guess it hasn't happened yet. Usually I don't mind the quietude of my apartment.

My brother is a different story, a thirty-year-old guy who bounces from girlfriend to girlfriend. Sometimes he snags two girls in one month and leaves them just as fast, so I've given up keeping track of his current sweetie. He got Mom's good looks and Auntie's sense of humour, so even though he has a reputation for loving and leaving, it makes him attractive to a certain set of females bent on conquest. They want to be the one who tames him. Good luck, I say.

"Girls aren't bags of potato chips," I told him. "You can't use them up and toss them out."

"They know what they're getting into when they go out with me," he said and shrugged. "I'm looking for specific things in a woman. I know what I can live with and what I can't. A month is enough for me to tell if someone would get on my nerves in the long run."

"So everyone gets on your nerves in the long run," I said.

He shrugged again. "Most people turn out to be annoying if you're with them for more than four hours at a time."

When my brother started playing girlfriend roulette in his early twenties, Mom and my aunt said it was a phase. So much for that. I thought he'd slow down when Mom and Auntie got sick, but I only saw him twice at the hospital. He touched their hands, spent a few shadowy minutes in the corner, then he was gone.

My brother reappeared at the funeral with his latest girl. He cried while she patted his back. I didn't know whether to believe his tears.

Two weeks after Mom died, everyone at the archive walks around me like several quiet satellites. I appreciate the blunt rhythms of my job.

Scan books. Check the scans and correct distorted text. Put the files on the library's online archive. It's one thing that hasn't changed since the double death, makes it slightly easier to deal with everything else.

Like sorting through their belongings.

After dinner Dad and I sift through their clothing. Some things can be donated to Goodwill, but I don't know what to do with refitted pants and blouses and skirts, the things with odd slits or snaps or buttons to account for the section of organs and skin that bound them together.

"I can't be without your mother," my aunt joked darkly three weeks before they died. "I'd need to get a whole new wardrobe and it's not worth the hassle."

So what to do with fifteen extra wide skirts built for two? They're too big for placemats and too small for tablecloths. I take my uncle's suggestion and have a couple gin and tonics, enough to put me in a haze, because the last meals I had with Mom and Auntie are too vivid, especially the ones six months ago before that final diagnosis.

My mom and aunt agreed on many things, they had to, and one of them was hating doctors. Once they made up their minds, they formed a brick wall opinion. You could argue and plead and cajole and they would smile and nod and do exactly what they wanted.

This is why, when Mom started coughing a lot, she covered the fits with a smile big as red wax lips. My aunt said they'd be fine.

I said they should schedule an appointment with a doctor.

My aunt rolled her eyes. "We've been to more than enough doctors in our lives."

"If you don't go you might end up dead," I muttered, though I couldn't imagine that happening.

"Please pass the potatoes," said my mother.

My mom and aunt were a little like Eng and Chang Bunker, those Siamese twins who married sisters and had tons of kids and lived in farms side by side. But Eng and Chang devoted their bodies to science after they died, and Mom and Auntie refused to do that.

"The doctors have studied us more than enough to know what's connected where," my aunt said.

But they must have talked about Mom's coughing fits in private. I'd kill to know what they said, who argued what, because they scheduled an appointment when Mom was wheezing so bad that even her prescription inhaler didn't provide relief. They wanted a stronger drug. They got a death sentence. But I think they knew it was coming.

I took two weeks off work, used up my vacation time and sick leave, but my boss let me since she knew the circumstance. Mom and Auntie and I went to the art museum to see Degas paintings, the zoo to see kangaroos and koalas, and we visited their favourite Lebanese restaurant every day for lunch.

A long good-bye is a mixed blessing—you can say all the things you want to say, you can make all the arrangements you need to make, you can have good times, but those moments are mixed with grieving. You can't help but start the process before you have to.

When Eng and Chang Bunker died it was a lot faster—one twin passed three hours before the other, and the remaining twin didn't want to be removed from his brother to save his own life. It's a decision that's hard for anyone to understand. But I know if my auntie had made another choice, I wouldn't have had my mom around for those last weeks. That's what I think about as I lie awake in their huge bed. I tell myself the trade-off was worth it. I tell myself it wasn't my decision. I roll over and clamp a pillow over my head to shut out any more thoughts.

Even if I'd given them my two cents, it wouldn't have mattered.

I call my brother's cell phone, get his voicemail and leave a message asking him to stop by the house for dinner tomorrow and to see if there's anything from Mom and Auntie he wants to keep.

He doesn't call back.

I leave one message a day for two weeks, then I get pissed enough to stake out my brother's apartment and accost him when he's coming home. Probably from a date.

"Hey," he says when he slides out of his cute little Japanese car and I barrel out of my secondhand station wagon.

"Where have you been?" I cross my arms in classic older sister stance.

"I have a life," he says. "I have work. I have Jen." His latest girl.

"Did you get my messages?" I put my hands behind my back but he doesn't notice my stare as he examines his key ring.

"I get a lot of messages and I have to deal with the ones from work first." He walks away from me to his apartment door, but I trail along.

"You should help us sort the stuff from Mom and Auntie," I say. "Don't you want anything to remember them? Don't you even care?"

He whirls around so fast I nearly knock into him.

"Of course I care," he says, "but I have a shitload of memories. I don't need their junk. I have enough of my own. I need to haul half of my stuff to Goodwill. Clothes and books and furniture and just . . . crap I don't need."

He whirls back around. "Are you coming in for a fucking drink or not?"

"I didn't know I was invited," I say.

"You're my fucking sister. It would be impolite if I didn't invite you in for a drink."

I'm not sure when my brother started caring about politeness, but I'll take what I can get.

"How's Jen?" I say while he gets a couple beers from the fridge.

"She's good," he says. "Patient. She teaches second grade. I need a patient woman."

"A patient woman who's not annoying," I say.

"You got it." He pops the cap off my beer before handing it to me. My brother is a beer snob, only serves fancy microbrews, so when I'm at his place I know I'll get something good.

"If I see anything from Mom and Auntie that I think you'd like I'll save it," I say. "Something small."

"Sure, whatever." He plays with a little ceramic elephant statue on his coffee table.

"Are you doing okay?" I say.

"Fucking peachy," he says. "You want another beer?"

"I'm fine," I say, taking a pull, then holding the bottle by the lip and swinging it from my fingers like a pendulum. My brother walks the ceramic elephant across the coffee table.

Six weeks after my mom and auntie die, I walk into the lobby of their old bank for the first time in two months. There's a new person, a single person, inhabiting their window. I do an about-face and go back to my car and use the drive-through again.

At home I consider getting drunk with my uncle (Dad has still not told me or my uncle to leave), but he needs someone to guide him to bed and position the trash can on the floor just in case. Dad stays up late looking through the realty section of the paper. I have a hard time falling asleep, replay memories I haven't considered for a long time. When I was in elementary school I got teased because Mom and

Auntie looked like they did, but in third grade I learned how to ball my fists. When I came home with playground bruises and a note from the principal, Mom and Auntie were mad.

"You shouldn't get a reputation as a girl who beats people up," said Mom. She wouldn't listen when I explained that I was defending myself and defending them against words. I tried to tell them about it when I was nine and ten and eleven, but they just smiled and said to tell the other kids that sticks and stones would break my bones but names would never hurt me.

After six or seven trips to the office with a bloody nose, kids left me alone. But my brother didn't have it as easy. He was withdrawn, never talked back, so even the poor girl with the cleft palate who was stepped on by every other kid in their grade made fun of him. My brother was quiet as a marble statue. An easy target.

"The names didn't get to me," he said later when we were both in high school. "Why beat people up if they didn't get to me?"

I still don't believe him. How could those words not make him angry?

But I got even more upset a couple years ago when I tried to explain to Mom and Auntie how growing up with two mothers wasn't easy. They knitted their eyebrows identically.

"We've always felt accepted in town and at the bank," said Mom.

"You didn't deal with playground jerks," I said. "Don't you remember my bloody noses?"

"I guess that happened a few times," said Auntie, "but I didn't think it went on for long."

I was angry they didn't care enough to recall the rough times I had, or the stamina it took to live with them. I didn't want much, just a little acknowledgment, a hint of identification, a few words to suggest they knew my childhood hadn't always been easy. Was that too selfish?

After the bank fiasco I go to Mom and Auntie's favourite Lebanese place for lunch. Don't ask why. They ate here every Wednesday, ordered hummus and falafel and tabouli and got the whole meal for free because they brought people in. They had a hundred friends at the restaurant between the wait staff and regular customers, so four servers stop to hug me and say how much they'll miss Mom and Auntie. I chew my pita and wonder what it would have been like if Auntie had shown up here or at the bank without Mom. How would everyone have looked at her? What would they have said after she left?

Before now I didn't consider how much of her decision was a matter of pride. Was she worried that people would whisper of her selfishness? No one could fault her for wanting to live, but that would have meant taking Mom's life early. Besides, without my mother, I don't know who Auntie would have become. They were connected in more ways than just the body.

When I get home and the For Sale sign is in the front yard, I blow up at Dad. He's in the kitchen making eggplant parmesan and doesn't blink when I barrel through the door screaming that he can't do this yet.

"Pretty soon no one will live here but me," he says. "Unless you want to move back in."

I pause because I like my drafty little efficiency apartment, but I want to come back here and remember the conversations Mom and Auntie and I had on the couch. I want to remember them tucking me into bed. I want to remember sitting outside their bedroom door at night with my ear tight against the wood, trying to hear what they said to each other when alone. I never could make out many words, but that didn't stop me from trying to poke into that small important space.

"I'm worried you'll regret selling the house later," I say which isn't entirely a lie.

"But this place is full of them," Dad says. "Everywhere I go I feel them watching me."

"Yeah," says my uncle. He sits at the kitchen table with half a bottle of red wine.

"Then why don't you leave?" I say to him.

"Your mom and aunt won't watch me anywhere else," my uncle says. "I want them to drive me crazy."

This sort of truth can only be spoken by a half-drunk person.

I call my brother to tell him the house is for sale. I don't expect a response, so I'm surprised when the doorbell rings just before seven and I find him on the front step.

"Are we having dinner or not?" he says. "We always eat at seven."

I step to the side and he breezes past me.

"Where did you come from?" says Dad.

"Want a drink?" says my uncle.

"Sounds good," says my brother and grabs a wine glass from the cupboard. At dinner we talk about everything but the For Sale sign in the front yard. My brother says the eggplant parmesan is great. My dad says he should come over more often. My brother says he might.

After dinner my brother follows me to my bedroom. I'm not expecting this. We sit side by side on my bed. I'm still not sure why the hell he showed up.

"How's Jen?" I say.

"History," he says.

"She was too annoying?" I ask.

"She thought I was too annoying," he says. "I was with her for two fucking months. She was pretty cool."

A compliment like that from my brother is close to a marriage proposal.

"I'm sorry," I say. "That sucks."

My brother rubs the blanket between two fingers and doesn't say anything for a long time.

"Why the fuck didn't Auntie think it was worth it to stay around?" he says.

"She didn't want to live without Mom," I say.

"What about us?" yells my brother. "Didn't she think we had fucking feelings? Didn't she think we'd want her to be alive?"

"Well, yeah," I say, "but living without Mom, it would have been—"

I pause. Then I start crying. He's asking everything I want to ask. That's why it hits me then, this overwhelming loneliness, the kind you feel when you're in a crowd of strangers getting shoved back and forth, surrounded by people, and totally isolated. Somehow being alone in a crowd is a million times worse than being alone by yourself. It makes the knowledge of your isolation worse.

That's what my aunt would have had to deal with every day.

"Fuck," says my brother. "I'm sorry."

"They're dead," I say. "We're supposed to fucking cry. That's what you do after someone passes away. It's fucking normal."

I've never seen my brother cry. Even now I don't know if that's what he's doing, but he wipes his eyes with his sleeve and pulls me close in a hug and I let my body shake against his. The house dissolves, and the only thing I feel is my heart beating in my fingertips and my brother's heart beating against my shoulder, the rhythms regular and strong and almost in sync.

COPYRIGHTS

"Bianca's Body" first appeared in *Hayden's Ferry Review*, 38 (2006)

"The Shell" first appeared in *Nimrod*, 52.1 (2008)

"Mr. Chicken" first appeared in the online edition of *PANK*, 5.06 (2010)

"Cyclops" first appeared in *Indiana Review*, 31.1 (2009)

"Seventeen Episodes in the Life of a Giant" first appeared in *CutBank*, 69 (2008)

"Snakes" is original to this collection

"Ears" first appeared in *Guernica*, 15 July 2010

"Combust" first appeared in *North American Review*, 295.2 (2010)

"Three" is original to this collection

"Butterfly Women" first appeared in *Oyez Review*, 38 (2011)

"Markings" first appeared in *Clackamas Literary Review*, Fall 2011

"To Fill" first appeared in *North American Review*, 292 (2007)

"Skin" first appeared in *Cream City Review,* 31.2 (2007)

"Holes" first appeared in Nimrod, 53.2 (2010)

"Things I've Been Meaning to Tell You" first appeared in *So to Speak*, Spring 2011

"Mothers" first appeared in *Gulf Coast*, Fall 2011

ACKNOWLEDGEMENTS AND GIFTS

A large trophy and several gold stars go to my parents, who have been my writing cheerleaders since I was six years old and started dictating stories to my dad. A lifetime supply of pens, coffee, and diet Dr. Pepper go out to Lawrence Coates and Wendell Mayo, my creative writing professors at Bowling Green State University. They read early versions of many of these stories, and their comments were instrumental in the revision process. Several gallons of mint chip ice cream go to my husband, Tristan, who was my editor even before we were dating, and who still suffers through the first drafts of everything I write. An attractive Chinese paper lantern goes to my Women's Studies professor, Jeannie Ludlow, whose course "Theories of Othered Bodies" launched me into doing much of the research I performed while writing these stories. Many hugs and ten pounds of Gummi worms go to my sister Kat, who shares my sense of humour and is the only woman I know to have knit herself a beard. Finally, a silver shower of gratitude goes to the literary magazine editors who first published several of the stories in this collection.

ABOUT THE AUTHOR

Teresa Milbrodt received her MFA in Creative Writing from Bowling Green State University, and her MA in American Culture Studies from the same institution. Her stories have appeared in numerous literary journals, and several have been nominated for the Pushcart Prize. She is an Assistant Professor of Creative Writing at Western State College in Gunnison, Colorado, where she lives with her husband, Tristan, and her cat, Aspen. When she's not conjuring gorgons and cyclopses at her laptop, she enjoys cooking, sewing, and questing for the perfect cup of coffee.

EMB
RACE
THE
ODD

PICKING UP THE GHOST
TONE MILAZZO

AVAILABLE AUGUST 15, 2011
FROM CHIZINE PUBLICATIONS

978-1-926851-35-8

BRIARPATCH
TIM PRATT

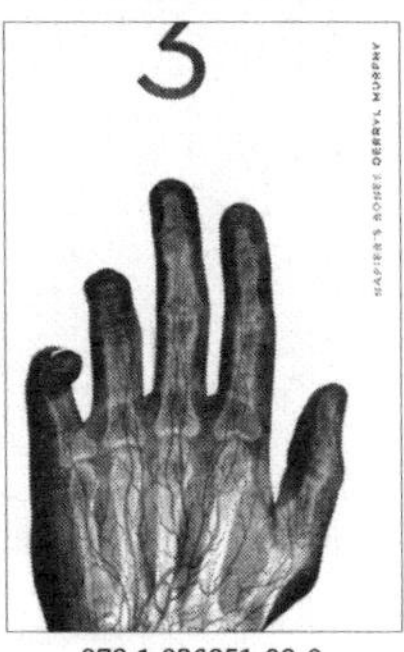

978-1-926851-10-5

TOM PICCIRILLI

EVERY SHALLOW CUT

978-1-926851-09-9

DERRYL MURPHY

NAPIER'S BONES

978-1-926851-11-2

DAVID NICKLE

EUTOPIA

978-1-926851-12-9

CLAUDE LALUMIÈRE

THE DOOR TO LOST PAGES

978-1-926851-13-6

BRENT HAYWARD

THE FECUND'S MELANCHOLY DAUGHTER

978-1-926851-14-3

GEMMA FILES

A ROPE OF THORNS

"I'VE REVIEWED ALMOST A DOZEN OF THEIR RELEASES OVER THE LAST FEW YEARS . . . AND HAVE NOT BEEN DISAPPOINTED ONCE. IN FACT, EVERY SINGLE RELEASE HAS BEEN NOTHING SHORT OF SPECTACULAR. READERS IN SEARCH OF A VIRTUAL CACHE OF DARK LITERARY SPECULATIVE FICTION NEED LOOK NO FARTHER THAN THIS OUTSTANDING SMALL PUBLISHER."

–PAUL GOAT ALLEN, BARNES & NOBLE COMMUNITY BLOG

CHIZINEPUB.COM CZP

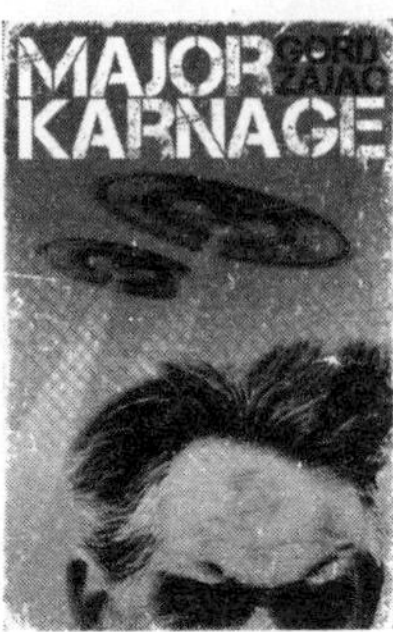

978-0-9813746-6-6

GORD ZAJAC

MAJOR KARNAGE

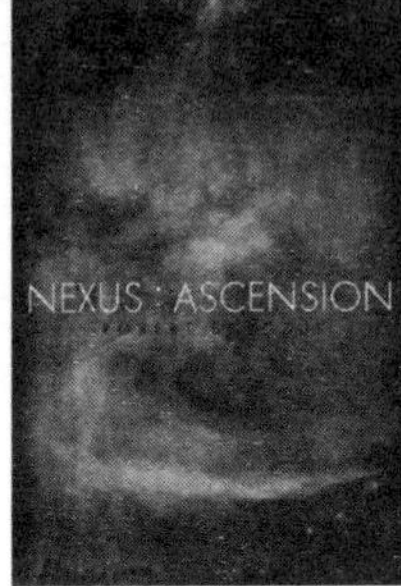

978-0-9813746-8-0

ROBERT BOYCZUK

NEXUS: ASCENSION

978-1-926851-00-6

CRAIG DAVIDSON

SARAH COURT

978-1-926851-06-8

PAUL TREMBLAY

IN THE MEAN TIME

978-1-926851-02-0

HALLI VILLEGAS

THE HAIR WREATH AND OTHER STORIES

978-1-926851-04-4

TONY BURGESS

PEOPLE LIVE STILL IN CASHTOWN CORNERS

"IF I COULD SUBSCRIBE TO A PUBLISHER LIKE A MAGAZINE OR A BOOK CLUB—ONE FLAT ANNUAL FEE TO GET EVERYTHING THEY PUBLISH—I WOULD SUBSCRIBE TO CHIZINE PUBLICATIONS."

—ROSE FOX, *PUBLISHERS WEEKLY*

ALSO AVAILABLE FROM CHIZINE PUBLICATIONS

978-0-9812978-9-7

TIM LEBBON

THE THIEF OF BROKEN TOYS

978-0-9812978-8-0

PHILIP NUTMAN

CITIES OF NIGHT

978-0-9812978-7-3

SIMON LOGAN

KATJA FROM THE PUNK BAND

978-0-9812978-6-6

GEMMA FILES

A BOOK OF TONGUES

978-0-9812978-5-9

DOUGLAS SMITH

CHIMERASCOPE

978-0-9812978-4-2

NICHOLAS KAUFMANN

CHASING THE DRAGON

"IF YOUR TASTE IN FICTION RUNS TO THE DISTURBING, DARK, AND AT LEAST PARTIALLY WEIRD, CHANCES ARE YOU'VE HEARD OF CHIZINE PUBLICATIONS—CZP—A YOUNG IMPRINT THAT IS NONETHELESS PRODUCING STARTLINGLY BEAUTIFUL BOOKS OF STARKLY, DARKLY LITERARY QUALITY."

—DAVID MIDDLETON, *JANUARY MAGAZINE*

CHIZINEPUB.COM CZP

978-0-9812978-2-8

CLAUDE LALUMIÈRE

OBJECTS OF WORSHIP

978-0-9809410-9-8

ROBERT J. WIERSEMA

THE WORLD MORE FULL OF WEEPING

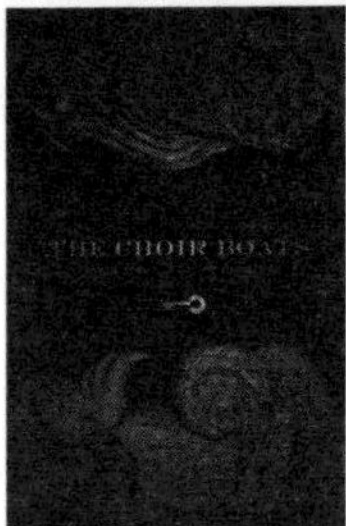

978-0-9809410-7-4

DANIEL A. RABUZZI

THE CHOIR BOATS

978-0-9809410-5-0

LAVIE TIDHAR AND NIR YANIV

THE TEL AVIV DOSSIER

978-0-9809410-3-6

ROBERT BOYCZUK

HORROR STORY AND OTHER HORROR STORIES

978-0-9812978-3-5

DAVID NICKLE

MONSTROUS AFFECTIONS

978-0-9809410-1-2

BRENT HAYWARD

FILARIA

"CHIZINE PUBLICATIONS REPRESENTS SOMETHING WHICH IS COMMON IN THE MUSIC INDUSTRY BUT SADLY RARER WITHIN THE PUBLISHING INDUSTRY: THAT A CLEVER INDEPENDENT CAN RUN RINGS ROUND THE MAJORS IN TERMS OF STYLE AND CONTENT."

—MARTIN LEWIS, *SF SITE*

ALSO AVAILABLE FROM CHIZINE PUBLICATIONS